About the Author

R. E. Boucher is a teacher with a joint honours' degree in English and Music. She is an accomplished musician and *The Electi* marks her first foray into literature. In her spare time she loves travelling, learning new languages and performing with her local Musical Theatre company. She lives in Dorset with her wife, Tash, their dog, Barkley, and their pet tortoise, Boots.

The Electi

R. E. Boucher

The Electi

Olympia Publishers
London

www.olympiapublishers.com
OLYMPIA PAPERBACK EDITION

A CIP catalogue record for this title is
available from the British Library.

ISBN: 978-1-80074-833-0

This is a work of fiction.
Names, characters, places and incidents originate from the writer's
imagination. Any resemblance to actual persons, living or dead, is
purely coincidental.

First Published in 2023

Olympia Publishers
Tallis House
2 Tallis Street
London
EC4Y 0AB

Printed in Great Britain

Dedication

For Tash. For always.

To Jas,

Be a Trebble

Maker!

love
Rach
x

To Jess,

Be a Trebble
Maker!

love
Kash x

Chapter 1

Wrong Side of the Tracks

Eloy & AJ — Trebs

It was the year 2062 but the village of Littlebourne was a place lost in time. The old part of the village had been abandoned in the twenty-forties when its businesses had gone bust and the post-war riots had destroyed what was left. The newer part of the village had been built just before the war and centred around the main road which stretched from one end of the village to the other. At one end of this road lived the Electi community, in their modern manor houses and high-end apartments with glistening glass roofs and automated security systems. Down the road, away from the sparkling chrome garages and upscale coffee bars was a designated 'Treb zone' and considerably less wealthy. Ageing blocks of flats filled every available space and the brightest lights shone from the local fast-food restaurant 'Burger Moon'. The two opposing classes of Electi and Treb were created by the new government of Anglia, formerly known as the UK. This organisational shake-up was a result of the first Nuclear War in 2035, which led to global chaos and the destruction of well over half the planet. Though the UK was largely spared from the catastrophe, society would never be the same.

Twins Eloy and Alejandra 'AJ' Kahn lived in a ground-floor flat in the Treb zone of Littlebourne. Their front window looked onto the roundabout at the bottom of the main road which, at the Treb end of town, was covered in anti-Electi graffiti and sporadic piles of litter. Their back window looked onto their very modest shared garden and the train tracks, used primarily for freight trains carrying food from mainland Europe to New London. On paper the twins were classified as Trebs, the lower class and Eloy deeply resented this. AJ, on the other hand, took pride in her commoner status and liked to try and 'shake up the system' whenever she could. At this moment she was using her holophone to hack into her school's assessment system, in an attempt to improve her grades. Her brother Eloy, already with straight As, was playing holo chess with their best friend Mizuki. Their holophones were generated from the microchips installed in their hands. These chips were used for everything from paying for lunch to unlocking their lockers at school. They were installed at birth for every Anglian citizen with the promise that the health department would use them to track things such as radiation levels, ensuring everyone's safety and continued good health. Suddenly both of their holophone screens and their lounge's holovision were taken over by the mandatory seven p.m. broadcast. AJ cursed under her breath as the voice of President Ignatius Impero-Regnum filled the small room.

"Good evening, beloved citizens of Anglia, and welcome to your seven-p.m. broadcast. I am pleased to inform you that your government has today taken further steps to de-radiate the mainland zones of Europe, previously ravaged by the war. The outer fringes of the mainland, our Anglian colonies, are being

used productively as factories to supply you, the citizens of Anglia, with food and goods."

"If you can call this food," Eloy interjected, staring despondently at his 'simulated bacon sandwich' flavoured meal drink.

"This is your monthly reminder to charge your microchips — remember — they are installed for your safety. Take note of daily radiation levels and wear your respirators if you need to go outside. Please also remember that any dissension or perceived aggression towards Electi citizens will not be tolerated and will be met with utmost force. This is for the safety of all Anglian citizens. This has been President Ignatius Impero-Regnum for the Anglian Government — serving you, to create a better world."

As the broadcast ended, Eloy punched the nearest cushion.

"You can't let him get to you," AJ sighed. "Besides, the new 'simulated potato' fries are pretty good!" Eloy grimaced in disgust, flicking his blonde hair out of his face as he did so. "Well at least without real meat or dairy Mum doesn't have to worry about breaking her veganism," he muttered, though he secretly wished that he could taste a real bacon sandwich. "She said it used to be much harder to find vegan stuff when she was a little girl."

"Yeah, how weird! I can't imagine being able to choose from all that food they used to have before the war. I bet cheese was great. All the old people rave about it," AJ mused, still flicking her fingers over her holophone screen at a speed too fast for human eyes to register. As Eloy returned to his game of chess, his mind still on thoughts of food, the twins' parents walked through the front door, visibly exhausted. Their father Marcus worked for the police but was having a harder and harder time finding job satisfaction. His usual day-to-day task seemed to be stopping anti-Electi protests that, in all honesty, he wanted to be a part of. As a Treb citizen, he deeply sympathised with the anti-Electi rebel groups and hated having to not only stop their protests but arrest them for their daring behaviour.

During the artificially intelligent robot boom, his job was temporarily taken over by a prototype AI robot called PC Bottley. Marcus was sure it would render his family homeless but he needn't have worried. PC Bottley severely injured seven Electi citizens in the first half-hour, claiming that they were inherently evil and couldn't be rehabilitated, leaving Marcus' job security intact. His wife Leyna taught at the local Electi school. Her job was also briefly taken over by an AI robot named Mr Bottington but it managed to tie up and dangle thirty Electi children from the roof in their first maths lesson, claiming that they were 'unteachable monsters' and Leyna was promptly called back into work. Mr Bottington was given a wig and re-allocated to lunchtime supervisory duties. Marcus and Leyna kept a photo of robots Bottley and Bottington on their bedroom cabinet, in part to remind them of their victory in an age of machines but also to remind them of the fragility of their employment — it acted as a powerful motivator in two stressful and difficult career paths. As the twins' parents entered the flat, they let out a mutual sigh.

"Rough day, Dad?" asked Eloy.

"Six protests," he moaned, "and your mother got another yellow card at work."

"Oh no, what happened?"

12

"Apparently, the writing of my four-year-olds is not up to the standards of the academy." Leyna Kahn collapsed onto the sofa beside her daughter AJ and began braiding her hair. "To be honest, I think it was a bit much asking them to write about the social reforms of the mid-21st century. They just want to play in the mud."

"Sometimes I just want to play in the mud," Marcus joked, throwing his policeman's hat onto the couch and leaning against the door frame, his long jet-black hair brushing his shoulders.

"Are you going to be okay, Mum?" asked Eloy nervously.

"Oh, petal, they've given me eleven yellow cards now. If they were going to fire me — they'd have done it already. They're just trying to keep up with the results from the ESA schools. They'll never do it though. Everyone knows the American grades are fixed." Leyna had first started teaching in a Treb school but was called up to the Electi academy as part of the 'Superior Teacher Training Program'. She hadn't wanted to go but she didn't have a choice. The main reason her superiors hated her was that she was probably the best teacher in the county. "Well, my loves," she sighed as she kissed AJ on the head. "I think I'd better get started on my work for the evening. Lots to do before tomorrow! I've got to get my little mud-slingers translating Latin by lunchtime!"

As she retreated into her bedroom with the ancient family tablet computer, the family dog, Sully, padded sleepily into the room. Sully was, as his name suggested, a rather sullen and grumpy looking dog. He was a Lhasa-Apso crossed with a Shih Tzu crossed with something nobody was really sure of. He looked almost exactly like a teddy bear, only, if the teddy bear was permanently annoyed and platinum blonde. Despite his grumpy nature, Sully was always able to cheer the family up when they needed it most. As Marcus went to the kitchen to find something to eat, Sully lay down in front of AJ and rolled on his back playfully.

"Oh, good boy! Who's a good boy?" She giggled. Sully sneezed as though in reply while playfully batting his ears with his paws. As Marcus busied himself in the kitchen, Eloy once again resumed his chess game with Mizuki. He was certainly the more academically gifted of the twins but lacked the physical prowess of his sister, who regularly broke the school sports records. As AJ returned to hacking the school grades system, Eloy rolled his eyes. He knew that no good could come from one of his sister's technological schemes. Last time, when she had tried to hack into the cafeteria to change the lunch menu options, she accidentally set fire to one of the fridges.

"Yes!" AJ punched a fist in the air and Marcus peered around the corner.

"Success?"

"Yep, my grades are now As for days!" She cheered triumphantly, doing a little dance with her feet on the lounge floor. Eloy rolled his eyes again but refused to look away from his game of chess.

"Some of us work hard for those," he grumbled, failing to hide his bitterness. Marcus shot a disapproving look at his daughter but couldn't help but be proud of her tech skills. After all, he had taught her himself. He looked at his son who was deep in thought over his next chess move and felt an equal sense of pride. He privately wondered what kind of a world his children would grow up to live in. With everything going on he worried there might not be much of a world left for them.

Archie & Eva — Electi

Meanwhile, in the country's illustrious capital city, Evangeline Impero-Regnum brushed her long brunette hair out of her face as she tried to concentrate on her social etiquette homework. While her Electi status afforded her a higher class of private tutoring, she still resented having to belittle Trebs as part of her studies. She read the first question to herself.

"Question 1. How do you politely dismiss a Treb attempting to engage you in conversation? A. Pretend to see a friend nearby. B. Wipe their recent memory with your Electi microchip. C. Report them for harassment."

Eva sighed and flipped to the last page to look up the answer.

"Any answer except A is acceptable."

Eva sighed. A further barrier to her concentration came in the form of her two brothers, Atticus and Archibald, who were loudly trying to beat each other at disuku, the nation's favourite sport.

"Must you play that while I study?" She shouted through the door, her well-groomed eyebrows furrowed into a frown.

"Dear sister," drawled Atticus, as he dodged a moving laser, "are you daring to criticise your superiors?" Taking advantage of his brother being distracted, Archie lobbed the holographic disc into the post-box-shaped goal.

"Gooooooaaaaaaal baby! The Archmaster reigns supreme!"

"You are not my superior, Atticus," Eva replied, smiling at her favourite brother's victory. "You can't even beat Archie at disuku!" At Eva's taunt, Atticus' eyes narrowed as Archie tried to stifle a laugh. Just as Atticus began to threateningly raise his arm, their father walked in. Even without seeing him the three teenagers instantly knew when their father was nearby. The whole room seemed to darken and the air grew heavy. Archie thought it was psychological, but Eva was half-convinced their father emitted his own personal force field from his microchip. At his entrance, each of his three children quickly ran to the study room wall and stood to attention.

"Greetings, President Ignatius Impero-Regnum," they chorused in perfect unison, each with painful memories of the consequences of not doing so. Ignatius surveyed his children through circular spectacles while subconsciously straightening his tie. His suit was, as always, perfectly steamed and showed no signs of creasing even in the usual areas of elbows and knees. It almost looked as though he had stepped out of a factory, such was the consistency of his daily appearance. A charcoal grey pinstripe suit was always his preferred attire, though he sometimes opted for a navy blue when the occasion called for colour. When looking at old family photos it was impossible not to notice the strong resemblance between Ignatius and his father, the enigmatic Atticus I, creator and founder of the 'Electi' name and society.

"Children, your tutor will be here in a moment. Please prepare the room for your history lesson. I'm sure I don't need to remind you that my government is facing yet more pressure to submit superior grades than our American cousins and I expect you to contribute to that. I cannot listen to President Moon tell me yet again how his son Umberto is scoring full marks on the standardised tests, I just cannot." He trailed off, jealousy dripping from every word. Guiltily, the Impero-Regnum children immediately busied themselves clearing the study room and — Archie most of all — worrying about their sub-par test scores. Ignatius kept looking at his watch as though they were holding him up. In truth, they probably were. As the President of Anglia, he was about as busy as a man could be. As soon as the children were ready, he nodded curtly and exited the room, to be replaced by a small, dusty-looking woman with pinched features. She motioned them to their desks and opened her shabby black suitcase. It might as well have emitted a cloud of mothballs as it opened, such was the age of the documents inside. Mrs Totterton was the children's private history tutor and Archie was fairly certain the main reason for her having got the job was the fact she had probably been alive, for at least the last two hundred years. She must have been the only person they knew who still used physical books to read from and wrote using a pen and paper. As she found the relevant page of her favourite volume, Atticus rolled his eyes.

"Here we are." Mrs Totterton cleared her throat.

"Now. Ahem. Let us summarise our recent history again, shall we? There is nothing so important as our recent past." Their faces fell. They had been over this what felt like a thousand times or more.

"Master Atticus, shall you lead us?" Atticus stood reluctantly, took the book from his tutor and began to read in his trademark monotone drawl.

"The most defining event in our recent history was NW1 — Nuclear War 1," he began. "As tensions between East and West grew, a new generation of nuclear weapon was launched by a coalition of Eastern countries, taking out the western states of America. As retaliation, the remaining states, later renamed the ESA (Eastern States of America), struck back and inadvertently destroyed over ninety per cent of Asia. The nuclear fallout left most of Africa, Australasia and mainland Europe as a barren, radioactive wasteland. The world map was redrawn, centring around the only two countries still inhabitable — the ESA and the UK. The entirety of the UK, including Ireland, was re-named 'Anglia' to mark a fresh start in the new world. As the nearest stable nation, Anglia claimed the least radiated areas of mainland Europe as its colonies in return for the promise of funding to make them inhabitable, in time. Anglia continued to gain colonies and employed the native survivors to de-radiate their land. This colonisation and subsequent use of the local inhabitants harkens back to the height of the British Empire in the first millennium."

"Very good," Mrs Totterton interrupted as if he had just recited the alphabet. "Now Archibald dear, continue." Atticus half-threw the book at his brother resulting in a disappointed scowl from Mrs Totterton.

"As a result of the massive planetary destruction millions of now-refugees flock to the ESA and Anglia. This leads to the destabilisation of both countries and governmental shutdown — with the monarchy overthrown in Anglia amidst violent protests against war-related poverty. More protests and riots follow, both in favour of and against the acceptance of refugees into the country, destroying much of the country's key sites and infrastructure. Ultimately, two far-right anti-immigration governments are elected — The Electi in Anglia and The Moon Party in the ESA — founded, of course, by tech giant Sean Moon and his son Corey."

"Lovely, now, Master Atticus, please continue for us." The book was passed back, gently this time as Mrs Totterton followed it with her bird-like eyes.

"The head of the new Anglian government — our father Ignatius Impero-Regnum — becomes President of Anglia. Immigration into the country is immediately frozen, appeasing much of the native population who have, until now, been forced to house many refugees in their own homes. As overpopulation becomes a major issue any non-Anglian Nationals are deported to the Anglian colonies and put to work in the newly constructed factories to create food desperately needed in this new, agriculturally ruined world. President Ignatius, head of not only the Electi governmental party but of the society from which its name is taken, begins to implement steps for introducing a bi-classification system for Anglian citizens. The Electi society began by his own father Atticus, already contained thousands of influential members. By turning this society into its own class, President Ignatius attempts to address the severely polarised state of his country. In creating two separate classes with separate rules, he hoped to be able to better serve the opposing factions of Anglian citizens. As the bulk of the dissension in Anglia came from its poorer citizens, the president bestowed upon them the title of Treb, promising them their own schools, hospitals and even residential areas. This promise carried a requirement, however, that Treb citizens would no longer protest the government's hard-line anti-immigration and hyper-surveillance policies. As the nation reeled from the war with many families left homeless and ill from the radiation, the deal was accepted by referendum and the Treb class assigned to all non-Electi members. The Electi class was opened up to the public and offered certain privileges to the richer citizens of Anglia, in return for a yearly subscription fee which would go towards re-building the county and its colonies."

"Good. Archibald, your turn." Archie suddenly jumped as hearing his name forced his head to slide off the arm upon which it was lazily resting.

"Uhm, yes, sorry. Where were we?"

"The class system," Evangeline interjected, her annoyance at not being asked to recite facts she knew at least twice as well as her brothers hard to miss. "How Grandfather's school club became a governmental party and then its own class. It's fairly important." She was seething now, not only at Mrs Totterton's inherent sexism but at the subject matter itself. Atticus held out the book to Archie but he refused it, confident he could 'wing-it' at this point and hopeful of cheering up his sister.

"Yeah so, the Electi becomes the superior societal class. At first, it's just our family, their university friends and the biggest business leaders in Anglia but now thousands can apply if they can afford it. Electi are given priority on all public services and receive preferential treatment in almost every aspect of public life, including jobs and education. Schools, businesses and now, towns are segregated into the better maintained Electi areas and disadvantaged Treb zones. The money promised to Treb citizens mysteriously disappears leaving thousands homeless. In an attempt to regain public loyalty, the government fits all of its citizens with state-of-the-art microchips for their safety and security. Little do the Trebs know the Electi ones are waaaaaay cooler. The Trebs thought they would be taken care of, but the government just screws them over — and they no longer have the power to do anything about it as the government becomes, essentially, a dictatorship. Trebs suck, Electi rule, blah, blah, blah."

"Archibald the Second, you are to respect your family history!" Mrs Totterton snapped. Privately, neither Archibald nor Evangeline much respected their family history. It was only Atticus who seemed to think that creating a segregated society just after a nuclear war was a fair and just idea. "All three of you will re-read *Anglia: How One Nation Survived NW1* by tomorrow!"

"Now you've done it," muttered Eva, still resentful of not having been asked to read. Privately, however, she couldn't have been prouder of her little brother. He was finally beginning to realise what she already knew — that the Electi were not the heroes of history their father would have them believe.

Chapter 2

Over the Burger Moon

Eloy & AJ

The next day, the twins were taking their usual route to school with their best friend Mizuki, who had recently dyed her hair a soft, pastel lilac as part of her ongoing drive for self-expression. AJ was fascinated.

"You're so lucky! My dad would never let me dye my hair like that," she exclaimed through her respirator. Due to increased radiation and pollution levels, it was unsafe to be outside without wearing one.

"My parents have really loosened up lately," Mizuki replied, tossing her lilac locks over her shoulder. "It's cool in some ways, but they're both so busy all the time that I hardly ever see them anymore," she sighed. Mizuki-Hoshi Koizumi-Grey was the child of one Electi and one Treb parent which meant that, without a sizable amount of money to pay for the yearly subscription, she couldn't qualify for full Electi status. She did, however, receive better treatment than her Treb friends. She was a year older than the twins, but they were in the same school year. This was because the twins had been two of only eighteen children born in Anglia amid an infertility crisis and had to be slotted into the year above at school. Their parents regarded them as 'little miracles' and had chosen names accordingly (Eloy's name meant 'chosen one' and Alejandra meant 'saviour of mankind'). Eloy privately thought that his sister had gotten the better deal, but at least his name was easier to spell. Mizuki had first befriended the twins when their nursery teacher had failed to pronounce any of their names correctly. This was a problem that continued to plague them as they grew.

"What colour would you dye your hair anyway, AJ?" Eloy asked.

"I'm thinking like an electric blue," she replied thoughtfully. Mizuki nodded in approval and Eloy squinted as he tried to picture it on his sister.

"I could see that working for you," he replied. "Me, I can't be bothered with any of that."

"That's because you got Mum's gorgeous blonde curls!" AJ teased with jealousy. "Whereas I look exactly like Dad!"

"Well, I think you look great," Mizuki smiled at her. AJ smiled back. Her friend always knew how to make her feel better.

"What's your first class today, Mizuki?" enquired Eloy, as they entered the school building and placed their respirators in their lockers.

"Economics," Mizuki sighed sadly. Through her Electi mother, Mizuki was excused from Treb classes such as cookery, custodial services and manual labour, in favour of courses 'more suited' to her part-Electi status such as Economics and Business Studies. While Mizuki loathed spending time with other Electi students, who all bullied her for only being half-Electi, she did at least appreciate not having to take the dreaded 'cookery' class. As their school was sponsored by the country's premier fast-food chain — Burger Moon — their 'cookery' classes consisted of unwrapping and warming simulated beef burgers and faux-potato fries. The lack of any viable way to farm 'real' food since the Nuclear War meant that the majority of available sustenance consisted of 'simulated meal drinks' grown in laboratories. Whilst most Trebs settled for these, not least because they were by far the most affordable option, Burger Moon successfully took advantage of the human desire for realistic food and created fake burgers, fries and other fast-food staples out of lab-grown food products. It may not have contained anything from an animal or plant, but they took the trouble to make it look real, and that seemed to be enough. The restaurants themselves were mainly run by artificially intelligent robots but cookery classes taught the children the basics of running a fast-food kitchen for the few human jobs still left in the sector. The school claimed that it prepared them for later life, but AJ and Eloy had slightly higher ambitions for themselves. Eloy wanted to be a politician and change the system, but Trebs weren't allowed onto the training program. AJ wanted to be captain for the Anglian disuku team: The Anglian Angels. Disuku was not only the nation's, but the world's favourite sport and AJ was obsessed. Unfortunately, Treb schools didn't have the budget for disuku training facilities. The pitches alone required thousands of pounds worth of lasers and holographic projection software. AJ and Eloy could only dream of their bright futures as they replaced the grease in the chip pans, sweating through their Burger Moon baseball caps.

"Special order!" shouted the class teacher, a particularly sweaty man called Mr Parfitt. "Those AIs are working faster than you lot!"

"That's because they don't experience heat like we do," AJ

muttered under her breath, but not quietly enough.

"Are you back-chatting me, girl?" Mr Parfitt snapped. He was from a well-to-do Electi family, but they had been stripped of their status when his father had committed fraud, and now Mr Parfitt, his parents and his uncle Winston all lived in a small house in Littlebourne, disgraced and dangerously bitter.

"My name is AJ, not 'girl'." At this point, Eloy grabbed AJ's arm in warning and shook his head. She couldn't help it though. The way Mr Parfit talked down to or, worse, leered at the girls in his classes just enraged her.

"One more word and you'll be out of my class, girl!" He warned. AJ took a breath and looked at her brother's hand on her arm. He was right, of course, if she'd been sent out, her parents would be called and she couldn't stand disappointing them. Not when they worked so hard to get her into one of the better Treb schools in the area. She nodded at Mr Parfitt and returned to the chip pan.

"We've got two of the school's trustees coming in and they are particularly keen to see how the Burger Moon sponsorship is making them money. We need two of our very best Moon Burger Deluxes with the side salads. Realistic looking vegetation only, please. They also want smoothies so, AJ, you're on a freezer run."

AJ grimaced. The freezer, in which the pre-blended smoothies were kept, was notorious for locking students inside. Then, once they managed to escape the freezer-of-certain-death, they had to warm the smoothies in an old fashioned and extremely temperamental microwave. Most of these had been banned due to health and safety concerns but the school seemed more interested in cost-cutting than student safety. While Eloy began to fry two of the more realistic burgers, AJ headed for the freezer. Propping the door open with a mop, she dashed inside for the nearest two smoothies. Suddenly, a clatter told her that the mop had given way and the freezer door closed with an ominous click.

"Oh no, no, no!" AJ shouted as she ran back to the door. "Someone, please help! I'm inside!" AJ could hear other students outside the door. "Hey, can you let me out? It's really cold in here!"

"That's because you're from the Middle Ages where it's hot and full of sand. You need to be better adjusted to Anglia." AJ's heart sank.

"I think you mean the Middle East," she replied, angrily. "Although I was born in the same hospital as you, Rebecca — the one down the road." Rebecca Weston wasn't the brightest girl in their year, but it didn't seem to matter, as her best friend Ann always did her homework for her anyway. Ann was at the door now, giggling gleefully.

"You know what she means, half-breed." AJ felt her face turn red and her blood pounded in her ears.

"I'm just as Anglian as you are, I just look better for it!" AJ shouted and kicked the door. That may have been a mistake as her foot instantly crunched inside her second-hand sneaker. Hopping in silent rage, AJ retreated to the back of the freezer to wait for Eloy to notice she was missing. Luckily, it didn't take long, and Eloy's concerned face was soon visible in the opening of the freezer door.

"AJ, are you okay?" AJ emerged holding two smoothies, trying to hold back her shivers and her hurt.

"I'm fine," she replied coolly. "Thanks for the rescue. That stupid door…" She didn't want to tell Eloy what had happened. Eloy was always so calm and collected, but when people made fun of their heritage it was a different story. Unfortunately, AJ was never very good at hiding things from her brother.

"It was Rebecca again, wasn't it?" he asked. "It's a hate crime, AJ, we have to report it!"

"And what happens when we do, Eloy?" AJ replied defensively, shoving the smoothies into the microwave. "We get sent to the headteacher who tells us to 'stop causing trouble' and Rebecca gets to feel even more superior." Eloy sighed but he knew she was right. Rebecca and Ann walked behind them, giggling.

"Chilly, are we?" They grinned. Eloy slammed his hand down on the counter, but AJ stopped him from retaliating further. As they walked away, Eloy muttered to himself, "We're Anglian. We're from here." AJ patted her brother on the arm.

"Rebecca thought we were from the Middle Ages," she laughed. Eloy stared at her, open-mouthed.

"She did not!"

"That's what she said — no lie! The Middle Ages!"

"Well, then," Eloy replied, his spirits improved, "we best get back in our time machine and bring back the plague just for her!" AJ chuckled, happy to have picked up her brother's spirits as well as her own.

"Unless you have a real time machine, though, you're going to want to save those burgers you're cooking pretty quickly," she interjected as the smell of burning burger filled the kitchen.

"It's that trademark charcoal-grill taste!" Eloy shouted as he sprinted back towards the fryer. AJ smiled. At least with her twin, she was never alone in the world, and never without someone to make her smile.

As their father's seven p.m. broadcast drew to a close, the Impero-Regnum children made their way to the dining room to sit down for dinner. As was customary, they stood behind their chairs until their father Ignatius arrived, allowing him to sit first. Then, Atticus would sit, followed by Archibald, Lady Margot and finally, Evangeline. There were two younger Impero-Regnum children, Antoinette and Euridice, but they lived at a prestigious boarding school in the countryside with their nannies. Ignatius and Lady Margot refused to have children in the house until they were old enough not to break anything. It was no surprise, given the sheer amount of glassware and priceless art adorning the walls. The dining room alone featured several, paintings by Vincent Van Gogh — some of the only surviving examples since the war.

The family butler, Samuel, led the kitchen staff silently through with today's offering. As the richest family in the country, the Impero-Regnums had the kind of money that could buy genuine meat and vegetation. They owned one of the only existing farms in the world on one of the few fertile patches of land available, on the Isle of Wight. The farm provided for them alone and the cost of running it, along with transporting the produce to their home, ran into the millions each month. The technology required to keep the plants and animals alive was so expensive that Lady Margot often wondered whether it was worth it just for some higher quality sustenance, but as the silver plates were lowered in front of them, her doubts subsided. Steaming portions of fresh roast chicken on a bed of green vegetables and mashed potato were placed before each of the Impero-Regnum family members. They waited for Ignatius before picking up their cutlery, as was tradition. Ignatius surveyed his food with some distaste.

"What, no carrots today, Samuel?" He inquired, disappointed.

"I'm so sorry Sir, but the carrots didn't survive this month — it is becoming more challenging to keep the soil uncontaminated—" Ignatius held up his hand to stop his Butler.

"I don't want excuses, I want colour, Samuel. This looks like the sort of meal I would feed our dog — not the food of Anglia's finest family!" Samuel paled and bowed.

"I'm so sorry, Sir. I will relay your displeasure to the farmworkers immediately." He scuttled out of the room clutching his chest. The poor man had lived through four heart-attacks since joining the family and Lady Margot was becoming concerned that he was about to have his fifth.

"Evangeline," Ignatius began, "tell the servants to throw this away — we're going out." Eva held in a gasp of horror. At a time when such food was so scarce, she hated it whenever her father wasted it. The last time she had tried to vocalise this, however, Ignatius forced her to eat nothing but budget 'Plain Flavoured' meal drinks for a fortnight. She became so unwell that they nearly called for a doctor, but after resuming her usual diet, she began to turn a normal colour again and her nausea subsided.

"Atticus, you may join us. Archibald and Evangeline, I heard that you were not on your best behaviour for Mrs Totterton today so you can eat whatever you can find in the cupboard and continue your studies." Atticus smirked triumphantly at his siblings before following his parents out of the room. Archie and Eva picked up their plates and took them into the kitchen, where a row of despondent faces looked at the floor. Eva looked behind her to check that her parents were out of earshot.

"Sophie," she whispered to the nearest servant. "Would you like to have some of this? It seems such a shame to waste it." Sophie's eyes widened in both excitement and fear. "But your father—"

"Doesn't need to know," Archie interrupted with a smile. The siblings retrieved the rest of the plates and lay them before the almost-tearful servants. Eva watched them with a kind of awe as they tasted real food for the first time in years.

"I wish I had that much appreciation for things," she said to Archie as they headed back towards the study.

"At least we appreciated it enough not to throw it away," he replied, smiling. The next morning, however, when Ignatius had ordered a servant to check the bins for scraps and found nothing, he became so enraged that he put Archie and Eva under house arrest.

"No more trips, no more outings and no more disuku for a week!" he barked. Archie and Eva held their heads low as their older brother smirked over their father's shoulder. Their mother looked at them with a mixture of disappointment and confusion. She couldn't understand why they both insisted on flouting the family rules when they knew, so clearly, the consequences. Still, she couldn't help but be proud that she had produced at least two children with a shred of humanity, even if she couldn't acknowledge it.

Chapter 3

Man's Best Friend

Eloy & AJ

The next day, Eloy and AJ were relaxing in the garden while their father, Marcus, cleaned the kitchen and their mother, Leyna, worked in the bedroom on her pupils' latest assessments. Sully, the family dog, was happily lying on AJ's legs as she scrolled through her social media page.

"I'm up to two thousand followers on XChange now!" she boasted. Sully gave a soft woof in reply, but Eloy scoffed.

"Two thousand is nothing nowadays," he muttered, unimpressed.

"Well, it's more than you have," AJ pointed out, bitterly.

"Yeah, but that's because I only let people I know in the real world become my followers," Eloy replied. "That way I don't have any weirdos stalking me."

AJ ignored him and carried on scrolling, while absent-mindedly stroking Sully's ears. Now and again, he would jump as if hearing something inaudible to everyone else, and AJ would give him a little cuddle to calm him down. He may have been a skittish rescue dog, but the family loved him for exactly what he was. Sure, he barked at night and was afraid of his own tail, but he was always there when they needed some company. They had found him wandering the barren heathland behind their flat one day and no one had claimed him. With little plant or animal life left in the wild to feed any stray pets, the Kahn family immediately took him in as their own. He had been a loyal companion ever since. As he settled down from one of his little frights, a loud bang like an explosion rang through the air. From the window, Marcus could see smoke coming from the heath in the distance. Before AJ could stop him, Sully had bolted and was tearing off towards the billowing smoke.

"Sully, no! Come back!" Marcus grabbed his respirator and ran out the back door after Sully, AJ and Eloy, who had already begun chasing their beloved pet. After bounding through the back garden and over AJ's rust-ridden bicycle, Sully deftly vaulted the back wall of the garden and raced towards the source of the noise, straight for the train tracks. Sully had excellent hearing but compensated for this with poor eyesight. AJ was closest to him, but as fast as her two legs were, they couldn't keep up with Sully's four.

"Boy, NO!" Eloy wasn't fast on his feet, but he was the first to spot the oncoming train.

Archie & Eva

"Where's Wendoline?" barked Atticus. He was rushing through the house in a fury.

"How should I know?" replied Archie.

"Probably in the kitchen." Since Mrs Totterton's haughty departure the previous day, the children had been spending their free time pretending to study, largely for their mother's benefit. She was losing track of the number of tutors she had needed to apologise to this week and her patience with her children was wearing thin.

"That hideous dog has mauled my best disuku shoes!" Atticus growled. Eva and Archie quietly giggled as their brother left the room. The two younger Impero-Regnum children had never been fond of the first-born. Once Atticus was out of sight Eva removed the book she had been pretending to read from their laps to uncover her E-Scroll. It was like an old tablet computer but ultra-thin, foldable and — most importantly — waterproof. The number of times Eva had dropped hers in the bath while trying to beat her cousins in an online hackathon was uncountable.

"So, if you enter the code and touch this icon here," she showed her brother, "you can bypass the parental controls altogether." She always made this kind of thing look easy, Archie thought to himself. Her pale fingers flitting expertly across the surface of the screen.

"I think I'll just stick to disuku," he grumbled. "I don't have the brains for this stuff."

"You do! You just don't want to use them! But it's fine, I don't need your help hacking into father's files." She winked as she said this, with a glint of mischief in her eyes, hiding a greater sense of purpose. Archie gasped.

"You're not? You can't seriously hack into father's data?"

"Why not? He hacks into ours." Eva's voice was cold with a trace of bitterness.

"He does not! Does he?"

"You know, Archie, you might be right. Maybe you don't have the brains for this stuff. *Of course* he hacks into our files — he tracks our microchips as well — you must know that!" Eva was exasperated by her brother's naive ignorance. Archie's mouth was open but no sound was coming out. "Okay," she began, "apparently you didn't know."

"You mean he doesn't trust us?" Archie looked pale.

"Duh." Eva was half smiling but the severity of the situation remained. At least until—

"WENDOLINE!" Atticus' voice blared out through the study room door.

"Well, you can't blame Father for not trusting Atticus," Archie grumbled. "Mental that one, honestly." He smiled at his sister, grateful for her constant companionship in a house otherwise bereft of warmth or affection.

"Got it!" Eva did a little victory dance with her feet, her heels clicking on the parquet floor.

"Got what?" Archie asked, bemused.

"There was this file I just couldn't get access to, and I've finally cracked it. I should have guessed the password. Father is so predictable."

"What was it? Electi4eva?" Archie laughed at his own joke as he often did.

"Don't be silly," Eva chided him. "It was 'Ch33se&W1ne'. His favourite rationed treats!" As Archie daydreamed about the last time he had tasted camembert, Eva continued to scan the screen.

"What's in the file, sis?"

"Something about Treb monitoring, through their pets! Wow, this is… I hope Father isn't involved in this. It looks incredibly illegal whatever it is."

"What? Like robot dogs and stuff?"

"Yeah, looks like it. Cats too — birds even. No fish though. Something about not being able to fully submerge the tech in water for over twenty-four hours." Eva continued reading. "They seem to be focusing on specific people — young people. About seventeen or eighteen of them by the looks of it." Eva kept muttering to herself as she read. "What's Acertine poisoning?"

"Eva, do you ever worry that… that Father might not be one of the good guys?" Archie looked down as he said this. Eva looked grave.

"All the time," she replied.

"Wait, you don't think?"

"What?"

"Well, Wendoline? What if she's monitoring us?"

"Oh don't be preposterous, Archie! Father wouldn't want his own home monitored!"

"He might if he's the one monitoring it," Archie pointed out. Eva considered this.

"Good point. Let's go and find her. Hopefully, before Atticus gets hold of her and turns her into real sausage meat."

Wendoline was an extremely tubby sausage dog; kept at her grand size due to the large amount of rationed gourmet sausages she would consume on a regular basis. As Archie and Eva searched for her, she was in their mother's secret stash of biscuits munching her way through a pack of malted milks.

"Wendy! Wendoline! Here, girl!" Upon hearing her name, Wendoline hastily tried to cover her tracks by kicking the crumbs under a cabinet and plodding casually round the corner.

"Wow." Archie scoffed at her candour. Wendoline burped loudly. "Well, if she's a robot," Archie began, "I'm not concerned. The only thing she's monitoring is our grocery supply." Eva conceived that her little brother was probably right but wanted to be sure.

"Here, girl!" Wendoline waddled over to Eva's outstretched hand and licked it. "That's it, good dog." As Wendoline inspected her hand for treats, Eva waved her other, microchipped hand over her tubby body. "Got it!"

"Got what?"

"I scanned her for software. The results are on my E-Scroll, come on!"

"You have got to tell me where you get these apps, Evie. My chip only tells me when I've forgotten to brush my teeth, it's so annoying!"

They retreated to the study, Wendoline following lazily behind and still optimistic for some kind of a snack. "Here." Eva pointed to the screen. "No software detected. No signal either. Yep, one hundred per cent dog all right." Wendoline finally caught up with them and burped again.

"Classic, Wendoline," Archie sighed.

Eloy & AJ

As Leyna marked her students' work with her headphones in, Polish folk music from her homeland blaring out, her family were still chasing their dog, Sully. AJ had managed to cross the tracks before the oncoming train, but Marcus and Eloy were stranded on the other side of a barrelling freight train. It seemed to go on forever. Eloy lost track of the number of carriages as he worriedly looked for Sully and his sister. Struggling after trying to keep up with his much more athletic twin, he clutched his chest as the final carriage sped away and scanned the barren heathland for movement. There were a few dead trees, scorched bushes and the occasional pile of litter, but not too many places for a small dog to hide.

"There!" His dad pointed to a bush beside the tracks in which his sister was cradling Sully in her arms. They ran over the tracks as soon as the train was safely away. Sully had got himself caught in a bush full of thorns in his haste to discover the source of the strange noise. A clump of his fur was still attached to one of the branches and he was whimpering softly as if in pain.

"Oh no, is he okay?" Eloy's voice cracked as he knelt beside them. He looked forlornly at the fluffy blonde bundle.

"He's still breathing, I think it's just a flesh wound," replied AJ as she checked him over. "But there's something here. I don't understand." She turned the dog over in her hands and Eloy could see a patch of missing fur. Instead of skin beneath it, however, there was something smooth and shiny and a flashing light.

"What the…" Eloy began.

"I know right?" AJ looked at the light, confused. "I'm pretty sure this isn't what dogs are supposed to look like on the inside." Marcus looked closer, pulling back more of Sully's fur.

"Wait," he interrupted. "I've heard about this. It isn't safe to talk here. We need to get back to the flat." Marcus picked Sully up, his legs dangling helplessly in surrender and the three of them jogged back to the kitchen, closing the door behind them and shaking the dirt from their boots. Gently, Marcus lay Sully on the wonky table and AJ stroked his head to calm him as they examined his missing patch of fur. Eloy examined the area with curiosity.

"Did he have an operation or something? Is his microchip bigger than ours?" His questions were only half-listened to as Marcus checked Sully over.

"No, no, he hasn't had an operation," Marcus replied gravely. "His chip is the same size as ours and besides, it's in his neck." Sully's missing patch of fur lay between his right eye and his nose. As the three of them took turns to soothe and examine him, Sully lay reluctantly and surprisingly still. Occasionally he kicked his back leg out in a pathetic sort of protest.

"Why is there no blood?" asked AJ, confused and relieved in equal measure.

"What's this?" Marcus lifted what at first seemed to be a flap of skin but turned out to be silicone to reveal a small lens. "Oh no," he breathed. "Quickly, children, go to Eloy's room!" As Marcus beckoned his children out of the kitchen, he shut the door behind them. The twins, thoroughly confused, waited for their father in Eloy's room. They could hear Sully barking in the kitchen — he had been locked in and sounded very displeased by the whole situation.

"Dad, what the heck is going on?" demanded AJ. Her jet-black hair was sticking out all over the place after their outdoor escapades and she angrily brushed it away from her face.

"Right, there's something you need to understand," Marcus whispered. "There were rumours, at least, I thought they were, about the Electi government monitoring Treb activity through... through their pets. Selling robot dogs and cats in place of real ones. Fitted with cameras and microphones and artificial — albeit low-level — intelligence to make them appear real."

"Oh... my... god." Eloy collapsed onto the bed as he tried to comprehend the fact that his dog was a government spy-bot.

"What do we do?" AJ asked resolutely.

"Nothing," Marcus urged. "If they know we've found out we'll be rounded up and sent to the factories. Trust me I've seen it done. Trebs ask too many questions and..." he trailed off, remembering friends he'd once known who had dared to question the government and mysteriously disappeared soon afterwards without so much as a postcard. "We must act as though nothing has changed. Though we'll have to make sure we're careful about what we say regarding the government. They'll be listening, they've *been* listening," he corrected himself. A panicked look flashed across his face as he said this, and the twins exchanged a worried glance. "Look, I need to go to work. Sort some things out, talk to Bruce. You two fix Sully up with some felt or something and explain to your mother — out of earshot — what's happened. I'll be back later." As he rushed out of the front door their mother, Leyna, came out of her bedroom, humming to herself with her headphones still in. She turned her music off at the sight of their horrified faces.

"My petals — what on earth has happened?"

Chapter 4

Curiouser and Curiouser

Eloy & AJ

As Leyna stood with her headphones askew, confusion all over her face, the twins weren't quite sure where to begin. AJ thought it best not to lead with the fact their dog was a robot but to soften the blow by saying he had run away but that he was 'all right now'. As she began to speak however, she was interrupted by a loud bang, not unlike the one that had scared Sully outside in the first place.

"What on earth?" The twins looked at each other and raced back out towards the train tracks before their mother could stop them, grabbing their respirators and locking Sully safely in the kitchen. The smoke was coming from what they thought was an abandoned public toilet. When they reached the door, they read the sign *'Danger: Electrical equipment stored within — Danger of DEATH'*. Finally catching up to her children and motioning them to stand well back, Leyna hesitantly opened the door. Through the crack, they could see a lot of flashing lights. Leyna crept inside.

"Mum! What if there's a fire?" Eloy shouted. "Something just exploded in there!"

"This was supposed to be empty," Leyna's voice came through the doorway. "There's an entire office in here!" The twins waited nervously as their mother looked around inside and breathed a sigh of relief when she emerged with what looked like several folders and an E-Scroll. AJ whistled, she had never seen an E-Scroll up close before and was desperate for a chance to use one. Leyna gave her daughter a look that clearly said 'don't even think about it' as she closed the door behind her.

"What's that Mum?" Eloy asked.

"These buildings were supposed to be old public toilets but that must be a cover-up — and not a very convincing one when you really look at it," Leyna replied, eyeing the antenna and satellite dish on the side of the building. "I suppose I just never thought to look that closely." She worriedly considered how long this building had been operating under potentially nefarious circumstances. She continued talking as she led her children back to the house. "Someone's shoved a load of paperwork and tech into a metal can and set fire to it. I got what I could rescue without burning myself, but your father needs to see this. Whatever it is, I doubt it's legal." As the three of them walked back into the flat, AJ suddenly remembered Sully, who was barking grumpily in the kitchen awaiting their return.

"Oh, um, Mum? There's something you should know about our dog."

The walk to school on Friday morning was a battle through torrential acid rain — a regular weather pattern of modern-day Anglia. The twins, in their matching yellow government-issue rain protection suits, sheltered beneath their mother's polka dot umbrella wrestling against the wind. Their best friend Mizuki stayed perfectly dry beneath an enormous golfing umbrella and white custom-designed rain suit. As they walked through the rainstorm, Eloy attempted to convey the previous night's events to Mizuki.

"So then we find out that our dog is a spy-bot!" Eloy shouted through their rain suits, "And Mum breaks into this burning building while AJ and I are outside freaking out!"

"Wow! What did she find inside?" Mizuki looked around to make sure nobody was listening. "You know I heard a Treb hacker group tried to break into the building so there had to be something important in there. I wonder if they got anything?"

"Mum didn't tell us what she found, she only said it probably wasn't legal," replied AJ as she wiped the iridescent rain from her visor with her sleeve. "Oh, for goodness' sake." She had finally given up on her mum's umbrella and given it to Eloy, darting under Mizuki's umbrella with her instead. Eloy had half expected Mizuki to kick his sister back out into the rain but she was too deep in thought to mind being dripped on. The rain suits protected against the acid rain but once it hit your visor it was nearly impossible to see through. Acid-proof umbrellas were the only solution other than staying indoors, which wasn't an option for the average Treb citizen with work or school to get to. The increasing rain made it impossible to continue their conversation until they'd arrived at school, by which time Mizuki had even more questions.

"So what else did your mum say? Did she know any more about your dog being a robot?"

"She was pretty confused, but then, we all were. I mean we knew Sully wasn't quite right, but nobody could have guessed he was running on Saturm 25 Home Edition! Dad still hasn't come back from work. If that's even where he is." Eloy was worried.

"We superglued some of Mum's fake fur boot lining over

his lens so hopefully whoever is watching just thinks his fluff is in the way. But at least this way they can't watch us anymore. I mean, that dog was in the room when I got dressed!" AJ shuddered, more from the thought of being spied on than from her cold, wet rain suit.

"So, you just have to keep acting like he's your pet and you don't even know?" Mizuki tied back her pastel purple hair and hung her umbrella on a nearby stand while she tried to untangle her friends' unbelievable story.

"Yeah, we just have to pretend we don't know anything. It's weird though." AJ trailed off as she watched a crowd of people pass by and decided they had better keep their voices down. She needn't have worried as the school bell interrupted any conversation they might have continued. The twins threw their rain suits into the decontamination hatch by the reception desk and headed to their cookery class while Mizuki headed to her Business Studies class. After an hour and a half of oily torture, they were finally released for break-time. Eloy thought it was a joke that they had to pay for the food they had just prepared as he grabbed his salad.

"How does a salad have two thousand calories in it? I mean, it's ninety per cent green stuff!"

"Quit complaining," AJ replied through a mouthful of fries. "Just get the chips instead — they have the same number of calories but taste ninety per cent nicer!" As AJ enjoyed her synthetic French fries, she saw a Treb boy walk past with a white bottle and felt a pang of guilt. At least in the Treb world AJ and Eloy's parents earned enough to afford food that actually looked like food. Many Treb children at the school could only afford the standard white and flavourless 'meal drinks' provided by the government to its poorest citizens in an attempt to appear charitable. They sat down in the courtyard next to Mizuki who was sipping a gigantic pink milkshake and furrowing her brow. AJ caught herself staring at her friend's tattoo sleeve again. It wasn't a real tattoo of course, as Mizuki was only sixteen, but every morning, Mizuki drew elaborate patterns and motifs all down her left arm. The sakura cherry blossoms and beautiful dragons were all inspired by her Japanese heritage. It was one of the most beautiful things AJ had ever seen.

"I've been thinking," Mizuki began. "What if my cat's a robot too? I mean, I know Mum's an Electi but Dad's a Treb, so you never know."

"Hunka-Munka — a robot? Wow, do you think they'd use cats as well? Crikey." AJ leant back in her chair as she wondered what other domesticated creatures might be packing modern technology. "Do you think maybe gerbils too? Oooh, imagine the tech you could stuff into a guinea pig." The others laughed. While AJ wasn't blessed with a wealth of common sense, she made up for it with a terrific sense of humour.

"How would you find out?" Eloy pressed her. "I mean, you can't just go home and say, 'Hey Mum, hey Dad, I think we should tear our tabby open and look for metal!'" He laughed at his own joke again.

"Obviously I wouldn't do that! I'd be clever." Mizuki leaned in closer and lowered her voice.

"You know those micro-cameras you can get? I'll just feed her one mixed in with her dinner. Then I'll see exactly what's inside her!"

"Ew, Mizuki, that's gross! Cat innards!"

"Or synthetic cat innards. Either way, I need to know."

"When are you going to do it?"

"I'll ask my mum to order me one on Zoom2U. With her Electi account, she can get it delivered within an hour, so I can do it tonight. I don't want that tubby tabby spying on me for any longer than is necessary."

Archie & Eva

The Impero-Regnum children were waiting for their technology teacher, Miss Perl, to arrive when Wendoline, waddled in. She flopped down onto one of her many child-sized chaise-lounges and began to snore, her caramel fur glistening in the bright lamplight.

"Stupid thing," Atticus grumbled. "I wish I could just sleep and eat all day and get away with it. I'm sick of these evening classes."

"Well, why don't you?" Archie offered. "I'd certainly be grateful to have to see less of you." Atticus was about to hit his younger brother over the head with a table lamp when their mother, Lady Margot, entered.

"Your technology lesson is cancelled this evening, children. Miss Perl is... indisposed. You will be given a new tutor in the coming weeks." Archie made a noise of surprise and rose to his feet.

"But Miss Perl was the only decent tutor we had!" he protested. "She was young, she was relatable... she was really pretty." Margot gave her son a disapproving look.

"Well, she's been let go." She turned on her heel and left the room. Wendoline snored herself awake with a surprised jolt and waddled out after her, in the hope of more sausages. Eva sighed and tried not to think about the millions of starving Anglian Trebs as her obese dog turned the corner.

"What now?" Archie moaned, but his siblings ignored him. Atticus was looking at his hair in the mirror and Eva turned to her holophone, apparently deep in thought. "Seriously does nobody want to know why she got fired?"

"Of course I do, Archie, but if you'll give me five seconds. Look, I've found something," Eva sent a webpage to her brother's holophone. "Here." Archie read the news article, trying to ignore his sister's patronising gaze.

SABOTAGE AT DATA-RETRIEVAL STATION BY UNDERGROUND HACKER SECT

"Yesterday evening, at 19.25, a government data-retrieval station was broken into, hacked and destroyed by the rebel Treb group calling themselves 'The Trebble Makers'."

Archie chuckled. "That's quite clever!" His sister motioned him to read on.

"A letter was posted to Electi headquarters signed with their signature star, informing the government of their intent to carry out further attacks if their demands were not met. The government has declined to disclose these demands. The data-retrieval station was situated in the village of Littlebourne and was used to collect information on the local environment and its recovery. The leader of the group, Siri Perl, is now on the run, facing the death penalty for her crimes."

Archie's jaw dropped. Atticus let go of his mirror and it smashed on the floor. Just as he was about to let out a barrage of curse words that would have made his mother blush, their father stormed in.

"What do you know?" he demanded. "She must have told you something! Devious little snake!" His eyes seemed to spark with rage as he glowered at his retreating family.

"We don't know anything, Father, you must know that?" Atticus protested as he cleared up the broken glass.

"I don't know anything anymore!" he ranted. "In my own home. MY OWN HOME!" He picked up the table lamp previously meant for Archie and tossed it against the wall whereupon it shattered, adding to the broken glass already on the floor. Lady Margot hurried in at the commotion.

"Darling, what in the world is going on?"

"I'm confiscating all of your holophones," he barked. "Give me your hands. NOW." The children begrudgingly presented their microchipped hands, allowing their father to scan their chips and remove their holophone privileges. "Yours too," he sneered at his wife. The look in her eyes was a mixture of fear and loathing as she reluctantly gave her husband her hand. As he left the room, Eva took Archie's trembling hand in hers.

"It's going to be okay," Eva whispered to her brother. "We're going to be okay."

Chapter 5

Curiosity Nearly Killed the Cat

Eloy & AJ

Their afternoon classes passed in a blur as the trio's heads collectively span with questions about robotic pets and secret cameras. Their 'modern technology class' — ironically named as all the school's technology was at least ten years old — was spent theorising about other animals that might be kitted out with cameras. AJ was still set on guinea pigs whereas Eloy thought that birds would make the best spies due to their higher vantage point. While animal life was generally extinct, a surprising number of people had managed to shelter their pets with them during the war, meaning that, while difficult, it was still possible to own domesticated animals. Of course, they came at a price and generally were only affordable by Electi citizens. After school, the three of them went their separate ways — Mizuki back home to conduct her micro-camera experiment; Eloy to the holo chess club and AJ to her athletics club. It was important to their parents that the twins received a well-rounded education to give them the best chance in life. It did mean, however, that it was usually dark by the time they got home. School days were getting longer with new Electi legislation, in an attempt to keep up with the rising grades of the ESA schools, and the twins were always exhausted before they even reached their after-school clubs. They still managed to excel in their respective fields, however. Eloy remained the champion of the holo chess league and AJ could run faster than anyone else in the school. Once, Marcus even encouraged his daughter to go easy on the others — in case they became suspicious. AJ couldn't understand what there was to be suspicious of and resented any implication that she should give less than her best, so Marcus let it go. But he always looked a little worried when she was smiling on the first-place podium every Sports Day.

When the twins finally arrived home from school, any thoughts of the insides of Mizuki's cat quickly vanished from their minds upon seeing their father's face. "Sit down kids. I need to tell you something." Silently, Eloy and AJ sat at the kitchen table opposite their father, wondering what else could go wrong besides their robot dog and a burning building in their back garden. "It's about that building that caught fire. What your mother found inside — it was government tech. Bruce and I managed to recover some data from the laptop and found some pretty frightening stuff."

"It just gets better and better."

"AJ, this is serious. We're on a watchlist. Because of when you two were born — it shouldn't have been possible because of the infertility crisis. So, they've been monitoring us. That's why that building was kitted out with tech and why Sully was found by us. They wanted us to find him so that they could…" he trailed off and looked out of the window to check that Sully was still playing outside and out of earshot. "We've got to be extremely careful. If anyone ever found out I had this information—"

"But we didn't steal it!" Eloy protested. "Mum rescued it

from a burning building!"

"I know but they'll never believe we weren't part of the hacker group that broke in. We're too involved now. So, I'm going to hide it. I can't tell you where — that way they can't question you if they find out. But we need to be extremely careful."

Nobody spoke for some time. A notification on AJ's holophone broke the silence. "Oh, it's Mizuki. She's done it."

"Done what?" Leyna asked.

"She fed Hunka-Munka a micro-camera to see if she's a robot. Turns out that no, she's just a regular cat, but from the looks of her stomach, she's been eating one too many simulated fish fingers. Mizuki's going to stick her on her mum's treadmill." Leyna looked surprised for a moment before bursting into laughter. Marcus, while trying to maintain the severity of the situation, broke soon afterwards and began to chuckle.

"Honestly," he said, "you've got to laugh really." He smiled at his family and they embraced. "It's going to be okay. We have each other."

"Plus, we're going to the finals tomorrow!" AJ sang as she spun around in delight. "The Anglian Angels versus the ESA Elites!" Being the only two remaining stable nations on Earth, an international disuku game was a hugely popular occurrence. Mizuki's mother, being an Electi, had managed to secure early-release tickets for Marcus to take the twins and her daughter.

"Oh, that's right! Goodness, I nearly forgot about that! Well, then we're going to want an early night. Up early for the train tomorrow!" The twins kissed their mother and father on the cheek before heading off to brush their teeth. As they left the room, Marcus and Leyna looked at each other.

"Do you think we should tell them?" Leyna asked her husband. He looked away.

"No. No, it's safer if they don't know. Not until they have to."

In the bathroom, AJ sat on the edge of the bath as Eloy brushed his teeth. Her microchip was beeping at her, but she was ignoring it.

"You need to brush too, or it won't stop," Eloy garbled through a mouthful of toothpaste. AJ sighed and picked up her toothbrush.

"Why us, Eloy? Why do you think we were born?" Eloy spat out the rest of the toothpaste and rinsed.

"Well," he began. "Sometimes I think that it's because Mum eats so healthily — when we can afford to — you know? I sometimes think that it was just luck. But really, who knows? I'm just glad we were born." AJ nodded in agreement as she hastily brushed her teeth. "I don't see why we need to be monitored, though, I mean it's not as though we planned to survive an infertility crisis! Do they think we're dangerous or something?" Eloy asked as AJ spat out her toothpaste.

"Maybe," she began. "Or maybe we have some sort of special cure in our blood that would improve the birth rate again? It never fully recovered, did it?" she asked.

"No, it didn't — but then why not just call us in for mandatory testing? They've done that with loads of things before, like for the people who survived that pandemic in the 2020s." Eloy headed towards his room and AJ followed behind.

"It is weird that we are the only fifteen-year-olds in school — in the village even. Don't you ever think about it?" she mused, leaning against Eloy's door frame.

"Well of course I do, AJ, but it's a rabbit hole I'm not sure I want to go down. I'd rather think about things I can understand. Like chess and political science." He laughed at AJ's expression. "What do you think about then?" he asked her.

AJ thought for a moment. "Disuku, being in a rock band and Sophie Lavine." She gave her brother a mischievous smile. He was confused.

"Wait… Who's Sophie Lavine?"

"Kids, go to bed! Our train leaves at seven thirty tomorrow morning!" Marcus' voice from the other room put an end to their conversation and they said their goodnights, both now full of excitement for the following day.

Archie & Eva

The Impero-Regnum children were under even stricter house arrest since the discovery that their former tutor was a traitor to the government. Their classes for the day had been cancelled and their father was doing damage control on the Trebble Makers attack. Eva decided to use her free time to write a letter to her father explaining why he should not have taken her holophone and that, frankly, he had trust issues. Atticus and Archie were playing disuku again. Archie may have been banned from the sport but, as far as he was concerned, what his father didn't know couldn't hurt him. Besides, Atticus couldn't play it on his own and the last time he had tried to play with the butler, poor Samuel had nearly lost an eye. Disuku was a game that originated in the early twenty-thirties, just before the war, and was now easily the most popular sport in the world. The pitch was a large cuboid enclosed in either plexiglass or a force field depending on your budget. The area was filled with moving non-lethal lasers and the object of the game was to get the disc (disuku) into the goal without being hit by a laser. If you were, the disuku was flung into the air and free to be claimed by the opposing team. The disuku was holographic and projected by a wrist device worn by the player. The Impero-Regnum's personal pitch was stadium size, which made it difficult when the usual five-person team consisted of one teenage boy. Atticus liked to use brute force to knock Archie out of his way, but Archie was fast and often managed to dodge both his brother and the lasers.

"Goooaaaaal!" Archie bragged as the disuku flew elegantly into the small post-box-shaped goal. "What is that now, ten points to me, two to you? Oh dear, brother, I believe that means I win!" Atticus was not happy. Usually, he would express this feeling with his fists, but he was currently stuck between the outer force field of the disuku pitch and their gymnasium wall.

"I'd run if I were you, Archie," called Eva from the study next door. Archie agreed, as Atticus was looking angrier with every minute he was stuck, and Archie retreated to join his sister.

"Eva," he asked. "Do you think Dad's gone... a bit... you know..."

"Crazy?" she offered.

"Now that's unkind. I just mean that he's behaving even more erratically than usual."

"He's just under a lot of stress. But yes, I have concerns." It was at that moment that Atticus, red-faced and seething, burst into the room and charged at Archie.

"Be right back," Archie joked and dashed out towards the garden.

"Atticus, STOP!" Eva called sternly. Atticus turned to look

at his sister, daggers in his eyes. "You're behaving just like Father," she scolded. "Can't you ever learn to calm down?" Atticus walked towards her, his fists clenched. "Atticus, please, don't hurt me." Her voice was wavering now. Luckily, Archie couldn't resist coming back to see why he hadn't been pursued.

"Oi! Atticus! Leave her alone!" This was enough. Atticus turned and chased Archie out of the room, leaving Eva shaking in her seat.

"That's it," she breathed. "I've got to get out of here."

"Well, here's your chance!" Eva jumped as her mother waltzed through the door in a scarlet floor-length gown. "Where are your brothers?"

"Probably killing each other. Why?"

"Your father thinks it would be good publicity to be seen at the disuku finals."

"You mean we'd get to leave the house?" Eva's eyes glittered.

"With your father and me, yes." Her heart fell. She knew their father wouldn't let them out of his sight. But it was something at least. As Lady Margot went to fetch her warring sons, Eva folded up her E-Scroll and put it into her pocket. "She's going to need my help," she sighed and followed her mother towards the garden.

Marcus & Leyna

"They were watching them, weren't they?" Leyna asked, nervously. "Do they know? Do they know what they can do?" Marcus put a hand on his wife's arm.

"There's no evidence of that. But they are certainly suspicious." He looked grave. "We may have to relocate.

Things are heating up at work and I'm not sure how long I can keep everything buried. Their security and monitoring are just getting better and better."

"I just want to keep them safe." Leyna held back tears. "We've been so careful."

"I know," Marcus whispered. "It's okay, we won't move unless we need to. We're so settled here." He stroked his wife's arm. "There's something else," he added. Leyna looked up, curious. "There may be others. Others like Eloy and AJ."

Leyna gasped. "We have to find them!" she exclaimed. "Marcus, we have to find them."

He nodded. "I know."

Chapter 6

The Disuku World Cup 2062

Eloy & AJ — Archie & Eva

It was an early start. The twins boarded the seven thirty train to New London with their dad and their friend Mizuki. It was a half-hour journey from Littlebourne and they passed the time by playing games on their holophones and updating their fantasy disuku line-ups. AJ also couldn't resist snapping photos of the passing landscape and uploading them to her Xchange social media profile. She and Mizuki were in constant competition for the most followers and AJ was currently winning. As they ascended the hill to the sparkling city, AJ looked eagerly out of the window, her hands pressed against the glass window. New London had been built on top of the remains of Old London, which had been bulldozed after being largely destroyed by the war and post-war riots. The historical buildings had been preserved in secure force fields to prevent further damage and underneath the new city lay a vast network of tunnels used by the city's all-Treb municipal workforce. AJ loved looking for any remnants of the old city which could be seen on the outskirts.

"Look! You can see an old supermarket!"

"Pah," Eloy scoffed. "Can you believe people used to spend hours shopping — in person?"

"Yeah, it's pretty weird. Think of all that wasted time! I

don't know what I'd do if I needed something I couldn't get from Zoom2U." AJ watched the old city slowly grow into the new, dazzling capital that had been built after the war. Tall, golden buildings gave little indication of the post-war slump but instead served to 'show off' to any other surviving nations that 'we're doing just fine in Anglia, thank you very much'. AJ gazed in wonder at the crowds of (mostly Electi) citizens going about their daily business; zipping from building to building in great glass tunnels to shield them from the ever-increasing spells of acid rain. Eloy was still peering backwards as the last remnants of Old London disappeared from view.

"Oh wow, an old car dealership! No cars though." Due to alarming pollution levels, all non-electric cars had been destroyed in a last-ditch attempt to save the dying planet. Many Electi citizens used self-driving electric E-cars, but the Trebs were lucky if they could afford one.

Electi citizens were also permitted to use the ultra-high-speed monorail service, which was far more efficient than any car, while Trebs were restricted to the train. Marcus had an E-car for work purposes but was not allowed to use it elsewhere, and they had become far too expensive for him to afford on his or his wife's Treb salary.

Meanwhile, in the president's private monorail car, Archie and Eva were doing their best to ignore the rest of their family by playing virtual cards on Eva's E-Scroll. "Snap!" Eva cried out happily.

"Wait, we were playing snap?" Archie asked. Eva sighed at her little brother and folded up her E-Scroll. They didn't live very far from the stadium, but the government monorail line dropped them off directly into their private box. This box encircled the entire pitch and was on the third floor. Their father liked to look down on his citizens, both literally and figuratively. In this presidential box there was a dining table and chairs; three Chesterfield sofas overlooking the pitch; a private kitchen with their personal chef; an old-fashioned chess table (their father liked to play); a virtual-reality gaming booth; a bar; a seventy-two-inch holovision and a private bathroom. There was even a chaise lounge for Wendoline, who always enjoyed her outings to the stadium as the chef would give her scraps of liver and black pudding. The game wasn't due to start for several hours but Ignatius liked to arrive before, as he called them, 'the riff-raff'. Several hours later, as the Impero-Regnums were tucking into their three-course breakfasts and making themselves comfortable, the Kahn family were walking towards the CT&T disuku Stadium from the train station. The closer they got, the louder the billboards became, blaring out their trademark phrases, 'CT&T — Anglia's number one holophone service provider' and 'CT&T — Giving you coffee, talk and technology!' AJ scoffed. "Everyone knows that Moon Media are better."

"Not in this country," Eloy replied. "They're big in the ESA but CT&T controls the Anglian market."

"Ugh," Marcus groaned, "Enough tech-talk you two, it's nearly game time!" Marcus led the way through the Treb turnstiles with the others following behind. He sent his children to find their seats while he grabbed them all some food from one of the many Burger Moon kiosks surrounding the stadium. He had ordered it on his holophone but unlike the Electi level, Trebs didn't get table service.

Archie peered down over the pitch from the family box. He whistled.

"Look at all the people! I've never seen it this full!" His eyes darted between the lower Treb level seating and the upper Electi level seating. It was impossible not to notice the differences. While the Electi level provided plush armchair-style seating and a variety of restaurants, the Treb level consisted of metal benches and fast-food kiosks. Archie wrinkled his nose.

"Depressing, isn't it?" Eva commented. Archie jumped. He hadn't noticed his sister walk up to him.

"Um, yeah. It just seems wrong. All this segregation."

"Children, back from the edge!" called Ignatius. "Don't let the riff-raff see you spying on them or we'll have a riot on our hands."

"Did you see that?" Eloy pointed up to the president's box. "I think the president's kids are here!"

"Well, I'd be surprised if they weren't," AJ muttered apathetically. "It's the match of the year. Everyone who's— ouch!" AJ stopped as a falling apple core hit the side of her head, shattering one of the lenses in her glasses.

As AJ brushed the broken glass from her lap, Eloy glared up at the giggling group of Electi men above them. "Ugh, they're like children. Don't they know how much glasses repairs cost on Treb medical care?"

"They're not like children," protested AJ. "Children aren't so cruel." She looked up at the men as she said this, a steely gaze in her eyes. Mizuki giggled but couldn't help feeling torn. Her half-Electi status had helped her to secure tickets for the event but she was still only permitted in Treb areas. This meant she never missed the anti-Electi commentary and was,

59

occasionally, on the receiving end of it.

"Here you go, team!" Marcus passed a jumbo box of faux-chicken nuggets to Eloy and Mizuki, while he and AJ each had a Moon Burger Deluxe. "AJ honey, what happened to your glasses?"

"Don't ask," she mumbled through a mouthful of burger.

"Oh, Evangeline, you simply must try the foie gras! It's to die for!" Atticus drawled, gravy dripping from his mouth.

"I'm watching the pre-game show, Atticus! Emily Chel is singing the international anthem!"

"Suit yourself." Atticus and Archie were no longer on speaking terms after their fight and Archie was sporting a black eye. He walked over to his sister and looked down at the entertainment below.

"Hey, Eva, do you think we'd be able to see her better from the lower level?"

"Well yeah but we can't go down there, you know that. We'd be recognised."

"Not among the Trebs. We're never allowed amongst them, so they'd never think it was us! Plus, you know they have fast food down there! I never get to try it, please, Evie?"

"Are you insane? Father would crucify us!" Eva looked horrified.

"Not if he doesn't find out — he's in the backroom playing chess with Corey Moon," Archie muttered. "They're probably rubbing their hands together discussing how much money they are going to make from streaming the game exclusively to Moon Media customers. Not to mention the huge number of people ordering from Moon Burger while they watch the game. It's a good day to be Corey Moon."

"Corey Moon is the President of the ESA, Archie — every

60

day is a good day to be Corey Moon." Eva pointed out sarcastically.

"Good point," Archie conceded, "but what a distraction, eh? Father will never notice we've gone!"

"But even if we do make it down to the lower levels, our clothes don't exactly look like they come from the Treb section." Eva mused as she began to consider the possibility of her brother's scheme.

"Aha!" Like a magician's assistant, Archie presented Eva with two Anglian Angels vest tops and matching baseball caps. "I also have sweatpants!" He grinned, beaming with excitement. Eva was so impressed with her brother's rare display of forethought that she did something rather out of character.

"You know what? Let's do it." She smiled.

"Really? You never want to join in on my schemes!" Archie hadn't thought Eva would agree, and was momentarily panicked that he, therefore, hadn't thought out any further stages of the plan.

"That's because your schemes are usually stupid, Archie. Now come on before I change my mind!"

Eloy tried not to knock over his bucket of nuggets as he stood up for the international anthem. It was a decent tune, but the words seemed a little hollow in his opinion.

'With the new era's dawn
  From a war born of scorn
  Two great nations rose up and took charge.

The Moon and the Star,
  Built a world better far,

And restored the great order at large.'

Eloy took a nugget from the box, popped it into his mouth and replaced his hand over his heart, conscious of the repercussions of being seen not doing so. As the anthem ended, AJ tapped her brother on the shoulder and gestured to the exit. Confused, Eloy followed.

"What's up? We're missing Emily Chel."

"I wanted a milkshake."

"And why do you need me for that?"

"I need you to carry my ice cream," AJ pleaded.

"You're unbelievable," he muttered, reluctantly following his sister. They walked towards the nearest kiosk and joined the queue. In front of them were a boy and a girl of about the same age. Eloy couldn't help but look at the girl, her long brunette hair glinting in the iridescent lighting. The pair were discussing the paradox of having kiosks of the rival Moon Media business within the CT&T stadium.

"I suppose it's about keeping your enemy where you can see them. CT&T know they've got a monopoly on the media over here, but they also know that people love Moon burgers. It's just good business sense. But what I don't understand," the girl went on, "is why you're making us eat from one of them."

"Because Father never lets us eat fast food and it's my favourite!"

"Mine too!" AJ interjected. Eloy looked witheringly at his sister. She always liked to try and make friends at inappropriate moments.

"What's your favourite?" the boy asked AJ. "The Moon Burger Deluxe or the Full Moon Fries?"

"Duh — both!" she replied grinning. While Eloy shook his

head, the girl in front of them met his gaze.

"Siblings — am I right?" she offered.

"Uh, yeah. How did you know that?"

"Lucky guess… and you two do look awfully alike. My name's E—" she stopped abruptly. "Enid. I'm Enid."

"Eloy. Pleased to meet you." They exchanged shy smiles. Eloy went to ask Enid if she was from around here, but a large tub of mint chocolate ice cream was shoved into his hands. "Come on, Eloy, the game's about to start!" Eloy turned around to say goodbye to Enid, but her brother was pulling her away.

"Oh, AJ!"

"What?"

"That girl…" he trailed off as Enid disappeared into the crowd, his heart feeling much lighter than usual.

"Archie, we need to be more careful!" Eva scolded as they sat in a dark corner with their Moon Burgers to watch Emily Chel.

"Me?" Archie scoffed. "Oh, excuse me, I'm Enid, pleased to meet you!" he mocked.

"Well, I couldn't very well tell him my real name now, could I? Besides, I've never met a Treb before."

"You fancied him, didn't you?"

"Oh, shut up!" Eva kicked her brother under the table in her annoyance, forcing him to lose his grip on his lunch.

"No! My burger!"

"Oh, have mine. I've lost my appetite anyway." As Archie happily munched his Moon Burger, Eva thought about the Treb boy. Father had always told her Trebs were dangerous. That they only wanted violence and the destruction of the Electi. But this boy — she had only seen sweetness in his eyes. Once Archie had finished his feast and the pre-show entertainment had concluded, they returned stealthily to the Electi-only area where they changed back into their normal clothes. As they tiptoed through the service corridor that led to their private floor, Evangeline suddenly stopped.

"What's up?" Archie asked, confused by the sudden interruption. Eva was looking curiously at a metal panel which seemed to be coming away from the wall. Through the small gap, Archie could see a sliver of light and a staircase.

"What do you think is up there?" Eva asked aloud.

"Dunno," shrugged Archie. "Probably just electrics and stuff. Before he could stop her, however, Eva had swung the panel open on its door-like hinges and crept through the gap. Archie reluctantly followed, sneaking past the metal panel, up the stairs and into what turned out to be a long corridor with low ceilings. "Woah," Archie breathed, "this must be a secret level in between the Electi level and our box."

Eva nodded in agreement. "That must be why the ceiling is so low." The walls were covered in old paper posters, depicting the influx of refugees after the war. Archie stared in disbelief at one particular poster which depicted the refugees as werewolf-like creatures, attacking and killing what appeared to be Anglian citizens. The poster's slogan read 'The Electi Government: The only line of defence in the new world'. "What is all this?" Archie asked.

"Government propaganda," Eva replied, deep in thought while looking at a poster of her father. "After the war, Father used these to try and rally support for his government.

"…and people believed it?" Archie was shocked, gaping open-mouthed at a poster depicting foreign children as viruses coming to infect Anglian children.

"People were scared," Eva stated sadly. "The war changed

everything — people thought they were going to die. I suppose the fear was that the refugees would bring the radiation with them?" she offered.

Archie walked to the next poster, passing a room filled with what looked like surveillance equipment and live feeds of some sort of prison facility. He would have stopped to investigate but a poster of an angry mob of zombie-like creatures caught his eye. "It's so gross, surely people can't have seen other people this way. Like they were animals. Monsters, even?"

"You mean the way Father looks at Trebs?" Eva's voice was as cold as the empty corridor. "Father built his government out of fear. Fear of the unknown and the 'different'. That's what keeps it going. The constant fear that there won't be enough resources — so he plays the Trebs against us, keeping us afraid and looking to him to provide for his Electi citizens. You know something, Archie, I really am starting to think that we're on the wrong side here." As Archie considered this grave possibility, a door slammed nearby. Footsteps began to grow closer and after a quick panicked look at each other, Archie and Eva silently retreated to the entrance of the corridor.

"What was that place?" Archie asked.

"I don't know," Eva replied, deep in thought, "but we need to get back upstairs before Father notices we're missing. They stashed their disguises in a duffel bag and began climbing the stairs to their family box, but before they could reach the top, a shadow fell over them.

"Well, well, well I can't wait to hear what you've been up to!" Atticus was standing in front of them, folding his arms and grinning smugly. Archie muttered something unrepeatable and Eva scowled. As Atticus led his disgraced siblings back upstairs, their minds raced to try and think up a plausible excuse. Their father was, predictably, furious.

"What the hell were you thinking? You could have been seen — you could have been kidnapped! Do you have any idea of the paperwork I could have faced?" His eyes appeared to be sparking again.

"Paperwork?" This was too much for Eva. "So, if we'd been kidnapped, the biggest concern on your mind would have been paperwork?" Her father's eyes narrowed.

"With the way you are acting, can you blame me?"

"I hate you," she whispered.

"Excuse me, Evangeline?"

"I hate you!" This time she screamed it so loudly that Archie thought it must have been audible from the Treb level.

"In the back room, now. Both of you!" Ignatius strong-armed both of his children into the windowless room in the corner of the box and locked the door. Archie sat down and sulked in the corner, silently blaming his sister's sudden courage for their predicament. Eva sat by the door, refusing her urge to cry. She had always known that their father hadn't really cared about them, but she couldn't stand by and be treated this way anymore. Her outburst, however, was certainly going to have lasting repercussions.

Eloy and AJ returned to their seats just as the game began, with the customary siren and laser show. AJ's eyes sparkled. This was her dream — to represent her country and lead her team to victory. She knew all the player's moves and knew what they would do before they even did. The Anglian Angels made a promising start. Team Captain Natasha Jay managed to dodge four of the ESA Elites and six lasers to make it to the scoring zone. Unfortunately, just as she went to shoot, the remaining

ESA Elite player slammed into the side of her and she fell into a laser, forfeiting possession.

"Foul! That was a Foul!" AJ was incensed. The AI referee allowed it and play carried on. By halftime, the score was 4-0 to the Elites and it didn't look good.

"They always win," muttered Mizuki. "It's not our fault they have better training facilities over there!"

"And more money to spend on the sport," Marcus added. Meanwhile, AJ was staring down one of her least favourite Elite players and wishing the pitch lasers weren't quite so harmless. The siren sounded for the second half and AJ could hardly watch. The Angels suffered three more goals against them and with ten minutes to go, the Angels goalkeeper Owen Dobson was hit by a flying elbow pad and knocked unconscious. It was a humiliating defeat, and it was with heavy hearts that they left the stadium and headed back for the train. Meanwhile, on the top floor, Eva and Archie were let out of their temporary prison and escorted back to their private monorail car. Nobody was speaking and Ignatius looked as though he wanted to hurt someone. Only Atticus seemed to be in a good mood as his disgraced siblings were marched towards their seats.

"Don't you just love a family outing?" Archie smiled weakly.

Chapter 7

Suspicious Minds

It was the end of winter and finally, the bitter ash snow and freezing acid rain were starting to subside. Christmas — now less of a holiday than a welcome excuse to stay indoors and splash out on simulated roast turkey flavoured meal drinks — had been a merry affair in the Kahn household. Sully had even been given a blue woolly hat which the family secretly hoped would muffle any sound from reaching his internal microphone.

The Impero-Regnum family had, of course, dined on their usual five-course Christmas dinner, the centrepiece of which being the 'turducken' — their private farm's prize turkey, stuffed with both duck and chicken. Eva thought this was an affront to all the poor citizens of Anglia, as well as the poor birds who had to die to create it. Their technology lessons had been taken over by a young man with red glasses with whom Archie developed an unlikely friendship, considering his authoritative role. They seemed to share the same sense of humour, much to the annoyance of Atticus and Eva.

The Treb school term began in a haze of optimism as the days grew longer and the pavements cleared of snow. The twins still engaged in hushed conversations with Mizuki about the mystery of the burning building and Eva continued to warn Archie of their father's questionable exploits, but life continued with the dull monotony of modern-day Anglia into early Spring.

It was every Treb's least-favourite class — CPU (City Protection and Upkeep). This was essentially a glorified form of community service in which Treb students were required to patrol, clean and maintain their designated public 'zones'. Once again, Mizuki had used her half Electi status to avoid this, but Eloy and AJ spent every Thursday afternoon scrubbing graffiti from the walls of the closed-down Indian restaurant.

"Ugh. Racist idiots," Eloy grunted through his respirator as he frantically brushed off the words 'Go home'.

"I mean how stupid can they be? India doesn't even exist anymore!" The twins took their anger out on the dilapidated building, silently wondering why they were even bothering to clean a place that wasn't even in use.

In the post-war financial slump, many businesses had closed. Especially, suspiciously, businesses owned by immigrants. It wasn't a coincidence and it was, in fact, an open secret that life had become more difficult for those wishing to live in Anglia who hailed from overseas. The pay gap was widening with the government using a tactic of low pay and racist propaganda to force any foreigners out. More than anything, this contributed to the highest level of homelessness Anglia had ever seen, with the old village of Littlebourne a local refuge for those with nothing left.

AJ and Eloy walked past the shelters sometimes, their hearts aching for the families forced to live in the ruins of the old buildings without so much as a respirator to protect them from the elements. They saw some of them at school, slowly wasting away from the radiation. It was heart-breaking — but what could they do? Their parents could barely make enough to pay their rent as it was. "Can you imagine?" AJ mused. "If everyone with any foreign blood was chucked out? There'd be no one left!"

"Well, we'd be the first ones kicked out. A Polish mother and a Pakistani father — we'd have no chance." As they continued scrubbing, a pristine white E-Car full of Electi teenagers sped past. The twins ignored their abusive words, but they couldn't avoid the flying smoothie.

"UGH!" It had hit AJ squarely in the back of the head. "How bad is it?" she asked her brother. "Tell me honestly," she pleaded.

Eloy hesitated. "I think it's one of those exclusive faux-avocado ones," he said, while carefully wiping some of the green goo from his sister's hair.

"Oh no, the green one that looks like slime?" AJ whined.

"That's the one."

"Fan-freaking-tastic." Her sarcasm wasn't lost on Eloy, and her foul mood continued well into their lunch break. When she sat down next to Mizuki, the force of her tray hitting the table sent her milkshake flying.

"No! Not my computer! This model isn't waterproof!" Mizuki hurriedly wiped away the pink liquid from her portable surface computer while AJ apologised repeatedly. "My data... I think it's okay."

"What data?" asked Eloy, intrigued.

"Well ever since the whole pet-bot fiasco," she began, "I've been doing a little digging into my mum's Electi files."

"Oh no," Eloy sighed, "What is it with you girls and hacking? Leave it alone! You'll only get into trouble." Mizuki ignored him and carried on.

"I found out that there are only a handful of people with pet-based surveillance — including you two." Eloy nodded. This made sense with what his father had told them about being amongst only a handful of Anglian children born in 2047. He wondered whether all of those children were under surveillance and if so, why. "I also found out," Mizuki continued, "that I am actually under a different kind of monitoring due to my friendship with you two!"

"What? Why does being our friend make them want to watch you? We're not that interesting," AJ joked.

"And what is 'a different kind of monitoring' exactly?" Eloy was troubled.

"Well I've been trying to decrypt the files all day but It's harder than I expected. I managed to work out that my location is being tracked via my chip, but I already suspected that much. There's also this shady project my mum is involved in. 'Project Libertas'. She's got a bunch of files about it but they're all in some kind of code."

"You ought to be careful looking at that stuff," warned Eloy. "If they're monitoring you, they aren't going to want you poking around in their files."

"Oh, they aren't going to know, it's just my mum's stuff. She's not very high up in the Electi order so it can't be all that secret — whatever it is she's doing." Mizuki wiped the last of the milkshake from her computer and stood up to leave for her next class. Unfortunately, she hadn't realised there was still a puddle of milkshake underneath her and she slipped over backwards, hitting her head on the edge of the table.

"Mizuki!" AJ quickly leapt down to her friend's side.

"It's okay... I'm fi—ouch."

"You need to get to the school nurse," AJ insisted.

"Yeah, yeah. Okay," Mizuki conceded.

"Do you want me to help you?"

"No, AJ, honestly, I'm fine. You need to get to history anyway. Tell Ms Draiken I'll be a little late, will you?" As Mizuki hobbled weakly towards the nurse's office, the twins made their way to their history class. History was a joint Electi and Treb class led by Ms Draiken, a short but stocky woman with permed ginger hair. She always liked to push the boundaries of the staff dress code and was currently sporting a full-leopard print romper suit, complete with a leather jacket and boots.

"Wow. Can you imagine if Mum went to work like that?" AJ asked, shaking her head in disbelief.

"Well, that's why she's at an Electi school and Ms Draiken is stuck here teaching us Trebs!" Eloy replied.

"Quiet please," Ms Draiken peered at them through her bright purple glasses. "Today the powers that be have decided we need to be reminded about the history of the Electi as a society, class and government. Riveting," she muttered. "So, everybody, follow this link and find the information page on your desks. I want all of you to have written at least one thousand words by the time I've finished painting my nails." With that, she promptly sat down and sniffed a half-empty bottle of red nail varnish.

The collective groan of the class reverberated around the mobile hut serving as a classroom. Eloy turned his attention to his desk. As a Treb school, their budget only extended to the old surface computers that had been there for years. They were good enough, but Eloy wished they could have had the full-booth surface computers of the Electi schools. With those, you were encased by three screens and could complete multiple tasks per surface. The old desk computers were still running on the old operating system — Saturm 8 School Edition — and suffered from frequent crashes if you tried to do more than one thing at a time. Eloy swiped open the document and reluctantly began to read.

Electi: Our Proud History

1964: Atticus Impero-Regnum I creates the 'Society of the Electi' at Oxford University. Atticus hand-picks members from the wealthiest and most influential students and professors. They host society dinners with influential and powerful people, including members of government, and as time goes by, the society grows.

As Atticus makes his way in the world of business and politics, he offers paid subscription to the society to those who can afford it. Many of its members are CEOs in the most powerful corporations and banks and many are important members of the government. Eventually, Atticus Impero-Regnum becomes Chief Whip and Electi society members make up 60% of the elected government. By 2035, following the war, his son Ignatius had succeeded him and secured the position of President of the Anglian government. At this time the Electi has over 750,000 members.

"Can you believe it?" AJ whispered. "All of this class division because of one guy?"

"One guy who decided that he was better than everyone else just because he'd been lucky enough to be born into money," Eloy muttered darkly, checking to see that Ms Draiken couldn't see them talking.

"Do you think we'd have been different if we were rich?" AJ asked, allowing her mind to wander into a world of all-you-can-eat buffets and front row seats at disuku matches.

"I don't know," Eloy replied, now thinking about the sort of careers he could access if he were rich. "I'd like to think we'd still have been the same down-to-earth, lovable people we are now." He smiled at his sister, but his break in concentration had cost them both.

"So," came the sarcastic voice of Ms Draiken. "The Kahn children feel as though one thousand words is too easy for them, do they?" Eloy and AJ abruptly stopped talking and Eloy cursed himself for his momentary lapse in vigilance. "Let's make that two thousand then. She smiled a wicked grin, showing each of her five gold teeth as she did so. "Where is that half-class girl — Mizuki something? She's over half an hour late."

"She's with the nurse Ms Draiken," Eloy replied. "She hit her head."

"Well it shouldn't take that long to sort out — is her chip not working? It'll shoot her some painkillers and she'll be fine. Honestly, all of this fussing nowadays — we don't even need a school nurse," she replied. "That'll be at least half an hour's detention after school to catch up."

"Ugh, what a dragon," AJ grumbled under her breath.

But Mizuki still wasn't back by the end of the day. The twins looked everywhere for her, but no one in the school had spoken to her since lunchtime, and the school nurse herself claimed never to have seen her.

"She must have gone home," AJ mused. "Still, we should at least check. It's unusual for her not to answer her phone."

"Yeah," Eloy was concerned. "Do you think this has

anything to do with what she was looking at on her mum's computer?" AJ didn't answer. They both knew the dangers of asking too many questions — their father was always telling them to be careful. Eloy couldn't shake the nagging memory of something Mizuki had said.

"I am actually under a different kind of monitoring due to my friendship with you two." What was it about them that made them so interesting to the Anglian government? Was it just because of their age — they couldn't help when they were born, Eloy thought to himself? He couldn't get his head around it.

They took the usual detour to Mizuki's building on the way home. It was in a much nicer part of the village as Mizuki's Electi mother brought in a great deal more money than any Treb ever could. The pristine pathway led up to a huge white cuboid of a building with tall windows. As AJ looked into the retinal scanner, with her finger on the fingerprint scanner, the main door opened. The twins walked into the modern, minimalist entrance hall with its white walls and grey carpet. They took the lift to the 34th floor and approached apartment 379. Mizuki's father was already at the door.

"Hello AJ, Eloy, is Mizuki with you?" Mizuki's father Simon was a tall, mousy-haired man with a warm smile. It had caused quite the stir when Miranda Koizumi, of the high-ranking Koizumi family, had married a Treb. Not only that but a Treb whose parents had once been arrested for protesting the Electi government, and were now serving time in the mainland factories. While his wife's income and status allowed them a more comfortable style of living, Simon had been blacklisted from subscribing to Electi status due to his parents' history. Since their union, laws on Electi citizens marrying Trebs had been tightened, and the government was in the final stages of banning it altogether.

"Hello, Mr Grey, we thought Mizuki might be with you. It's just... we haven't seen her since lunch."

"Oh," his warm smile faded. "Well, that's most unusual. Stay there, I'll get my coat." The door closed to be quickly re-opened by a now panicked-looking Mr Grey, who had inadvertently put his coat on inside-out. He was calling his wife on his holophone as he led the twins back out of the building and towards the school.

"Miranda? Have you heard from Mizuki? No. Well, she hasn't been seen since lunch. I hope this doesn't have anything to do with your missing data." The twins looked at each other, remembering their conversation with Mizuki over the spilt milkshake.

"You knew she'd been looking at your wife's data?" asked Eloy, nervously.

"Miranda, I'll call you back. Get in touch with your contacts in the force, will you? Okay, I love you too, we'll find our girl, don't worry." He hung up and looked forlornly at the twins. "Yes, I knew. She's good with technology but less skilled at covering her tracks. Her mother had to go to a meeting today and has been disciplined for her lack of vigilance. She's got her computer locked away now."

"Wait, so the government knew?" AJ's face paled.

"They know *everything*. You have no idea... if they have Mizuki..." Mr Grey looked horrified as he visibly tried to come up with a plan.

"What?" AJ stopped walking. "Why would they take Mizuki? Just for looking at a bit of data?" Mr Grey sighed heavily and turned to AJ.

"You don't understand, data is money in this society. They take their privacy very seriously and any intrusion is seen as a direct attack on the government."

The three of them spent the next hour searching the village but nobody had seen or heard from Mizuki, Just when Simon was about to give up hope, his phone rang again, but this time it wasn't Mrs Grey.

"Hello," Eloy could hear a cold, low voice coming from Mr Grey's holophone. By the look on his face, it wasn't good news. As the call went dead, Mr Grey's voice dropped to a whisper and he looked at the floor. His words came out so faintly that AJ wasn't even sure she had heard them correctly.

"The Electi... they have her."

Archie & Eva

After the Impero-Regnum's disastrous outing to the Disuku World Cup, Eva and Archie were in more trouble than ever. Their father had left on business with Corey Moon to visit the ESA, leaving them, Atticus and their mother at home. Privately, they were all glad to have a break from the tyrannical patriarch. After a particularly dull etiquette and mannerisms lesson, Eva was silently packing away the silverware when her microchip started buzzing. An ominous red glow emitted from her hand and her heart started hammering against her ribs. Though Electi and Treb microchips had come a long way, their original purpose was to serve as an early warning system in the event of another nuclear attack. The chips glowed red and buzzed to alert the wearer of any imminent danger, giving them a chance to find somewhere safe before the threat arrived.

"Children! The shelter! NOW!" Eva's mother's voice rang

through the house via the sound system and Eva immediately ran towards the back doors of the study. As she turned the handle, she heard a familiar snuffling coming from underneath the sofa. She hesitated — she knew she might only have seconds before a strike but... she couldn't leave her pet, could she? Wendoline's low whine made the decision for her, and Eva dove under the sofa to retrieve her frightened pet. As she ran back towards the door, she was forced backwards by an invisible field of energy and propelled into the air by a huge gust of wind. Her back hit the wall and everything went dark.

"Eva! Eva, where are you?" Archie tore out of the Impero-Regnum's underground bunker to search for his sister, despite his mother's protests that the danger may not have passed. He ran through the kitchen without pausing to witness the destruction caused to the family home. Pots were scattered, the pantry door was off its hinges and the dog's basket had been catapulted on top of the fridge. He ran through to the study room and let out a small squeak as he saw Wendoline wedged between the coffee table and an upturned plant pot. With some difficulty, he dislodged her and laid her on the floor.

"Wendy, Wendy! Come on wake up Wendy!" Wendy snorted. "Oh, good girl! Good girl. Where's Eva, Wendy? Where did she go?" Wendy blinked sleepily and looked towards the corner in which Eva had fallen. Archie went over to investigate just as Atticus entered the room.

"Archibald, did you find her?" Archie was kneeling in the corner looking at something in his hands. Atticus walked towards him but stopped abruptly when he saw what Archie was holding.

"Evie's bracelet," breathed Atticus. "I don't understand."

"Where could she have gone?"

The boys looked back towards their mother, her hands trembling and tears rolling down her face.

"My Evie… my little girl."

Chapter 8

Suspicious Hearts

Eloy & AJ

Eloy and AJ arrived home feeling hopeless. After the ominous phone call, Mizuki's father had sent them home, his eyes full of fear.

"Oh there you are, you're very late!" Marcus hugged his children but stepped back after seeing their forlorn faces.

"Mizuki's been taken." The usually upbeat AJ was holding back tears.

"What?" Marcus led them to the kitchen where they sat silently at the table. Sully walked in with his favourite squeaky toy, Mr Ducky.

"Not now boy," Eloy soothed.

"So what happened?" Marcus asked. AJ couldn't speak. She looked at her brother.

"We last saw her at lunch. She was talking about some data she'd found on her mum's computer."

"She what?" Marcus tried to hold back his shock as his children were clearly very shaken.

"She just wanted to know more about the—" Eloy paused and mouthed 'robot pet thing'. Suddenly remembering Sully was in the room, AJ quickly picked him up and dropped him into his basket in the lounge, closing the door behind her.

"Good thinking, AJ. What in the world was Mizuki thinking? She knows how extensive the monitoring is!"

"She reckoned she was onto something. Something called Project Libertas." At Eloy's words, Marcus gasped.

"Stop… stop talking. This is big, Eloy. If they think she's involved… I mean, I had no idea Miranda had that kind of clearance."

"How do you know about it, Dad?"

"I um," he paused. "No one can know. It's to do with my work."

"With the police?" AJ was confused.

"Yes, I… I need to talk to Bruce about some things. Just lay low for a while. Please? And don't speak to anyone about this — I mean it!"

"Okay, Dad, we promise." Marcus looked worryingly unconvinced as he grabbed his coat and headed for the door. Eloy and AJ exchanged baffled glances as Sully re-entered the room, still holding Mr Ducky purposefully. After losing a quick round of rock, paper scissors, Eloy went outside to play fetch with him. AJ, her head still spinning, headed into the hall. She found her mother tidying her bedroom, which was often far messier than her brother's.

"Oh, you don't have to do that, Mum. Sorry I've just got a lot on my mind at the moment."

"We all have, my petal, don't you worry. Has Dad gone back into work?"

"Yeah," AJ replied. "Is he okay?"

"Your dad is very busy right now, honey. He's… he tries to help a lot of people — with his job."

"Well of course he does," AJ replied, "he's a police officer!"

"He helps more people than he's supposed to, honey. More people like us. Trebs, you know. Those rebel groups — they're not trying to hurt anyone. They just want life to be better for us. Your father… he keeps them ahead of the police — when he can. But if his bosses found out — well with Sully being what he is… he just needs to make sure he isn't at risk." Leyna emptied an armful of meal-drink containers into a bin bag and sat down on her daughter's bed.

"At risk of what, Mum?" AJ looked at her mother through her newly repaired glasses, searching for answers in her worried expression. Leyna wrestled with her own thoughts before deciding her daughter was old enough to know the truth.

"At risk of being arrested, my love." AJ looked confused.

"Why would Dad be arrested for helping people?"

"He's helping rebels, my love. Dissenters of the government – traitors, technically. That makes him a traitor. And, as you know, people who get arrested these days… they don't ever come back." At her mother's words, AJ rushed to the bathroom. Leyna stood up to follow her but Eloy waved his hand and pulled her aside.

"Mizuki's been arrested, Mum." Leyna gave a high-pitched gasp and clapped her hand to her mouth. AJ could be heard being sick in the toilet.

"Oh, AJ, darling I'm so sorry, I didn't know about Mizuki. I'm sure she'll be okay! I didn't mean to upset you…" Eloy sat down next to his mother.

"It's okay, you were just telling the truth. Remember that boy in the year below us? His whole family disappeared after he was found filming some Electi kids breaking into a Treb house."

"Well, he did upload it to his Xchange page," Leyna added,

sadly. "Silly boy."

"No," Eloy shook his head. "The Electi kids were the ones in the wrong — not him."

"Well of course they were," Leyna sighed, "but every Treb knows the danger. We must be careful. What on earth did poor Mizuki do to get taken?" She searched her son's eyes but he looked away. "You weren't involved in it, were you?"

"No," Eloy mumbled. "She did this all on her own." AJ now appeared, woozy and wobbling, and Leyna led her to sit on the bed.

"Mizuki," she cried out, through tears and continuing nausea.

"I know, petal, I know." Leyna stroked her hair while Eloy went to fetch her a drink of water.

"Not from the tap!" Leyna called out.

"I know, I know!" Eloy replied, heading for one of the bottles in the fridge. He never understood why their mother was so averse to tap water, especially considering how expensive the bottled water was. She always said it was because, while pregnant, she would only drink bottled water and herbal tea — which she credited as being part of the reason the twins were born despite the infertility crisis. AJ gratefully sipped at the water while the three of them precariously sat on the edge of her bed.

"Mum," she began, "I'm scared."

"I know, petals." Leyna put her arms around her two children and gently pulled them against her. "Me too."

Marcus

Bruce's doorbell rang just as he was finishing his TV dinner.

83

"Hold on!" he called in his warm, gruff voice. "Oh, Marcus, it's you. Everything all right?"

"Not really. Can I come in?" Bruce ushered his friend and colleague into his self-proclaimed bachelor pad. Images of supermodels lined the walls and his French bulldog, Batman, was curled up in an armchair, snoring loudly. Marcus sat down next to him, giving him a wary glance as he realised he may be part of the monitoring program. Bruce spotted his look and reassured him.

"He's not bugged, mate. I had him checked after you found out about your pooch. Specialist x-ray — very hush-hush. He's just a regular Frenchie."

"Oh good call, good call."

Bruce couldn't fail to notice that Marcus had lost all of his regular confidence, as he fiddled with his hands and glanced nervously around.

"The kids, they know about Project Libertas."

Bruce was silent for a moment. "How?"

"Their friend Mizuki — she dug into her mum's files and found something. Now she's missing."

"Well, that can't be a coincidence."

"Exactly."

"Do they know about our involvement?" Bruce's usual bravado was gone, and his face was several shades paler than usual.

"There's no reason they should. The only person I've told is Leyna and you know she wouldn't blab. Helping out the rebels is a criminal offence; she doesn't want me arrested. She's proud we're helping them anyway."

"What was Mizuki's mother even doing getting involved with that? I thought it was level five clearance and above?"

"Miranda must be higher up in the order than she lets on. I thought only the president and his inner circle were working on tracking Project Libertas down." Marcus paused. "Unless Miranda is part of that — which would be odd, considering she married a Treb. You would've thought that would have restricted her position."

"Unless she's spying on him," offered Bruce. Batman snorted in his sleep and unconsciously kicked his leg out, making the already tense men jump in fright. "Jeeze, Batman, calm down will ya?" Batman opened one eye and snuffled.

"I'm going to try and track down Mizuki but I think she'll be in the White Tower — especially if she really did find out about the project." The White Tower was what regular Treb police officers called the top-secret prison in the capital. They knew about it — they'd seen glimpses of security cameras or heard whispers of it — but they didn't have the clearance to go there. It was used for the most treasonous criminals and high-level data breachers. Rumours of its brutality ranged from laser cell bars to acid-rain shower torture.

"We're going to have to be even more careful." Marcus continued. "I think we need to tone down our role in Project Libertas. Just while we locate Mizuki."

"But they need us!" protested Bruce.

"Yeah but my kids need me in their lives and not rotting in some factory on the mainland!"

"Point taken."

Bruce threw his plate into the dishwasher and made for the door. "Come on, we've got to get to the station."

Eva

Eva awoke to the sound of birdsong and the feeling of grass beneath her arms. She groggily felt around her with her hands. More grass. *'But,'* she thought, *'there's no natural grass left in Anglia, and radiation killed off the birds.'* She opened her eyes and gasped. She was beneath a beautiful blue sky — clearer than she had ever known a sky to be. There were fields of vegetables, fruit and flowers and the air smelled of something beautiful but unfamiliar. The sun was so bright her eyes lit up with white dots when she blinked, and she desperately tried to remember how she got here. She couldn't even remember the last time she'd been outside — her father had always told her it was unsafe. But this, Eva thought, was breath-taking. The last thing she remembered was her chip glowing red as she ran towards the door with Wendoline in her arms. She looked around for her pet, but she was nowhere to be seen, and this definitely wasn't her home.

"Where... where am I?" At her words, a familiar face appeared above her, hand outstretched. "Welcome to Project Libertas."

"I'm sorry," Eva stammered. "Project *what?*"

"Project Libertas. We've been tracking you for some time, Eva." Siri Perl, Eva's old technology teacher stood above her, smiling. She had changed her look considerably since working as the children's tutor. Her once black hair had been dyed varying shades of blue and purple and fashioned into long, beautiful locks. Her umber skin glistened in the bright, Spanish sun and her new nose piercing glinted playfully as she spoke. As Siri held out her hand, Eva nervously rose to her feet.

"Ms Perl — what are you doing here? We thought you were on the run!"

"I am, Eva. This is a haven for people like me. People who

understand the way things are. People like you."

"I'm not sure I do understand." Eva was puzzled and suddenly realised that she was outdoors without a respirator. "The air — Ms Perl it isn't safe!"

"Please, call me Siri," she soothed, "and don't worry Eva, the air here is perfectly safe — we are far away from Anglia." Everything here was like a dream. Eva guessed that she must have been knocked out from the blast and she would wake up any moment with Wendoline licking her face smelling of sausages.

"Come. Follow me." Siri took Eva's hand and led her to the top of the hill on which they stood. From its peak, Eva saw an entire village, bustling with people. The valley below, cleverly concealed by the surrounding hills, had been arranged into a spiral pattern, with the main pathway moving inwards towards a central structure. Makeshift houses had been constructed along the path, with a selection of what looked like market stalls and meeting places scattered in-between. People were leaning over campfires, cooking delicious-looking food, much of which Eva had never seen before. Families sat together talking, playing games and singing and Eva was shocked to see that nobody was staring at a holophone or E-Scroll or even wearing a respirator.

"What *is* this place?" Eva pinched her arm to be sure she wasn't dreaming.

"The short answer?" Siri thought for a moment before continuing. "It's a community for Trebs who escaped deportation to the factories, arrest by the government or some other Electi-fuelled danger. As far as the Anglian government knows, all the people before you are 'missing presumed dead'." Siri looked at Eva as she surveyed the scene. Eva squinted at the people milling around the village and tried to imagine them as terrifying fugitives from the law. They certainly didn't seem dangerous. Many of them were children. She turned her attention to the large building in the centre of the valley, adorned with a blazing golden star, the logo of the rebel group known in Anglia as The Trebble Makers. It was a deliberate play on the newly-updated Anglian flag – a silver star surrounded by darkness – a symbol of Anglia being the sole European survivor of the war.

"What's that?" Eva asked, pointing to the tall building, which looked like a wooden tower block with leaves on top.

"That's our base of operations," replied Siri. "It's where we keep all the tech. That's how we communicate with Anglia and check we aren't being monitored." Siri led Eva down the hill and was approached by a middle-aged man in a state of panic.

"Siri, it's the Treb police officers in Anglia — something's up, they've had to go dark."

Siri looked concerned by this and whispered to Eva, "This is what happens when we leave men in charge for a few days!" Eva was ushered into a corrugated metal hut and offered a plate of food before Siri was rushed off to the central tower. Despite being only eighteen years old, Siri seemed to be in charge of Project Libertas and Eva was privately impressed. As she wondered how her former tutor had come to lead such an extraordinary group, she looked down at her plate and gasped.

"Fresh oranges! I've never even seen those before!" Her family's occasional supply of real food from their farm on the Isle of Wight did not extend to Mediterranean or tropical fruit and Eva was in heaven. As she took huge bites from everything on her plate, Eva couldn't believe how sweet the fruit tasted. A kindly woman, Eva guessed around thirty years old, smiled and offered her a banana.

"We grow it all here. The Spanish sun is wonderful for crops." So she was in Spain. Eva's face fell.

"But Spain was destroyed by radiation from the war! We're not safe here!" Eva nearly dropped her plate of food in panic.

"Hush my child, we're perfectly safe. The radiation didn't reach this part of the island. Sure, global warming turned the climate from Mediterranean to tropical but what's a little heat when there's all this delicious food!" She gestured out of the window at the lush greenery. "Your government likes to pretend things are worse than they are outside of their own country."

"But, why?" Eva didn't understand. Every day they were being told that mainland Europe was a barren wasteland, with the government working hard to de-radiate the outer fringes. Yet here she was, on a Spanish island surrounded by lush, uncontaminated life.

"Imagine," the woman began, "if people knew that Europe was becoming safer. People from the Treb class your father so despises. They would all flock here, away from Anglia and then who would clean their toilets and flip their steaks? That's why we started this project and the Trebble Makers. Someone has to stand up to them and demand they stand down."

Eva blushed. She was always somehow held accountable for her father's views even though she had never agreed with them.

"If they were given the choice to stay in Anglia under that oppressive regime, or to build a new life out here — which do you think they would choose?" The woman turned away for a moment to unwrap something from a blanket. When she turned back to face Eva, she was holding a small panda cub.

Eva gasped, "But pandas are extinct! How?"

"Our team in Asia. They don't have the facilities there to

care for them yet, but they recovered four pandas from a cave in the Indonesian jungle. They survived the war. We've got tigers, zebras and tortoises here too. The last ones left in the world. It really is a paradise." The woman pointed to the window of the hut, through which Eva could see fields upon fields of happily grazing animals. She let out a slow, steadying breath. She had never seen such creatures before — unless you counted the holographic versions in New London's holo-zoo.

"But then why don't you tell people?" Eva asked. "They could come out here and help you!"

"We tried. As soon as the government heard our communications, they arrested our four founders and dispelled our message as a lie. That was at our first base back in Belgium. They sent in the army. Only a handful of us made it out alive." The woman explained sadly. Eva looked guiltily at the floor.

"My father's government... killed people?" The woman looked at her with sympathetic eyes as she fed the panda cub from a bottle.

"I'm sorry you had to find out this way my child, but the Electi's need for power and control outranks anything else... Even human life. They won't let their Treb servants go without a fight. They didn't want them all running off to greener pastures and leaving the Electi to fend for themselves. No, they keep dissenters in their hideous factories in their Anglian colonies and not one of the poor souls know that if they just walked a few kilometres down the road, they'd find freedom."

"Can't you save them?" Eva was horrified. She had always been told that the factory workers had all volunteered to make the journey to the mainland and that they were well compensated and cared for. The way this woman was talking made them sound more like prison camps.

"We've tried rescuing them, darling. But we've lost too many. The army guards their living quarters twenty-four hours a day and there are twenty-foot walls all around the factory cities. The only reason we're safe here is that we have help on the inside from a small group of Treb police officers," she explained.

"What kind of help?" Eva's head was spinning. It was too much to take in. Her father was a murderer, her family was hundreds of miles away and she was stuck in Spain in this hidden utopia.

"I think that's enough questions for today. Here." She handed Eva the cub. "Take a lie down with Tian. She has a very calming effect on people. She was born here so is hopelessly domesticated — poor thing. We'll train her up to live in the wild again when it's safe, of course. For now, though, she's safer hidden away. She wouldn't survive out there the way things are."

Eva lay on the nearby mattress with the panda. She began licking her arm and nuzzling her. She was clearly used to being around people. Eva felt perfectly safe with the cub as she let her exhaustion send her off to sleep, her head still buzzing with a thousand questions.

Chapter 9

Brave New World

Mizuki

The last thing Mizuki could remember was AJ's face. She had slipped on her milkshake, she remembered that much, and AJ was next to her. After that — darkness. She felt around her but for some reason, she was unable to move. Her head felt dizzy and heavy — was it from the fall or had she been drugged? It felt as though she was in a vehicle of some kind as she could feel the bumps of the road and the changes in speed. She tried to pull the hood from her head, but her hands were tied. It was then that she began to panic. She tried to call for AJ, but nobody could have heard her. She tried kicking, but her feet just hit cold, hard metal and after a while, it hurt too much to keep trying. She tried rolling, to try and free her hands, but there wasn't enough room. After what felt like hours of attempted escape, the car came to a stop. Mizuki quickly tried to decide whether it would be safer to play dead or to take her kidnappers by surprise and jump out when her temporary prison was finally opened. As the click of the car's boot met with sudden, bright sunlight, visible through the thin fabric of her hood, Mizuki decided to plump for the former option. No amount of kicking and flailing would protect her from the person now lifting her out of the car's boot and over their shoulder. Through a gap in her hood, she was able to make out a large pair of men's trainers and floor markings that seemed familiar to her — though she couldn't quite place them. The man carrying her ascended a flight of stairs before going down what looked like a service corridor. It was dark and Mizuki tried desperately to make out any signs that might hint at her location, but all she could see was a concrete floor. Eventually, they came to a stop and Mizuki was flung onto a hard floor. Her hood and restraints were removed but she stayed motionless until the sound of footsteps had retreated. Cautiously, she opened her eyes. As blinding light seemed to burn her retinas, she gasped. Bars separated her from the rest of the room — but no ordinary bars. These bars were made of white-hot lasers and, Mizuki presumed, deadly to the touch. She shrunk back into the corner of her cell and began to cry. She hadn't meant to cause any trouble. She was just so sick of being ignored by her parents, ridiculed by her Electi classmates, and judged by her Treb ones. She thought that if she could uncover something useful, then maybe she could make a difference and become more than just the 'half-Electi, half-Japanese' girl everyone else seemed to see. As she stared at the bars, she felt a pang of guilt in her stomach. What would her parents say? Did they even know where she was? She curled up in a ball on the thin mat in the corner of the room and tried to stop crying. "Someone?" she whispered. "Please help me."

Eloy & AJ

Mizuki had been missing for four days. Eloy and AJ had been banned from speaking about it and levels of paranoia within the Kahn household were verging on dangerous. Marcus spent most of his time at work, using his resources to try and find Mizuki without his bosses noticing, but with no luck. Meanwhile, a national emergency had been declared due to the kidnapping of the President's daughter, Evangeline Impero-Regnum. While the twins weren't as personally worried by Eva's disappearance as Mizuki's, they still felt sorry for her. "I mean, imagine if I went missing," AJ theorised. "What would you do?"

"Aside from having five minutes of peace?" Eloy's joke fell flat as they both looked at the floor. "No, I get it. Her family must be as worried as... well, as worried as we are about Mizuki. But then it serves them right for taking her," Eloy added bitterly. As Eloy began to feel guilty for his last comment, Leyna came through the front door and immediately tripped over the dog.

"Oh, Sullivan what are you doing sleeping on the doormat?" Sully gave a low woof in haughty response before slinking off to find Mr Ducky.

"Are you okay, Mum?" AJ called.

"Yes, I'm fine, darling, thank you. How was your day?" AJ told her mother about the extra security measures brought into their school due to the kidnapping. Every student had to have their bags searched, before going through a scanner and washing their hands with a detection solution. All before entering the building. In the middle of their mathematics lesson a group of police officers had stormed in and dragged out a twelve-year-old girl with ginger pigtails. AJ had tried to stop them, but Eloy pleaded with her to just stay sitting, or she would be next. Reluctantly, she had obliged. She couldn't live with herself if she put her family through that kind of worry.

"It's even worse at my school," Leyna replied. "Treb teachers are shadowed all day by an Electi official — even to the bathroom! I suppose they must think there's some sort of grand plot to kidnap Electi kids." She sighed and sat down heavily. "I mean really — we don't *want* their children — they're all rude, entitled little brats anyway. What would I have to gain from kidnapping one of them?"

"The ransom money?" suggested AJ. Leyna considered this briefly before replying that it wouldn't be worth it. As AJ laughed, their lounge's holovision screen was once again taken over by the seven-p.m. broadcast. President Ignatius Impero-Regnum's face filled the screen and Eloy had never seen such fire in his eyes before.

"He looks mad," he muttered quietly.

"This isn't going to be good," Leyna replied, worriedly.

"Good evening citizens of Anglia. This is your seven p.m. broadcast. Tonight there will be a slight change to proceedings as I will be announcing a new, temporary curfew for all Treb citizens."

AJ shot to her feet.

"What? You can't do that!" Leyna motioned her to sit back down.

"He can't hear you, honey."

"Until my beloved daughter Evangeline can be found, no Treb citizen will be permitted outside of their homes after the seven-p.m. broadcast. This will be enforceable from this evening."

Leyna gasped. "Is he joking? Does he seriously expect every Treb to be able to make it home in the next three minutes? What a joke." She shook her head angrily.

"Due to recent circumstances, armed police will be patrolling Treb areas from seven p.m. Any resistance will, as always, be met with utmost force. This is for the safety of all Anglian citizens."

"Oh great," Eloy moaned, "more unpaid overtime for Dad then."

"If anyone has any information regarding my missing daughter, they are to report to the police immediately or face severe penalties. This has been President Ignatius Impero-Regnum for the Anglian Government — serving you, to create a better world."

"That man," AJ began before Leyna stroked her arm.

"I know, I know." They sat in silence for a few moments before, suddenly, Eloy shot up from his chair, staring at his holophone with a frantic look in his eyes.

"What's wrong darling? You look pale."

"It's Dad!" Eloy gasped. "He says he's on his way home and we need to see something. It must be about Mizuki!"

Eva

"Good mooooooorning Project Libertas!" Siri's voice rang out of the speakers that were spread throughout the village. *"Today's top story — Evangeline Impero-Regnum has joined us! Somewhat against her will so let's all be nice to her and make her feel welcome, please. Do try and remember that she is NOT representative of the Electi order and is, in fact, one of us*

— even if she doesn't know it yet."

Eva raised her eyebrows. She didn't feel like one of these people. Besides, they'd kidnapped her. Tian the panda cub stretched and strolled outside. Eva hoped this was okay as she didn't have the strength to follow her. Siri continued, *"Our Treb police team in Anglia are currently lying low so be on high alert everyone — if the army is coming, we won't know about it until they get here. However, to our knowledge, the Electi still believe this island to be uninhabitable, and therefore have no reason to look for us here."* Eva began to wonder which island she was on. She'd never been to Europe. She'd visited the ESA plenty of times with her family, but they always took the Atlantic Monorail. She'd never crossed an ocean by any other mode of transport, so how had she even got here? *"This is your daily reminder to wipe your microchips! There are leaders on hand to help you with this, at any of our wipe stations."* Eva looked down at her hand. Her chip was still there, but had it been wiped? Why were they wiping their chips — they kept people safe, didn't they? *"This is vitally important, people. If even one of you forgets, they can track you to our location and shut us down. Please wipe your children's chips too, if they have them. Alternatively, if you wish to have your chip surgically removed, you can see our on-site doctor Dr Kyap. This is Siri Perl, signing off, reminding you to have a Treb-tastic day!"* Tian sauntered back into the tent and butted her head against Eva's leg.

"Don't mind her, she's just hungry." The woman Eva had met yesterday walked into the tent with a bottle for the panda cub. Tian seemed grateful and quickly shuffled over to the woman for her breakfast.

"My name is Carmen." The woman turned to Eva. "I'll be

taking care of you here. I also look after the animals, so you may have some unusual company from time to time." Eva was happy for any animal-related company. "But Carmen, why am I here?"

"I'll answer that." Siri strode into the tent and threw Eva an apple. She nodded at Carmen who picked up Tian and exited the tent. "When I was your teacher, I sensed something in you, Eva. Something neither of your brothers possessed. Courage, bravery and most of all strength." Eva scoffed. Both of her brothers were much stronger than her and she had never been in any sort of situation where bravery was required, until now of course. Siri smiled at her confusion and continued. "It takes a great deal of strength to hold onto your own beliefs and convictions, even when they are not shared by those who raised you," Siri urged, sensing Eva's self-doubt. Eva began to understand.

"Everyone here seems so kind. We were always told to fear them… I mean Trebs… I mean…" Eva blushed as she stumbled over her words.

"We're just people, Eva. People like you." Siri raised her hand in a kind of frozen high five and Eva raised hers to meet it. Though the colour of their skin was so different, Siri's glowing gold tones warm against Eva's pale fingers, they were both human beings. They were both women. They were both, as it turned out, sick of men running their lives.

"I understand why you took me now," Eva began. "Not for a ransom, but to make a real difference. My father… I can't watch him make people suffer any more. Do you really think I can help?"

"You know that what your father is doing is wrong, Eva. We couldn't invite you here, we had to take you, and I am sorry for that. But we need you, Eva. You have inside knowledge and connections that could really make the difference in this fight. Our numbers are growing every day and soon we won't have room to house every endangered Treb who needs our help. Anglia is becoming a harsher and more dangerous place to live by the day and while setting up this community is a start; it won't fix the problem. We need to overthrow their entire system, Eva. With you, we can finally take all of them down."

"All of them?" Eva's eyes widened as she looked at her enigmatic tutor. "All of whom, exactly?" Siri replied swiftly, a triumphant glint in her eyes.

"The Electi."

Chapter 10

Abandon Ship

Archie

The Impero-Regnum boys had been confined to their bedrooms and, on the rare occasion they were allowed out, they were followed by two armed guards. Archie's two younger sisters, Antoinette and Euridice, had even been brought home from their elite boarding school on the coast so that they could be watched at all times. They stayed in a separate annexe of the house with their nannies, Constance and Patience, as Lady Margot refused to deal with children until they turned twelve. Since Evangeline's disappearance, Ignatius seemed to think that any of his children could be snatched at any moment and Lady Margot kept fainting in response to loud noises. Atticus was spending his free time trying to beat his guard at disuku while Archie, too upset about his sister to enjoy anything, was lying on his bedroom floor, staring out of the window. It was Eva's sixteenth birthday. Archie wondered if anyone else in this family had even remembered or if — he paled at the thought — she had even reached this teenage milestone. As the thick smog moved overhead, Archie tried to catch glimpses of the sky above to distract him from his fears. He couldn't remember the last time he had been outside — not just to his garden or the Electi-only public parks which were protected from the elements and radiation by a forcefield — but truly outside in the open air. He wished he had been able to go outside with Eva — she would have loved it, he thought to himself. He pulled out Eva's E-Scroll. There must be something on here to give him some clue as to where his sister might be. As he swiped through the apps, he heard his parents muttering outside the open window. They must not have realised he could hear them. Archie silently crept to the window and ducked down.

"Miranda Koizumi and that wet Treb she married are still in the interrogation pods, but I don't think they know anything. Nothing about Project Libertas or Eva. The half-class girl has given up speaking altogether. But I refuse to let them go until Eva's back — and even then!" His father's voice was angrier than Archie had ever heard it.

"Ignatius, darling. Someone must know something! You're monitoring every Treb and Electi citizen in the country for God's sake, from their movements to their conversations — how can she have just disappeared?"

"Well I don't know, do I, Margot? You stupid—"

Archie heard a sharp crack and hoped that it was a nearby table or wall his father had struck. He heard his mother whimper and retreat indoors while his father stood there seething, dialling someone on his holophone. "Theresa? Yes, I need transportation back to the stadium now. I need to speak to the prisoners personally." Archie listened to his father's footsteps grow quieter and suddenly realised what they had found that day at the stadium during the Disuku World Cup. As Archie's mind flitted back to the screens on the walls with bright bars, it all fell into place. The stadium was a prison. Archie had seen the prison cells on-screen in one of the hidden rooms while they explored the mystery corridor. Eva had been saying all along that their father was up to something, but Archie hadn't listened. He could have kicked himself — was this why she had gone missing? Did she know too much? But then, of course, his father would know — unless he was keeping it secret from their mother which, Archie considered, was certainly possible. Archie returned to Eva's E-Scroll, remembering something his mother had said and talking through his thoughts to Eva's stuffed dragon toy nearby.

"She said that he can track us — monitor us — but people don't know that! How can it even be legal? Is he tracking me?" he continued to mumble absent-mindedly while searching Eva's E-Scroll for answers. He paused for a moment, remembering the time he had run away, aged eleven, and his father's butler was able to find him within ten minutes. He looked at his hand, with his Electi chip shining through, gold and glittering beneath his skin. He typed his name into a search bar on the E-Scroll. Nothing. He thought about what to do next. Eva would know. She was always the first one figuring out complicated technology.

Archie heard the familiar slam of the front door and opened his bedroom door just enough to peer out. He looked at the permanently closed door to his father's office. They were forbidden to enter. But this was an emergency. Checking nobody was around, Archie tiptoed down the corridor, slipped through the office door and closed it silently behind him. On the wall were at least ten large holovision screens, displaying live footage of the house, exact locations of the family members (excluding Eva) and what looked like a camera feed to a prison, where a teenage girl with purple hair was being questioned by officials. There was also an unusual looking machine standing in the corner, with what looked like hundreds of wires plugged into it. Archie spent a few moments taking it in, before realising that if he was being tracked, he would need to be quick. He sat down at the computer interface and paused. What should he look for? If there was a way of finding Eva surely his father would have thought of it. He needed help. Then it occurred to him — Siri! His old technology teacher would have far superior tech skills to his father and must be able to find Eva. Archie typed her name into the tracker.

'Location unknown, chip deactivated: If chip reactivated, set to kill.'

As Archie read the on-screen message, he suddenly felt extremely sick. They could kill people using their chips. How could his father be involved in all of this? He had to get out. He ran out of the room, grabbed his respirator and tiptoed downstairs, intending on heading straight out the front door. As he tore through the entrance hall, he heard his mother talking to the servants and quickly hid behind a marble pillar. He was still under house arrest, after all. He couldn't let his mother see him, as much as it would pain her to have another child disappear. He crawled into the lounge, behind a sofa and, when the coast was clear, ran out the back door. As he approached the back wall to the garden, he remembered. His chip. He would be tracked. How could he go anywhere without his father knowing? Archie felt the weight of his choices. He could stay and do nothing or do what it takes to find his sister, his best friend, and the only other person he knew who seemed to see their father for what he was. He remembered in the back of his mind something Siri had taught them a few months ago about magnets messing with the chips. He snuck back into the kitchen, pulled the fridge magnets off the freezer and stuffed them into his pockets. He tiptoed back up to his father's study and brought up his location onto the screen. He held a handful of magnets over his chip, and almost immediately his locator icon began jumping all over the screen, fading in and out of view.

"Yes!" Archie sprinted to Eva's room, burrowed through her dresser and, finding what he would need, used several of her hair bands to lash the magnets to his hand. Taking a second to wrinkle his nose up at a photo of one of the Anglian Angels Disuku players he had found in her make-up drawer, Archie took one final look at Eva's empty room and headed downstairs. His mother was distracted by Wendoline who was flopped in the way of a cupboard door and Archie, sensing his moment, ran for the garden. Once outside he headed straight for the back wall of the Impero-Regnum mansion, avoiding his guard who was currently searching for him in the bushes. He was going to find his sister. With or without anybody's help.

Eloy & AJ

The Kahn family squeezed into the small master bedroom and crowded around the holophone screen generated by Marcus' chip.

"Here." Marcus pointed. AJ adjusted her glasses and squinted.

"Nah, I don't see it."

"Here." Eloy shifted to let AJ get a better look. As she looked, she could make out the pixelated outline of a familiar figure.

"Holy…"

"AJ!" Marcus warned.

"But it's Mizuki! That's definitely her."

"Are you completely sure, AJ?" Marcus asked sternly, "Eloy wasn't convinced."

"I'm sure, Dad." AJ had that steely look in her eyes which told Marcus not to doubt her. Eloy was too preoccupied with where Mizuki appeared to be to waste time questioning his stubborn sister.

"That's a prison. It's got to be. Look at those bars — they're so bright!"

"Laser cells," Marcus confirmed. "They don't use them in regular prisons. She's being held in the White Tower." The twins looked confused. "There were always rumours of a high-security prison in the capital — only Electi officers had clearance to know about it, of course. That's the only time I've heard mention of laser cells," Marcus explained.

"How are you even seeing this?" Eloy couldn't understand. "If you don't have the clearance, how have you got this footage?"

Marcus sat down and ushered his children closer.

"I think it's time I explain a few things to you both. Now that you're involved." Marcus rested his hand on his wife's arm and she stroked it to reassure him. "I'm what they call a PLA — Police Liaison Assistant. I help the rebel Trebs —the ones trying to find a solution. A peaceful solution, where possible. Project Libertas is their main base. It's off the coast of Spain on an Island that used to be called Mallorca. The Electi think it's a radioactive wasteland so they're safe there, for now. The Electi know about the project but not its location. Bruce and I... we help keep the rebels one step ahead by giving them a heads up on any mainland raids. I've had to break a lot of laws, mind.

That's how I'm getting this footage. I'm taking a lot of risks and it's only a matter of time until I get caught. That's why I've decided—" He paused and exhaled loudly. Leyna squeezed his hand.

"I'm going to Project Libertas. They have a boat going tomorrow from the south coast. I'll be safer there and far more useful to them."

"But Dad — what about us? You can't just leave us?" Eloy was trying to hold in his emotions but struggled to hold back tears. AJ took his hand.

"Don't be silly kids. We're all going. With Mizuki gone, I can't risk them taking you too. And it's only a matter of time before they accuse your mother of kidnapping the prime minister's daughter."

"But she didn't do it?" AJ was baffled. "She was only saying earlier about how awful all the Electi kids are!"

"It doesn't matter who took her, love." Leyna smiled. "They want a scapegoat and the wife of a spy is a perfect choice."

"But Mizuki! We can't just leave Mizuki.' AJ's voice cracked and tears began trickling down her face. Eloy was taken aback by his sister's uncharacteristic display of emotion. She was usually the strong one. Marcus took her hand.

"We can't help her from where we are, AJ. We must take this chance." His heart broke for his daughter, but Marcus knew the government would come after his family next. The Kahns spent several minutes in silence. Sully barking in the back garden was all that could be heard.

"Okay." Eloy stood up. "Are we doing this or not?" AJ, still torn between abandoning Mizuki and her own safety, watched on as the family began making preparations to leave.

Eventually, she stood up and walked weakly to her room. What material possessions should she even take to a rebel Treb base? She walked over and picked up the photo of the three of them that stood by her bed. She looked at Mizuki, her lilac hair captured as it ruffled in the breeze. AJ felt a pain in her chest she had never experienced before. She put the photo, her Anglian Angels kit and a few more clothes into a case. Her spare pair of glasses, toothbrush and toiletries went in next. She looked around at the rest of her possessions. Her bass guitar, video games and sporting trophies all caught her eye. These things that once defined her would have to be discarded — useless as she started a new life as a fugitive from the government and her own country. She took a moment to try and imagine what life might be like in this new promised land, but her father's shouts brought her out of her daze.

"Hurry up everyone, I think they know I found the prison feed — we may only have minutes!" As AJ closed the lid of her suitcase, she caught sight of something out of the window. It looked like an angry mob dressed in green uniforms that looked suspiciously like... AJ realised in an instant.

"Uhm, Dad! Police!"

"Leyna, kids!" Marcus' voice boomed through the house. "Get to the back door now!"

Mizuki

Mizuki sat, stone-faced, opposite the Anglian prime minister. Her spirit was broken and all that she had left was rage.

"I will ask you one more time, girl, what do you know about Project Libertas?" His shouts reverberated off the metal walls, but Mizuki didn't flinch.

"I told you," she breathed, her voice ragged from days without food or drink. "I don't know anything." Ignatius sneered and waved at her guards. They uncuffed her from the bench and hauled her back towards the acid rain shower room.

"No!" Mizuki cried, her voice desperate. "I told you, I don't know anything! I don't know anything!" Ignatius walked towards her and glowered.

"If you have anything to do with my daughter's disappearance, it won't just be a little drop of rain you have to worry about." He turned and walked away, Mizuki's cries all that could be heard in the cold, metal room.

Chapter 11

Escape

Eloy and AJ

Eloy was never the fastest in his class. Maybe his brain could win a race but not his legs. He fell behind as AJ and his parents sprinted ahead of him. When his mother turned back and saw him struggling, her eyes widened. The police were metres away. Luckily, more through wanting to join in than grasping any real understanding of the situation, Sully was running alongside Eloy and wasn't prepared to let a grumpy police officer ruin their perfectly fun game. He turned around, bounded into the police officer and bit him on the ankle. In the confusion, Eloy was able to pick up his pace and catch up with his family, gasping through his respirator. Meanwhile, AJ was almost a blur in the distance. Eloy never understood how she could move so quickly without even breaking a sweat. But then, AJ never understood how Eloy could solve complex calculations faster than their school's brightest teachers. Having opposing talents was what made them such a strong team.

"Which way, Dad?" called AJ from the front.

"The old village!" Marcus called back. AJ was confused but didn't dare argue. The old village was abandoned, home only to homeless Trebs who couldn't find jobs in an AI heavy workforce.

As AJ ran past the ruins of old buildings, she caught glimpses of families huddled under old bus shelters and petrol stations. "Left here!" called Marcus.

AJ skidded and turned abruptly left, coming face to face with an old car dealership. Once Marcus had caught up with her, he started pulling at a pile of what appeared to be debris in the corner. AJ stood dumbstruck. Eloy finally caught up with them all and stared, equally baffled, at their father. As Marcus pulled at the pile however, Eloy could start to see something shining underneath. "Oh my god, it's a... is that a car?" The family all started tearing at the pile now, with the sound of approaching police growing louder and louder. Eventually, they could open the doors and climb in, Sully making it just in time to leap onto Leyna's lap.

Marcus started the engine and hit the pedal. They accelerated through the broken wall of the shop and out onto the road, narrowly missing a police officer. The twins almost forgot they were in danger, staring open-mouthed at their father not only driving a car but expertly navigating it through ruined buildings.

"Dad... you're... you're driving! How did you even learn how to do that? No one's driven since the twenties!" Marcus wasn't listening as he turned the car to the left and sped off towards open land, formerly used as fields. The twins ducked down in the back in case of flying bullets. Marcus took deep, deliberate breaths as he concentrated on where he was going. Eloy noticed his father's left hand clutch his chest. He knew his dad suffered from anxiety. He was open about it with his family but had to keep it quiet at work, for fear of being demoted or worse. He was the strongest man Eloy knew, but his dad always told them that mental health wasn't the same as physical health, and conditions like anxiety didn't just pick on the physically weak. Leyna stroked the back of Marcus' head and reassured him. She knew how to help him during his panic attacks but only he could get himself out of them. Usually, he would close his eyes to calm down, but with who knows how many police following them, he couldn't risk it. He focussed his mind and forced his breathing to slow despite his tightening chest.

"That's it, Dad," AJ reassured him. "You've got this." Marcus smiled. It was passing, he could focus. As the sirens died away, Marcus was able to relax and drove them into a valley.

"Don't worry, kids, we're going to make it. They won't catch us now."

"Dad, how did you even get this? I thought all the old cars were destroyed! What even is this?" AJ was excited and afraid in equal measure.

"It's a four by four — Bruce salvaged it years ago in case of an emergency like this. We've got enough petrol in the tank to get us to Bournemouth and then it's plain sailing 'til Spain!" While the four by four glided over uneven terrain with ease, the police's self-driving E-cars were restricted to main roads, and it was only a matter of time before they were out of sight.

"I've deactivated our chips," Marcus continued, "so they can't track us. I've wiped Sully's equipment too — he's basically a regular dog now, just with a highly increased lifespan and weakness to water."

The twins looked around them at the open country. Charred trees stood like monuments amongst the barren plains and dried-up rivers. They travelled in silence for what felt like hours, each drifting in and out of exhausted sleep. Marcus, his focus never wavering, felt more relaxed the further they travelled from civilisation. Leyna alternated between stroking her husband's arm and Sully's ears as she helped Marcus navigate his way south. The twins awoke simultaneously as Marcus drove down a particularly bumpy dried-up river. AJ looked out of the window at the arid landscape.

"This used to be the New Forest," Leyna sighed. "My mother brought me here when we first came to England. It felt like home. So much life and beauty."

"It must have been beautiful." Eloy looked wistfully out of the window. Leyna turned to face the road ahead of them once more and let her thoughts drift back to her mother. She had bought Leyna over from Poland when she was only four years old, hoping for a better life. Unfortunately, levels of xenophobia in 2020s Britain were only increasing and they found themselves largely unwelcome. Leyna was bullied in school for her accent and her mother struggled to hold down a job as priority was given to British-born citizens. Leyna was still a happy child, though. Her teachers taught her that it was her differences which made her special and she valued her Polish heritage.

She had been shopping with her mother when the bombs fell. They were looking for a dress for Leyna to wear to her school's awards ceremony. She had won a prize for a song she had written and her mother was over the moon with pride. Leyna was trying on something in her trademark sunflower yellow when the fire alarm went off. No one reacted — of course. Her mother, however, hurried Leyna back into the changing room to get back into her own clothes in case they needed to evacuate. Leyna was just pulling up her jeans and chiding her mother's worrisome nature when the lights suddenly went out. The barely noticeable, but now strangely absent, music had also stopped. Everything had gone suddenly silent and Leyna thought for a moment she had passed out. The next sound she heard was her mother knocking on the door and hurriedly calling her name. She grabbed her things and opened the door to see that it wasn't just the changing rooms in darkness but the entire shop. Her mother took her hand and pulled her out into the main shopping centre which, to Leyna's continued confusion, was in total darkness. People around them were looking around in bewilderment and many were staring blankly at their mobile phones, which, from what Leyna could tell, had all stopped working.

They ran outside and looked down the high street. They were surrounded by people, all looking up and down the road to see that nothing had power. Leyna asked her mother if there had been a power cut, but she didn't know. There was something in the air that suggested something far worse.

They began walking home and took their usual shortcut over the common. As they walked, they saw people outside their houses looking around. Whatever had happened had clearly affected more than just the city centre. Leyna felt her mother's grip on her hand tighten and saw her look up to the sky. She followed her mother's gaze and saw an aeroplane flying overhead. Only, it wasn't flying. It was... As Leyna realised what was happening, her mother had already pulled her into a run. The plane was falling out of the sky and directly towards them. Leyna was running after her mother and trying to ignore the sound of the falling aircraft. Her mother swung her around and behind a nearby building just as the plane hit the ground metres away. The sound was deafening and the debris flew around them. Leyna hid in her mother's arms and tried to hold back panicked tears. Her mother whispered in her ear that it was time to run and they began sprinting for home.

They reached the main door to their flat but were intercepted by three of their neighbours — a Pakistani man and his young family. His wife smiled at Leyna and their son looked to be the same age as her. They told Leyna's mother that none of their electronics were working but a friend had told them he had an old radio which was picking up some information about what was going on. They followed the family to their friend's house and joined a growing crowd of people gathered outside. Leyna held her mother's hand tightly. The crowd was silent as a short, worried-looking man held up a battered old radio and a microphone to amplify the noise. Between the crackling, Leyna could hear a man's voice. *"We're getting reports that... yes, yes, there's been a nuclear attack."*

The crowd let out a collective gasp and a woman near them screamed and fainted. *"We're not sure where... they think somewhere in Asia... but it must have been multiple bombs because the whole planet seems to have gone dark. Wait... wait America too? Oh no, they're saying multiple states have been completely wiped out. We've heard nothing from China or Japan either... Korea, India — they're all radio silent. We were talking to our correspondent in Africa but his feed went dead after reporting a cloud of what I'm guessing was some form of radiation."*

It was now impossible to hear the voice, such was the level of panic amongst the crowd. The Pakistani man took Leyna's mother by the hand and told her to follow him. They returned to his flat and followed him into a back room, where he ushered Leyna and his son into a corner to play with some of the boy's toys. He picked up a yellow toy car and handed it to Leyna, who smiled and took it. She could hear her mother talking with the boy's parents but couldn't hear what they were saying. They sounded worried, though.

Leyna and the boy played for a while and his mother kept making cups of tea on an old camping stove. Shouts and noises from outside were growing more violent and suddenly they heard the crashing of breaking glass beneath them. As Leyna's mother dashed to hold her in her arms, the man went to the window and told them the looting had started. They hid in the flat for a few hours, Leyna lying in her mother's lap as she stroked her hair to keep her calm.

At about nine a clock, when darkness had fallen, the boy's father approached them looking panicked. He'd received word of people losing contact with those on the west coast of England and thought they needed to get underground. They followed him outside and saw crowds of people running towards them. Leyna shouted out and hid behind her mother. The man pushed them into the crowd and joined them in running alongside the mob.

The crowd came to a stop at the underground car park nearby, which Leyna could see had been partially boarded up by anything people could find. There was a small gap at the entrance which was already near to overflowing with people. Leyna and the boy were pushed towards the gap by their parents but they were blocked by a gang of men with various makeshift weapons. They looked the group up and down and sneered, telling them coldly that only British people were going to be saved. Leyna's stomach dropped. Her mother begged them to let the children in — the horizon was growing darker and Leyna could see something like an enormous grey cloud approaching from the distance, covering everything in its path. The people were desperate now and Leyna was falling from the weight of the people pushing towards the entrance. After one last frantic push, she hit the ground and everything went dark.

When she awoke, she kept her eyes shut tight, not wanting to see what horrors might await her. She felt around for her mother but recoiled at the feeling of someone unfamiliar to her. She reluctantly opened her eyes to see that she was in a dark room with what felt like a million people. The boy from the flat was next to her but neither of their parents were anywhere to be seen. The boy was crying.

Suddenly, back in the four by four, Leyna remembered where she was as Sully shuffled on her lap and Marcus coughed. She looked out of the window and saw that tears were rolling down her cheek. She quickly wiped them away with her sleeve. She couldn't let her children see her pain. Not now.

The journey to the coast was long — made longer by necessary detours to avoid CCTV detection — and Eloy had a long time to think. How had their lives so suddenly gone so off track? There were so many unanswered questions — why were they being monitored in the first place; why was Mizuki somehow linked to it; and what was this so-called 'White Tower' where she was being held? He knew his father's colleagues would be doing their best to find her, but he hated just leaving her like that and running away. As night fell, they stopped to fill up with the petrol Marcus had been keeping in the boot — "if the government knew I had this!" — and Leyna climbed into the back seat in-between her children.

"How are you doing my petals?" The twins looked blank. It felt like a rhetorical question. "I think it's time I explained some things to you. You're fifteen now, nearly sixteen, and you have a right to know."

"Oh, God," AJ spluttered, "we're adopted, aren't we? I knew I couldn't be related to Eloy by blood!" AJ was half-joking and her mother gave her a playful tap.

"No, you're not adopted. Of course you're not — you're the spitting image of your father!" Leyna rolled her eyes but was grateful that her daughter was still feeling strong enough to be silly. It was a good sign. "It is about you two, though. The reason the government was keeping such close tabs on you. It's because of when you were born." Eloy nodded, this was all familiar so far. "In 2046 there was a pandemic of sorts. People who got pregnant... their babies... they didn't grow properly. It continued into 2047, and when I realised I was pregnant I was horrified because all the babies in Anglia were dying before they were born. All the Treb babies, that is — only the Electi citizens could afford the specialist medication that stopped the disease. But something happened — you grew. You thrived! You were a sort of medical miracle and I think that scared the Electi a bit." AJ and Eloy looked equally horrified.

"But Mum," Eloy asked, trying to understand. "Why did we make it? Why did we survive?" Leyna smiled at her son and kissed his head.

"I don't know my petal, but I thank my stars every single day that you did. And your father and I are going to do everything we can to keep you safe — you're special. You're our whole world. I'm never going to let them take you." AJ thought for a moment.

"Mum," she began, curiously. "Is that why I can run so fast? And why Dad always asks me to slow down? Because they might find out about me?" Eloy gasped and interrupted.

"And why I can solve problems in my head faster than our

school computers — because the teachers at school always tell me it shouldn't be possible." Leyna inhaled slowly before replying.

"Honestly? We don't know, but there's got to be a reason you two are so gifted. Maybe that's part of it — but it's certainly not a part we want the Electi to find out about." AJ and Eloy leaned into their mother, heads spinning with fear and curiosity. Leyna held her children close, tears rolling down her cheeks once more. "You're safe. I'll keep you safe," she breathed. "Just like my mother did for me."

Chapter 12

Sun, Sea and Subterfuge

Archie

Once Archie had run far enough that his home was no longer visible over the horizon, he slipped his sister's E-Scroll out of his pocket. He opened up Moon maps and searched for her last recorded location. While their father didn't know where Eva had been, Archie knew that Eva always backed up her microchip to her E-scroll, so there was a chance it could tell him where she last was. After several failed attempts at guessing his sister's password, he breathed an emotional sigh of relief. He had typed his name into the password box, never expecting it to work, and yet there she was. The location dot was in a place on the south coast Archie had never heard of that was almost definitely under the ocean by now. He programmed the E-Scroll to show him directions. It was at least a day's walk. He couldn't exactly hitchhike — anyone who could afford an E-car could likely afford an Electi subscription and would know who he was. He adjusted the magnets strapped to his hand, making sure his location couldn't be tracked.

As he scanned the terrain around him, he saw a dark line breaking the concrete. He walked towards it, hoping it was some kind of pipe he could follow to a river where he might catch a boat. As he approached, however, he heard a rumbling in the distance. He looked towards the sound and saw it — a freight train, not unlike the ones privately run by his father to bring supplies from the family farm. This one was heading away from the city, however, so must be on its way back to the island.

Archie ran towards what he now knew to be a railway line and hid behind a junction box. As the train approached, he analysed his choices. The train was travelling South which was precisely where he needed to go, however, it had to be travelling at a minimum of a hundred kilometres per hour. He breathed deeply and psyched himself up. "Archibald Impero-Regnum, you can do this. You've been training your whole life for this. The disuku games — your speed and agility are your greatest asset. You can do this. You can almost, definitely, maybe, jump onto a speeding train." The ridiculousness of his last statement had turned his legs to jelly but he knew that he had to at least try.

Concentrating on standing up without wobbling, Archie watched the train grow closer. The first few sections carried shipping containers, but he could see that one was empty, providing him with a perfect platform on which to jump. He took a deep breath, ran towards the train and jumped.

Surprisingly, he had almost overshot and was thrown into the shipping container following behind the platform he was aiming for. He felt sure he was going to be flung back to the ground but felt something pinning his hand to the metal container, keeping him in place long enough to secure his footing. He looked up at his hand — the magnets he had used to interfere with his microchip were securely attached to the blue wall of the shipping container. With a triumphant 'Aha!' Archie adjusted what he hoped was not a broken arm and pulled himself into a relatively comfortable position. There wasn't a lot of room to manoeuvre but luckily the force of the speeding train was enough to keep him safely tucked into a small recess in the shipping container.

He followed the train's path on the E-Scroll and was overjoyed to see that the tracks they were on led straight to Eva's last known location — give or take a couple of kilometres' walk. Not quite believing his luck, Archie braced himself for the long, bumpy journey down to the coast.

Eloy and AJ

Marcus parked the car next to an abandoned train station and Eloy gently shook his sister awake.

"AJ, we're here." Due to accelerated global warming, much of the South coast was now submerged by the rising sea. Luckily Marcus knew about the elevated paths made by other Treb fugitives before them, crudely constructed with whatever floating debris was available. AJ, of course, saw this as an adventure, leaping easily over the precarious walkways to safety. Eloy, however, was trying to hide both his nerves and his general lack of balance as he stayed as close to his mother as possible. Carrying Sully over his shoulder and a collection of spades in his arms, Marcus followed the wooden planks and metal ramps over the flooded buildings to a cliff, the summit of which was now almost level with the ocean. His family arrived close behind him, Eloy visibly glad to be on semi-dry land once more. AJ looked at the sea, awestruck. She had never seen an ocean before. A few kilometres out, a vessel could be seen, growing steadily closer. It was all becoming real.

"Dad, how long will we be on the boat?" Eloy asked. None

of them had been on a boat before, and Eloy was easily nauseated.

"I'm not sure, son, but don't worry, the forecast isn't too bad for our journey. With all the storms we've been having lately, we've really lucked out for the next few days." As Eloy tried to take solace in this, Leyna was watching someone approach them.

"Marcus, is there anyone scheduled to join us?"

"I don't think so, my love. Why?" The four of them watched as the figure grew closer and closer.

"If it was someone official, surely they'd have backup?" Leyna wondered aloud.

"Maybe we should hide?" AJ offered.

"He'll have seen us by now," Marcus warned. "Everyone, get behind me."

As the figure grew closer, however, he didn't seem like much of a threat. He was tall, lanky and from the looks of his gait, completely exhausted. A few metres before they could make out the stranger's face, the figure collapsed. Marcus cautiously approached him.

"It's okay!" he called back to his family. "It's just a kid! He's passed out from exhaustion I imagine. AJ come and help me carry him!" AJ rushed to her father's side and helped lift the boy. As his face flopped to the side she gasped.

"Hey, Eloy! Eloy!" AJ had dropped the poor boy back on the ground in surprise.

"AJ what the heck are you playing at?" Marcus grumbled, now lifting him unaided.

"I know him! I mean, I met him — Eloy and I both did — at the Disuku World Cup! He was waiting in front of us at the Burger Moon stand with his sister! Eloy totally fancied her."

"AJ!" Eloy blushed as his sister and father approached.

"At least we know he's Treb then," Marcus replied. "Poor lad, trying to make it to the colony all alone."

"Well, he's not alone now," Leyna replied. Sully barked and licked the boy's face. "What's his name?"

"Uhm, I don't think he told us," AJ replied.

"He didn't. But his sister was called Enid." Eloy blushed again as he said this. "I wonder where she is, it's sad he's lost his family," he said thoughtfully, trying to draw attention away from the red glow that covered his cheeks at any mention of Enid.

"Well, we'll take care of him now. Come on, we've got a ship to catch." Marcus began loading their bags onto a large plank of wood he'd taken from one of the walkways.

"Wait," Eloy began. "The ship isn't coming to us? We have to get all the way out there ourselves?"

"It's too risky," replied Marcus. "We have to go out and meet it."

Eloy's face fell. "You're joking? We can't swim that far? I mean, maybe you and AJ can but—"

"Don't worry, petal." Leyna took his hand. "We're going on the raft. Your father and sister are going to be our little seahorses pulling us along!" AJ was unimpressed with this idea but proud of her family's belief in her swimming ability, so said nothing.

"Very funny," Marcus smiled at his wife. "You know you're rowing yourselves there!" He threw them each a spade to use as an oar.

"Oh," AJ smiled. "Now the spades make sense." She was relieved as Marcus found another plank of wood, negating any requirement for a long, cold swim. The family gingerly climbed aboard their wobbling rafts and Marcus laid the unconscious boy on the plank next to AJ. "Right, anyone know how to row?" AJ asked.

"Well, it's fairly simple," Eloy mused. "We just have to make sure we stroke together at the same time." It was his time to shine, he thought — brains over brawn. Although as they pulled themselves through the water, he realised that at least a fair amount of brawn would come in useful, as AJ and his father pulled far ahead of them.

"Come on, Eloy, we can take them!" His mother may not have been an athlete, but she had a mental strength to rival the best of them — she never backed down and Eloy felt safe with her. He pulled his oar back with all his strength, gaining courage as the ship in the distance grew closer.

"That's it my darling, I'm so proud of you." Eloy kept pulling, Sully at the front of the raft with his nose in the air, appearing to thoroughly enjoy the feel of the wind and sea-spray on his face. When they finally reached the boat, Marcus pulled them all up and over the side. A woman with a tablet computer approached them.

"I was expecting a family of four." She looked at each of them, trying to work out which was the stowaway. Her eyes settled on the pale, red-headed boy flung over Marcus' shoulder.

"We found him near the shore," Marcus replied. "He's Treb — just trying to get to safety, like us." The woman appeared satisfied and nodded.

"You can go below decks now. Stay together, there are lots of passengers today."

The Kahns descended the stairs and found themselves in the middle of an enormous crowd of people. Many were huddled together in family groups but there were some who sat alone. Each had their own reasons for running away. All of them were Trebs. AJ's eyes widened at the prospect of meeting new people, and she instantly walked over to a family with three young children and a dog. Marcus smiled at his daughter's gregarious spirit.

As AJ made new friends, Eloy found a secluded corner and settled himself down on top of his coat. Out of the corner of his eye, he saw what looked like a tattered old book sticking out from under some discarded meal drink bottles. Books were widely regarded as antiques in modern-day Anglia, but Eloy found comfort in the yellowing pages and old-fashioned ink. Not to mention the fact that his disabled Treb-Chip meant that he could no longer use his holophone to connect to the internet — what else was there to do? Leyna sat down next to him and rested her head on his shoulder as he began to read.

'Atticus Impero-Regnum I was born on the seventeenth of January, 1945, during the horrors of the second world war.'

"Oh great," Eloy mumbled, "another Electi propaganda 'history' textbook."

"It looks far too old to be one of those," Leyna mused as she flicked through the yellowed pages. "Keep reading."

'Very little is known about his childhood and parentage, although later in life, Atticus would produce a detailed family tree dating back to the thirteenth century. This ancestry has never been corroborated by additional records, however. It has therefore been suggested by some authors that Atticus' claims of historical nobility may be entirely unfounded.'

"Well, that wouldn't surprise me in the least," Leyna smiled. "He lies about everything else, why not his lineage?" They read on.

'Upon completing his first year of study at Oxford University, Atticus founded The Electi society, the name which his son would later adopt for his government and social class. This was an invitation-only society for university students of note — predominantly those from noble families or with connections in business. Through this society, Atticus went from being a relatively unknown figure to one of the most influential students in the university. After he graduated with a first-class honours in political science, he began climbing the ranks of the country's most influential media company, CT&T, changing the way that newspapers and television reported for years to come. Under Atticus' leadership, this company grew to eclipse all others, giving Atticus almost total control over the people of Great Britain as he used the media to further his own agenda.'

"I remember my father telling me about that," Leyna interrupted. "The newspapers began reporting more and more negatively on immigrants like us. The public began to turn on us and blame us for all the country's problems like the failing economy."

'After this, Atticus worked in banking, before and during several financial crises from which he somehow profited. After retiring, he settled down to start a family and had one child, a son named Ignatius. It was this son who would go on to be elected the first President of Anglia following the horrific events of NW1. His first act as President was to officially discontinue the monarchy as a British institution, cementing his role as sole

leader and figurehead of the country.'

"Oh, I remember that too," whispered Leyna as she read over her son's shoulder. "I was never particularly fond of the royal family personally. My mother was very complimentary about the late queen, but she died the year before I was born. I did feel sorry for them when Ignatius stripped their family of everything though — they could have just taken their titles — but to take their homes as well... Nasty business it was. Then again, the country was suffering while they ate five course dinners every evening, so I wasn't altogether surprised." Leyna shook her head as AJ sauntered back to the group, sitting down next to Marcus.

"Whatcha reading?" AJ asked casually.

"I'm not really sure," Eloy admitted. "It's really old and it doesn't seem to have a title. It has some brutally honest facts about the president though — it was probably banned."

"Cool!" AJ grinned. "I just met the most amazing family," she beamed. "This little girl, Alicja and her sister Zuzanna are adorable! Their parents are both from Poland so naturally, I was telling them all about you, Mum, and how your family are from Zakopane and — wait — am I giving away too much information?"

Leyna looked at her daughter and smiled.

"No more than you give away on your Xchange profile dear."

"Oh no! My Xchange page — without my holophone how will I update my followers?"

Eloy laughed at his sister.

"You won't, genius! You can kiss your followers, goodbye!"

"But, but — I was so close to ten thousand views on my blindfolded disuku goal video! So close..." AJ looked off hopelessly into the distance.

"It will be an adjustment living without technology," Leyna told her, "but it will be fun! An adventure! Like, camping!"

Eloy and AJ looked equally confused.

"What's camping?" they asked in baffled unison.

"What? Oh yes, of course. Well before the war, when there were still green spaces and forests, people used to go in these sort of fabric huts and stay in the great outdoors!" Eloy looked offended.

"You mean sleep? Outside? In the cold and wet? No thanks."

"Oh, petal, it was lovely! Sleeping under the stars and waking up with the deer. Some of my fondest memories are of camping with my mother." Leyna's heart thudded against her chest with renewed vigour as she remembered her.

"Where we're going is still wild and beautiful," Marcus added. "You won't have ever seen anything like it! It's a far cry from the concrete boxes you've grown up in, that's for sure."

"...and Mizuki?" AJ was still worried about her friend.

"Bruce is doing his best, love."

A muffled grunt behind them drew their attention and the previously unconscious boy stirred to life.

"Don't rush yourself." Marcus was at his side. "Take your time, son, it's okay, you made it.

"I... I did? Is Evie here?" The boy looked around sheepishly.

"Do you mean Enid?" Eloy asked. "Your sister? Were you looking for her?"

"Oh, um." The boy looked around, scanning the sea of faces. "Where are we exactly?"

"We're on a boat, on our way to the base, don't worry, you've made it. You'll be safe soon. Why were you running? No judgement, of course — we're all fugitives here!"

"The base?" The boy tried to sit up but thought he might be sick.

"Yes, son, you know, the Treb base — run by the rebel group. That was where you were trying to get to, surely?" Marcus felt the boy's head for a fever, but he was stone cold. His eyes were wide, and his mouth was open in a silent scream of horror. Archibald Impero-Regnum had just realised how much danger he was getting himself into. He was heading straight into the heart of the enemy camp, surrounded by people who probably wanted him dead. All of a sudden, he was beginning to regret his courageous plan.

Chapter 13

Welcome to the Jungle

Eloy, AJ & Eva

The weather grew clearer the further they travelled from Anglia and AJ couldn't believe how blue the sky could be. As the boat pulled up to a beautiful sandy beach, Eloy peered over the edge in wonder.

"Dad! Dad, can you believe it?" Marcus looked at his children, beaming. He was so happy they could finally see what the world could be like. Anglia had exaggerated the scale of the disaster to try and prevent a mass exodus to greener pastures, but the Electi government weren't exactly improving things by continuing to destroy their country with pollution and copious waste.

AJ was entranced by the dancing wisps of cloud overhead and Leyna inhaled the fresh, clean air, without the need for her respirator, as if trying to fill her whole body with it. They disembarked slowly due to the sheer number of people and the fact they still needed to support the boy they had found. Of course, they didn't know that this boy happened to be the son of the Anglian Prime Minister. That may have diminished their levels of generosity towards him somewhat. Archie blinked slowly in the bright sun and tried to come up with some kind of plan. A man in a large straw hat came to meet them at the entrance to the jungle.

"You'll need to stick close to me," he instructed. "It's easy to get lost in here — trust me — we grew it that way on purpose!" The group laughed along with him, mostly with relief that they were finally away from choppy waters and cold ocean spray.

As they followed the man through the jungle, the party gazed open-mouthed at the lush greenery and inhabiting wildlife. AJ thought she saw a sloth, but no one believed her, and a small green bird landed on Leyna's thick blonde hair, having mistaken it for a nest. When the trees cleared, they were at the mouth of a hidden valley, full of small metal huts and wooden shelters. The man led them each to a hut and gave them brief instructions about when and where to get food, bathe and sign up for work. Eloy wrinkled his nose up at the idea of bathing in communal lakes. AJ wrinkled her nose up at the idea of work. Both, however, were excited to explore their new corrugated aluminium home.

"Dad, look! Bunk beds! I call top!" AJ flung her bag onto the top bunk and stuck her tongue out at her brother.

"Real mature," he muttered. As they were unpacking, a tall woman with blue and purple hair walked in.

"Marcus! You made it!" Siri Perl embraced Marcus with relief. "We've never met but I feel like we've been friends for years," she continued, "you've helped us out for so long! I'm so sorry it got so rough for you back in Anglia. We always knew it might, though. At least you're here now."

Marcus nodded and looked sympathetically at his family. Siri seemed to have only just realised they were there and apologised profusely.

"I'm so sorry, I'm Siri." She offered her hand out to Leyna

and the twins. "I'm in charge out here. Ask me anything and... well if I don't know, no one does!" She laughed, hoping the others would laugh along but they didn't. They still weren't entirely sure of her. "Your dad, he's saved a lot of lives. Some many times over."

"We know," AJ stated proudly. "He's a hero."

"He certainly is."

There was an awkward silence as the Kahn family took in their new surroundings and realised that their old life was well and truly over. Siri smiled weakly. "Well, I'll let you get settled." She began backing out of the hut. "Meals are served in the central hall at seven and seven." She placed a hand on the door frame. "Follow the signs to the bathing lakes — we've got three now! Male, female and who cares!" She smiled hopefully.

AJ's face softened, Siri didn't seem so bad.

"I'll see you guys later!" Siri gave them one last reassuring smile before disappearing back into the bustling thoroughfare.

"I thought she'd be older," Leyna offered.

"Me too," Marcus replied. "But then I also thought she'd be a guy." The Kahn family finished unpacking and sat on the wooden bed in the centre of the room. "It's going to be okay," Marcus reassured them. "Honestly."

Archie had been shown to a long metal hut full of bunk beds with several other single travellers. He gingerly climbed onto a top bunk in the corner of the hut and closed his eyes. What on earth was he going to do now? Was Eva here — and if she was — would she even be alive? Surely the Trebs would have killed her by now, he thought to himself — and they'd kill him too if they got the chance. He silently vowed not to go down without a fight, but he felt weaker than he'd ever been and was severely doubting his capability of putting up any kind of defence. A tall boy took the bunk below him and Archie tried not to move. As long as he stayed calm and inconspicuous, he shouldn't be recognised. This would be easier said than done though — even their stint at the disuku stadium had been fraught with danger and Archie knew that this would be significantly more challenging. He decided to leave at nightfall and explore the valley in search of Eva. Until then, he closed his eyes and allowed himself to drift into the darkness of sleep.

Everyone except Eloy slept well that night — too exhausted by the journey to complain about the threadbare blankets or hard wooden beds. Eloy couldn't seem to shake the feeling that they were still in danger, however, and he awoke as the sun rose, creeping out of the hut with the intention of bathing in the lake while it was still empty.

Eloy followed the wooden signposts and was pleasantly surprised to find that the men's lake appeared to be deserted. More confidently now, knowing he was alone, he strode through the thicket to the edge of the lake. Once in the centre of the clearing, he could see the full expanse of the jungle — trees snaked up towards the sky for kilometres around, and beautiful birds of every colour flew overhead. The sound of splashing in front of him brought his gaze back down to eye level.

"Oh my god!" The girl's voice broke the silence as well as Eloy's appreciation for nature and she darted back below the water.

Eloy froze for a moment, unsure of what he was seeing. As a shy head of brunette hair peered hesitantly from the middle of the lake, he realised his predicament and quickly turned away.

"Oh, I'm so sorry!" he called out pathetically. "I thought

this was the men's clearing but then the signs are a bit, well, you know." He shuffled awkwardly, unsure of whether to run away or stay put.

"No, no! It's my fault!" The voice returned over the water. "There were people in the other lakes and I... I get embarrassed." The girl's eyes were visible now, as blue as the water surrounding them.

"I'll just go then," Eloy began, and he made dramatic motions to signal his retreat. Wild splashing made him turn back around though as the girl protested.

"No, don't be silly. I'm the one in the wrong—" She stopped abruptly, realising that more of her body was out of the water than was comfortable, and both she and Eloy turned redder than the nearby birds who seemed to be watching their exchange with amused interest. Eloy turned away again.

"Just don't look," the girl pleaded and slowly swam to the edge of the lake. Eloy could hear her just behind him but would never dream of turning around, no matter how tempting. His mother had taught him the value of respect and he didn't want to make the poor girl feel worse. As the girl began dressing Eloy was horrified to see someone approaching through the thicket towards the clearing. "Oh no, oh no!" the girl panicked, as she hurriedly pulled on the rest of her clothes. Eloy's stomach dropped as his sister's confused face emerged from the bushes. She took a few seconds to take in the situation before grinning broadly at her brother. Eloy swore under his breath.

"Well, well, well, Eloy!" AJ cooed with both eyebrows raised. "A couple of hours in paradise and you can talk a girl into anything!" Eloy walked towards her and held out his hand as if to shoo her away.

"It's not like that, AJ! She was just in the wrong pool and

I—"

"No, no," AJ interrupted in mock apology, "I'm not judging! I'm kind of jealous actually, I always figured I'd be the first to uh, well, there you go!"

"AJ, I'm telling you it's not like that!" Eloy was getting cross now, but the girl was dressed and walking towards them both. She turned to AJ with eyes like ice, swiftly removing AJ's oversized grin.

"Excuse me but no boy could 'talk me into' anything, thank you very much! I am a respectable woman and if I did engage in such activities — which I can assure you I do not — it would *not* be in the middle of a bird-filled jungle clearing in a lake filled with frogspawn!" AJ and Eloy were too dumbstruck to respond. "Your friend here was nothing but a gentleman which is far more than I can say for you, madam!" With a final huff, she scowled at AJ and stormed out of the clearing.

Silence clung to the twins for a minute or so before AJ broke it. "Wow." She looked at Eloy, a mixture of alarmed and impressed. "She's a bit posh, isn't she? 'Specially for a Treb, do you like that then?"

"Shut *up, AJ!*" Eloy pushed his sister enough to make her readjust her footing. "Don't you remember her? She's that girl from the stadium! And yeah, I like her, I really do, but I swear nothing—"

"I know, I know I was only teasing you. What are you doing in the girl's lake though?" AJ poked him playfully.

"AJ this is the guy's lake — didn't you read the sign?" Eloy was once again exasperated with his sister. AJ shrugged.

"Not really, no. But then I always think gender is more of a social construct."

"Of course you do," Eloy sighed.

After the morning's events, the twins hadn't felt much like bathing in the lake, and they returned instead to their ramshackle hut. AJ, of course, told their parents all about the girl and Eloy's shame — much to his embarrassment. When Marcus had finally stopped laughing, he turned to his daughter.

"I bet you were jealous!" he teased. AJ blushed.

"Nah, too posh for me," she replied with a coy smile. Eloy was confused.

"And, she was a *she*," he commented, half clarifying, half questioning.

"Um, no, that part was fine." AJ looked at her brother with scepticism in her eyes. "You know that, right?"

"Wait." Eloy turned fully to face his twin. "Wait, what? You like girls?" he asked, slowly.

"You didn't know?" Leyna was surprised. The twins shared nearly everything, and their parents had both known since AJ was eleven. They needed to keep it quiet in the outside world of course, as the Electi made no secret about their anti-LGBTQ+ policies and conversion programmes, but they were far from ashamed of their daughter.

"No, I didn't know!" Eloy replied hotly. "Why wouldn't you tell me?" He was hurt and having a hard time hiding it.

"It was never a secret, Eloy. I'm always going on about how beautiful Sophie Lavine in the year above is!" Eloy considered this. "And the Anglian Angels captain, Natasha Jay."

"I just thought," he paused, "I just thought you were jealous of them. I thought that you wanted to be like them." AJ gave him a look as if to say, 'I wanted more than that'. Marcus caught it and laughed.

"What am I going to do with you both? Two fifteen-year-olds on a utopian island surrounded by beautiful girls! You'll lose your minds." AJ grinned cheekily. Eloy attempted a smile, but his thoughts were still lingering on Enid. By nightfall, he would find her. He couldn't keep meeting her like this without at least asking her out. Although, he thought to himself, what on Earth would one do for a date on Project Libertas?

Chapter 14

We've Got Fun and Games

Eloy & AJ — Archie & Eva

Archie opened his eyes and blinked against the bright sun. He had slept through the night and missed his chance to find Eva under the cover of darkness. He cursed himself and peered over the side of his bunk. The hut was empty, besides him. His stomach growled. Stretching, he remembered something the guide had said about meals taking place in one of the central structures. That would be like walking into the lions' den — everyone would be there with nowhere to hide. His stomach, however, won the war with his head and with a loud grumble, Archie decided to risk it. As he left the tent, he was able, for the first time, to take in the sights and sounds of Project Libertas. It was nothing like Anglia with its dark skies and concrete monoliths. Out here the sky was bluer than anything he could ever imagine and there was even grass — as green as it was in the old movies he had watched with his mother. Archie felt a pang of guilt thinking about her. She would now be looking for two lost children with only her husband, Atticus, Antoinette and Euridice for company. Archie hoped that this would at least force her to be closer with his two younger sisters whom, prior to now, Lady Margot had never shown any particular interest in. Archie was thinking about his sisters when a girl of about seven skirted around the edge of a nearby tent and walked into him.

"Oops! Sorry, are you okay?" The girl was small and pale-skinned with a shock of ginger hair. Archie thought she looked like a smaller, cuter version of himself.

"Hi there! I'm fine, are you okay? Are you lost?" Archie crouched down to meet the girl's eyes, not wanting to intimidate her with his height.

"I'm not lost, I just—" She looked around warily. "I'm just looking for a place that... I can't remember where it is." Archie privately thought that this sounded exactly the same as being lost but he didn't want to embarrass her.

"I'm going to breakfast," he offered. "Is that where you're going?" The girl nodded shyly. "Okay," Archie smiled. "Well, I know that talking to strangers isn't a good idea, and neither is following them, but I'm going to walk a really safe way where there are other people, so you know you're safe." Archie pointed to the wide, spiralling path to the centre of the valley, lined with huts and busy with people. "Does that sound okay?" The little girl hesitated. She looked down at Archie's open hand with curiosity.

"Why is your chip like that?" She pointed at the magnets still lashed to his hand with one of Eva's hairbands.

"Oh, well, uh, I didn't want anyone to find me." Archie winced. If walking past hundreds of Treb rebels wasn't a risky enough plan, now he had told one of them he was in hiding. The little girl looked at him and giggled.

"You are silly, don't you know there's a lady that does that for you? You don't need to wear a bracelet. Come on, I'll show you." The little girl stretched out her hand.

Archie smiled. "Okay, but you show me the way, okay? I don't want people to think I'm kidnapping you."

The little girl took Archie's hand with surprising strength and began skipping down the main path. Archie had to jog to keep up and shot occasional smiles at intrigued passers-by, hoping he wouldn't be recognised.

As they approached the centre of the valley, Archie began to panic. His chip. They would know it was an Electi chip and worse — one of the most high-ranking in Anglia. Not wanting to alarm the girl with a sudden stop, he kept following her, desperately trying to think of a plan. The central tower loomed before him — it looked like a giant tree — built out of wood harvested from the nearby jungle, and topped with a canopy of leaves and vines, undoubtedly to make it less conspicuous to any unwelcome guests. As they entered through a large wooden archway, Archie was greeted by a divine smell. He saw that the rear corner of the ground floor hosted an enormous dining area, filled with what must have been nearly all the valley's inhabitants. Adults and children were eating happily — there was even a small dog feasting happily on someone's discarded table scraps in a corner. The little girl pulled Archie around to the wall of the building and showed him a long line of what looked like old ATM machines, from when people used to use real money.

"You put your hand in there—" she pointed to the hole "— and the nice lady turns your chip off!" Archie sighed in relief. It was automated — nobody would actually see his chip. Quickly, he tore the magnets from his hand and thrust it into the machine. The image of a smiling woman filled the screen.

"Good morning. My name is Doctor Kyap and I will be wiping your TrebChip this morning! One moment please." Archie winced — what if this didn't work on Electi chips? "All done — have a great day on Project Libertas!" The woman's

140

voice brought Archie back to his senses, and he delicately removed his hand.

"There you go!" said the little girl. "Oh, and look! I found breakfast all by myself!" She gave Archie a proud smile before skipping off to the collection of tables along the back of the room. Archie looked down at his hand. The shimmering gold of his Electi chip looked just as it had before, he could only hope that the machine had worked. Despite fearing for his life here, he didn't want to trigger an Electi raid on all of these innocent people. He doubted his father would show them any mercy if he even suspected that they had kidnapped him or Eva.

At breakfast, AJ was tucking into some roasted plantain and passing her soybeans onto Sully, having read about dogs and vegetarianism on an XChange blog post.

"As long as he gets his protein," she continued, "he'll be fine — it's just like Mum!" Leyna smiled. Living on an island with no option of meat certainly made her life as a vegan easy. Eloy was looking around in-between mouthfuls of potato, searching for Enid.

"Don't worry, you'll find her," Marcus quietly reassured him, not wanting AJ to hear and seize upon a fresh chance to embarrass her twin.

As it happened, Eva was, at that moment, dining on a particularly delicious bowl of satsumas (in her short time on the island she had developed a minor addiction to citrus fruits) in Siri Perl's private dining room. Siri herself never used it, preferring to dine amongst the citizens, but Eva had been encouraged to use it for her own safety. No one was quite sure yet how the daughter of a dictator would be received on Project Libertas. Eva peeled yet another satsuma and thought about the

141

food back home. While she was privy to a much wider variety of food than her Treb counterparts, none of it came close to the bounty of this paradise island. What her father wouldn't give to gain access to the fertile soil of this island, she thought to herself.

She turned to look through the window and down to the dining hall below. Watching the crowds tucking into their breakfasts, she felt a pang of déjà vu. This was just like sitting in her family's box at the disuku stadium. Looking down on the Treb citizens below and feeling an enormous surge of injustice, she made a decision. Who was she to be sitting in a private dining room? She was just like anyone else. Resolute, Eva finished her breakfast, walked out the door and marched down the stairs to the dining hall. Glancing around for a seat, her eyes fell on a little girl with ginger hair. She looked just like Archie and was currently taking bets on how many soybeans she could fit inside her mouth. As she squeezed in the fourteenth unlucky bean, Eva stifled a giggle. She really was just like Archie. Scanning the room, Eva spotted a familiar face. A young girl with dark hair and glasses feeding a small dog. She was the girl from the lake — very rude — Eva thought. Though, if the girl was here, where was that boy? Interrupting her train of thought, Archie, unaware of his sister's presence, appeared just inches in front of her, as he congratulated the little girl on her seventeenth and final soybean.

"Archie!" Eva was euphoric and not entirely sure that she wasn't hallucinating. "Archie, it's me!"

Archie's head whipped around wildly, too surprised by the voice to focus on its location. Realising that his sister was mere inches from him now, Archie let out a sort of scream and dropped to his knees.

"Evie? Evie it's you, you're alive! I can't believe you're alive! I swear I'll never make fun of you again. I'll be the best brother anyone's ever known." Archie had shuffled up to his amused sister and grabbed her around the waist. She was giggling at his hilariously exaggerated promises when she noticed that the other diners were looking suspiciously in their direction.

"Archie," she hissed urgently. "Stop, people are looking!" Archie looked up at his sister's panicked face in swift apology. As he stood up, he felt the stare of hundreds of eyes upon him. Hoping for a miracle, Archie took Eva's hand and began to walk her towards the main entrance of the compound. Whether it was pure luck or the fact she had heard the ominous silence, Siri Perl chose that moment to commence her first radio broadcast of the day.

"My fellow citizens!" Her voice boomed dramatically over the speakers in the hall and, Archie could hear, throughout the valley. *"Welcome to the first day of the rest of your lives!"* She paused for effect, giving Archie and Eva time to slip outside before any Trebs realised where they had recognised them from. *"Our scholastic program finally begins today! We now have enough educational leaders to run four camps — one for each skill set — but more on that later! Any person between the ages of seven and eighteen will need to enrol today at the education hut — that's the little wooden building near the lakes. There are signs, please ask any leaders for directions. Classes begin tomorrow!"*

Back in the dining hall AJ groaned. "Are you kidding me? Do we *still* have to go to school? Really? *No* to the internet but *yes* to school?" Leyna patted her daughter's arm

143

sympathetically.

"Sorry, petal, I'm kind of the reason for that. I signed up as an educational leader." Eloy laughed but AJ looked imploringly at her mother. "It'll be good for you love, just wait and see." Siri's broadcast continued, reminding citizens to wipe their microchips and advising of any new work opportunities.

"See, Mum and Dad have to work too," Eloy reminded a grumpy AJ who was now sulking with a smoothie.

"Yeah, they've got me as head of security on my first day!" Marcus scoffed, half boasting but equally nervous about the new position. "Hopefully there isn't too much crime on a tropical island."

The Kahn family finished their breakfast before returning to their hut, unknowingly passing Archie and Eva as they did so, who were hiding behind shelf full of fruit.

"So, you weren't kidnapped?" Archie asked again.

"No, I *was* kidnapped, they just didn't do it in a… in a… it's just different. The Trebs — they're not like Father says. They're just people like us. They need me here to try and change things. They want to make things better."

"Yes, yes, we all want that." Archie was exasperated. "But that doesn't mean you can just go around kidnapping people!"

"Desperate times, Archibald," his sister implored. Archie glowered.

"Please don't call me that," he winced. An alarm in the distance made them even more panicky, and Eva quickly led her brother to the hut she shared with Carmen, the head of animal care. Archie looked nervously around the room then froze when he saw the panda cub, playing happily on the bed.

"Evie, what the—" Eva picked Tian up from the bed and

playfully waved her in front of Archie.

"It's a big scary bear! Rawr!" Archie slowly backed away as Tian tried to playfully bat his nose.

"That's not funny, Eva. How does it even work, is it real?"

"Yes, it's real — look out the window, they've rescued dozens of animals from extinction and are working to try and keep them thriving. Well, not quite thriving but…" Eva opened the back door of the hut to a vast enclosure surrounding the entire edge of the valley. Archie stared at the various enclosures, some housing lions, some zebras and a whole area for what must have been at least twenty species of bird. He looked up and was surprised to see the open sky.

"Why don't they just fly away?" he asked, confused.

"They don't want to," replied Eva. The further away they fly, the less food there is. They're cared for here, there's little to no radiation and they're with other animals. A few hundred kilometres in any direction and it's a different story." Archie walked up to a smaller enclosure at the back.

"Aw, look — tortoises! I love these guys! Euridice used to have one, it was so cute. These are massive though! Wait, what are those things?" Archie pointed to a group of large pink birds in another enclosure. Eva looked nonplussed.

"Archie, those are flamingos. How do you not know what a flamingo is?" Archie looked embarrassed.

"Oh well, you know, there are no animals in Anglia, and I was sick that day you guys went to the holo-zoo. Plus, this is different, they're so real."

"They *are* real, dummy."

"All right, all right! Give me a minute to adjust Eva, this is all pretty unexpected!" As Archie looked around him, he could see enclosures for goats, foxes, hares, antelope and even, he squinted to see through a patch of particularly dense shrubbery, what looked like a brown bear.

"There you are!" Siri Perl emerged from around the corner, making Archie jump. "Wait a minute." Siri stared pointedly at Archie.

"Siri!" Eva interrupted. "You remember my brother Archie — he came here to find me." Siri's eyes widened in sudden realisation.

"Wait, so we have *two* Impero-Regnum kids now?" She looked as though she had just won the lottery. Archie looked terrified. "Oh, ho, ho!" She punched the air in excitement. "Now we've really got a chance — not just a chance — a sign! How did you even get here? Oh, who cares." Siri hadn't stopped to let Archie respond, and he was still standing frozen to the spot. "You must be the Electi chip that tripped the alarms!" Siri picked up her walkie-talkie, leaving Eva and Archie to wonder what on earth it was.

"Siri to base, false alarm. Repeat, false alarm." She returned the walkie talkie to her pocket and beamed at the siblings. "This is it kiddos, we're going to the camps!"

"Siri, slow down. What do you mean, the camps?" Eva could never quite keep up with her former tutor's train of thought.

"Well, let's just say your education is going to be a little... different from now on." The siblings looked suspiciously at Siri before tentatively following her towards the education hut. What on earth could they learn on a tropical island thousands of miles from home? Eva wasn't sure, but privately hoped that there would be more fruit once they got there.

Chapter 15

Camp Pride!

Eloy & AJ — Archie & Eva

The 'Education hut' really wasn't much to look at. It was a shabby wooden structure with peeling blue paint and a leaky roof. Inside, however, was much more exciting. Each of the four walls was draped in a different coloured banner and emblazoned with a large image of an animal. In the centre of the room was a patchwork throw and a scattering of cushions. Siri beckoned the gathered children and young people to sit.

"This," Siri began, "is unlike any school you have ever been to." AJ was somewhat relieved by this. "We're not training you to churn out data or moulding you into automatons to merge into a predetermined career." Leyna's eyes widened. After several years in the educational system, this was music to her ears. "At Project Libertas, we will train you to be the best that you can be, whoever that may be." The crowd looked nervously around and Eloy caught sight of Enid and her brother. His heart skipped a beat and he quickly looked away, silently euphoric that he had found her again so soon. "The hut is divided into four camps," Siri went on.

"I'm a parrot!" Leyna exclaimed happily.

"Camp Loro," Siri corrected her with an exasperated head shake. "It's Spanish. We gave the camps animal mascots to entice the little ones, not the adults!"

Clearly, AJ thought, Siri didn't know Leyna Kahn particularly well yet. She was most definitely a five-year-old at heart. It's what made her such a good teacher. "Each camp focuses on a specific skillset — each of these skills having been chosen to perfectly suit our mission," Siri continued.

"Our mission?" AJ asked sceptically.

"Why do you think we're here, honey?" Siri turned to AJ with an eyebrow raised. "We're not just playing happy campers and hoping it all goes away out here. We're all Anglia has left fighting for it."

AJ was uncharacteristically silent at Siri's blunt response. Eloy looked back at Enid who seemed far less daunted by this revelation.

"You will be given a list of qualities and skills attributed to each camp and will be asked which camp you think best suits you. I will be cross-referencing your answers with the information given to me by your parents and," she paused for a wicked grin, "your school reports." The room let out a mystified 'oooooh' and exchanged worried looks.

"Our school reports? How on earth did you get those?" Archie protested, half impressed and half horrified.

"What I can't do with a computer, nobody can." The group was silent at Siri Perl's steely resolve and, despite the bright colours and animal motifs surrounding them, they could tell that this would be far from a regular summer camp.

Once the initiation had finished and they had all been given their questionnaires, Eloy made a nervous beeline for Enid. Archie elbowed his sister as he watched his approach. "Hey, Evie, who's this guy?" Eva turned around and blushed.

148

"Oh, it's you." She tried to keep herself as calm and collected as possible under the watchful eyes of her brother.

"Erm, hi. It's um, I'm Eloy. Did I tell you that yet? Just, we keep meeting and um…" He stopped when he noticed the confusion in the girl's eyes.

"We… *met*… at the lake," Eva stated, trying to banish the humiliating memory. Eloy paled. She hadn't remembered him from the stadium. Maybe he hadn't been as memorable to Enid as she had been to him, he thought hopelessly.

"Oh, I remember you!" Archie chimed in. "From the Disuku World Cup! You were talking to Eva while I got my food! Didn't you have a friend?" Eager to eavesdrop on her brother's latest embarrassment, AJ walked over to join them. "Yes, yes you! You were there too!" Archie pointed at AJ with fresh realisation. Eva now remembered their previous encounter and began to turn a rosy pink.

"Oh goodness, um, well yes now I remember, and I think I need to tell you something. My name isn't actually Enid, it's—"

"Students!" Siri's voice boomed from the centre of the room. "Sorry to be a bore but you need to complete the questionnaires independently — that means on your own. I can't have you changing your answers to be in the same camp as your friend." As the four teenagers reluctantly scattered, Eva reached out to grab Eloy's retreating arm. "Eva. I'm Eva. Come and find me later."

The questionnaires, AJ thought, were oddly specific.

Q1. If you had to do any of the following chores, what would it be?

1. Clearing out junk emails

2. *Making a telephone call*
3. *Filling in forms*
4. *Mowing the lawn (Lawns were areas of grass usually found in back gardens that required regular maintenance).*

AJ ticked number four, always preferring physical tasks to mental ones. Eva ticked one, knowing anything technical would take her the least time; Archie two, confident that his way with words always helped when speaking on the phone; and Eloy three, used to filling in complicated scholarship applications for school. AJ found that most of her answers landed her in the number four spot and wondered which camp that would be assigned to.

Q11. If you could do anything for your birthday, what would it be?
1. *Virtual Reality Gaming*
2. *Surprise party*
3. *Escape Room*
4. *Laser Tag*

"Oooooh, *yes* number four!" AJ whispered to herself while hoping laser tag was one of the designated school activities. As they completed their questionnaires — Eloy finishing first, followed by Eva, AJ then Archie — they were directed to sit back on the carpet. As Eva walked past a younger child, she could see that her questionnaire was different to hers, and largely comprised of images rather than text.

"They had to make it accessible for all ages," Leyna whispered to her, after seeing her curious glance. "It works the same way though — in fact, it's easier to get clear answers from the picture-based quiz." The four of them waited in the middle of the room for everyone to finish their questionnaires. Eloy kept shooting nervous glances at Eva while she pretended not to notice. Archie, now sat next to AJ, pointed at Eloy and whispered,

"What's his deal then? Does he fancy my sister or something?"

AJ laughed, resulting in a disapproving look from Siri, before replying, "He's my twin brother; he's an idiot with a genius IQ; and yes, he definitely fancies your posh sister." Archie smirked at her response.

"Hey, you're funny. I'm Archie."

"AJ."

Archie thought about his next move and decided that the day had already been mad enough to warrant throwing caution to the wind. "I, uh, don't suppose—"

"Let me stop you right there." AJ turned to Archie, having heard this opener a million times. Archie looked taken aback. "I'm not your type. And you certainly aren't mine. I make a great wingman though." She winked at Archie, who was taking some time to process this message. "Now, this girl—" AJ pulled out a crumpled picture of Mizuki from her pocket. "She's my type."

Archie blinked slowly. "Ohhh, I've got it. I'm there." He nodded and tried to appear cool. AJ laughed. This was always her favourite part of her constant coming out. Archie gave her a wink, pointed to the picture and gave a thumbs up. "Nice."

AJ laughed, but couldn't suppress the pain she felt at still not knowing how Mizuki was faring back in Anglia. Archie slyly pointed to Siri while her back was turned, and whispered to AJ, "She's my type."

"Wow, okay. Dream big, dude." AJ scoffed and fist-bumped her new friend.

"Okay, kids." Siri was in the middle of the room and holding a stack of questionnaires. "Sorry we had to do this the old-fashioned way, but our technology is limited for now. I promise you we'll be up and running soon. But for now, let me introduce you to your camp leaders — Leyna Kahn." Leyna stepped into the section of the room emblazoned with parrots and gave a friendly wave. "Roshin Haverford." A young woman with the longest, most beautiful hair Eva had ever seen stepped into the corner covered with bears. "Rachel Bowers." A small, shy woman with multicoloured hair stood nervously in the coral-coloured corner of foxes. "And, finally…" Siri took four dramatic steps backwards to the corner of the room covered in tortoises. "Me." Archie grinned and elbowed AJ.

"Ahem," came an indignant voice from the speakers around them. The eyes of the students all turned to face a newly illuminated screen in the middle of the room.

"And I, am Puffles!" A small, green dragon appeared on screen, waving cheerfully.

"Ah," Siri interrupted. "Our newest software. P.U.F.F.L.E.S or, to put it less interestingly — the performance utiliser framework for lifestyle and entertainment systems — has been designed to replace the current Electi and Moon Media monitoring systems we all use to control our lives. Unlike the current systems, P.U.F.F.L.E.S won't use your data to try and control or manipulate you."

"I won't?" Puffles sounded incredulous. "I mean, I definitely won't!" he beamed reassuringly.

"We're still working out some kinks with his personality programming," Siri explained.

"My personality is perfect!" Puffles shouted insistently. "And now," he announced before pausing for effect, "thanks to my impeccable programming and test calculation abilities, your chips will now glow the colour of your camps." Puffles clapped his virtual paws twice and in an instant, everyone's wrists glowed brightly with beautiful pastel hues.

"I'm... I'm pink, great." Eloy was not impressed as he reluctantly walked towards the coral 'Camp Zorro'.

"I'm turquoise... that's... oh tortoises, how cute! My little sister had one of those." Eva skipped happily to join Siri in 'Camp Tortuga', glad that she already knew her teacher. Archie joined Leyna in the yellow 'Camp Loro', while AJ was proud to be sorted into the purple 'Camp Oro'. Bears certainly seemed to be the most impressive animal of the bunch. Once everyone was placed, Puffles clapped his paws again and the room went dark. Everyone fell silent as the walls lit up with holovision screens, instantly silencing everyone's excited conversations.

"She wasn't kidding about the technology," AJ whispered to anyone who would listen. But no one was listening. All eyes were fixed on the film now playing in front of them all. Footage from the nuclear bombings of 2035, interspersed with images of Treb protests and Electi dinner parties filled the walls. The younger children, frightened, clung to the older ones. Siri's pre-recorded voice spoke over the noise of screaming.

"I am sorry to do this to you. But hate and evil can only continue when people turn a blind eye. Well, not anymore. In this place, you will learn about many atrocities that you never knew had been committed. You will hear of secrets and lies created by the very people elected to protect you."

The footage of thousands of mothers protesting during the infertility crisis of the 2040s filled the wall. Eloy and AJ felt their skin prickle as they remembered what their mother had told them about the miracle of them being born during this period. Leyna silently wept as she watched the women crying in the streets.

"You will learn of the illegal arrests, assassinations and mass-murders committed by your government in the name of progress."

Archie inhaled, more than slightly offended. His father was a nasty piece of work, sure, but this was going a bit far, wasn't it? The footage cut to a jail cell with laser bars and the image of a young child in his mother's arms. They had no food and were being taunted by guards. Archie felt sick.

"We cannot turn a blind eye anymore. Once you have seen it. Once you believe it. Only then, can we stop it."

The image on the screen showed Anglia from above, a grey, smoky wasteland, before zooming out to show the rest of the world around it. The room gasped. Far from being the centre of modern civilisation, Anglia looked more like a dying island. The Electi had led its citizens to believe that everywhere else on earth — save the ESA — was uninhabitable. However, as the camera panned out, Africa could clearly be seen to be greener than it had been for centuries; parts of Europe appeared to contain patches of water and forest; even Australia seemed to be recovering. The world was fighting back. But why would the leaders of Anglia and the ESA hide this from its people?

"We will never unsee what has been seen. And we will never, ever stop fighting."

The screens went dark and the room was silent.

Mizuki

The light from the laser cell bars was all that brought brightness to the gloomy room Mizuki was imprisoned in. It had been months, but it had felt like years. She knew her mother and father were in the cell down the hall because she could see them being dragged past for questioning, but there was no way for them to communicate. Nothing could be heard above the buzzing of the lasers.

She thought of AJ and Eloy. Were they looking for her? She hoped not. She didn't want them messed up in any of this. It was all her own fault of course. She should never have snooped in her mother's secret Electi files. How could she have been so stupid? The hardest thing was knowing that she was the reason her parents were in there with her. She'd give anything just to let them go — they could keep her. She didn't care anymore. She had no fight left to give. Whatever happened though, no matter how many times they asked, no-matter how many times they tortured her — she wasn't going to give up any information on her two best friends. They were everything to her, especially AJ. AJ was the first person she had ever had any kind of feelings for that were more than friendship. When AJ had told her that she felt the same... remembering that moment was all that was keeping her strong.

She lay on the metal bed frame, wide awake, as she did

155

every night. She made a tune in her head out of the rhythmic buzzing of the laser bars. Through listening to the guards, she had learned that this prison was hidden inside New London's disuku stadium. She couldn't believe that only a few months earlier she had been in this very building to watch the disuku world cup. As she remembered that day, something broke her attention. She thought she could hear something. Something other than the buzz, buzz, buzzing that never ceased. She peered past her feet at the gap in the bars. There was something moving down the hall. Another sound brought her to her feet, it sounded like a landslide, what on earth was happening?

Suddenly everything went dark. But that must mean… the laser bars had stopped buzzing. They weren't even there anymore — the power must have been cut. Quickly, Mizuki made a desperate decision. She darted, full pelt, eyes closed, through where she knew the bars to be. She opened her eyes when she felt solid concrete beneath her hands. She had fallen onto the floor but was now outside of her cell and in the long corridor leading to her mother and father. It was still pitch black, so Mizuki called out in a whisper.

"Mum? Dad? Where are you?" She crawled along the floor, feeling around for any identifying features, moving slowly down the corridor. Before long, she arrived at what felt like a pile of bricks. She felt her way up the pile to discover that something or someone had broken straight through the wall. She could see lights in the distance on the other side. She looked back at the corridor and then out towards the lights. She had a choice to make. Should she save her parents or herself?

Chapter 16

The Electi Family

Eloy & AJ — Archie & Eva

Archie swore loudly before remembering there were younger children around him. Luckily, no one seemed to notice. The reality of what they had just seen on the holovision screens was still sinking in. The world leaders, Archie and Eva's father amongst them, had been lying about the state of the planet — pretending that Anglia and the ESA were the only safe havens — when in fact pockets of life were springing up everywhere. The camp leaders patiently explained what Siri had told them; that the leaders wanted to keep their citizens close to maintain control, and that settlements of people were beginning to be found all over the globe. If people knew that there were better, lusher places to live, the Electi population would lose all of their public services such as schools and hospitals — a sector worked, almost exclusively, by Trebs. The ESA had taken a similar stance, by instilling an even greater sense of patriotism in its inhabitants after the war, to the point that no one would ever dream of leaving their precious Eastern States of America.

The young people listened in horror as they were told that all over Europe and even on the very island on which they now sat, factories were being set up to harvest and produce goods to ship back to Anglia and the ESA to feed and provide for the richer, more powerful citizens. These factories, however, were manned by Treb slaves — dissenters and protesters who were shipped out by the Electi government and never to be seen again. The leaders explained to their nervous students that the president of the ESA, Corey Moon, was working with the President of Anglia to colonise any inhabitable land as soon as it became available. They would then exploit that land for resources to send back to their own countries, all the while leaving their citizens under the impression that their countries remained the soul oases in a dying world.

"How come they haven't found us here?" AJ asked, aghast.

"They believe that this part of the island is barren," her camp leader Miss Haverford explained. "We hacked into their mapping software. This way, they don't even bother looking out here. The emergence of factories on the northern shore is very troubling though and may mean we need to relocate in the future, perhaps to Africa." The camp leaders faced dozens more questions and were only granted a reprieve by the sound of lunch being served on the patio outside. The holovisions were powered down and the students were allowed out together, although few of them felt like socialising. The Kahn and Impero-Regnum teenagers sat together in silence, picking at their vegetable stir-fry in dismay. After several minutes had passed, AJ let out a long sigh and said,

"Well, I feel fantastic." Her sarcasm earned her a quiet noise of appreciation from Archie but largely fell on deaf ears.

"I guess," Eloy began, "they have to make us angry. Because, if we're angry, we'll do something about it?"

"I'm already angry!' AJ stood up and knocked her drink over, startling everyone on the nearby tables. Eloy looked up at his sister, alarmed by another uncharacteristic display of emotion. "We lost our house, we got shot at, we're never allowed to go home and my"—her voice cracked—"my girlfriend is either imprisoned or dead and—" AJ sat back down, now unable to hold in tears. As Eloy took in what was happening, as well as how close his sister and her best friend apparently were, he put his arm around AJ.

"I know. I know, I'm sorry. I'm so sorry. I'm worried about her too. I'm so scared."

Eva's eyes filled with tears. She didn't really know these people, but her father had done this to them. Her family had caused them this pain. Archie looked hurriedly down at his lap. What would the Kahns do to them if they found out who they really were?

"I uh, I didn't know about you and Mizuki," Eloy whispered comfortingly. "I'm really sorry, AJ."

"It was the day before she disappeared," AJ sniffed. "When you were in the bathroom, I finally told her how I felt and…" she trailed off sadly.

"And that went well I'm guessing?" Eloy smiled. AJ attempted a smile and nodded.

"I was so excited to tell you but then she went missing and—" Leyna had noticed her daughter's distress and came over to their bench. Eloy stood up to let her in, and perched next to Eva, trying not to blush as his hand brushed hers. Leyna sat down next to her daughter and began braiding her hair. AJ sniffed again but visibly began to calm down.

"My petal," Leyna kissed AJ on the head. "You're stronger than all of us."

"Oh yeah," AJ scoffed. "Really strong, crying like a wimp."

"There is strength in showing your emotions AJ, you know

159

that."

"But I can't take it any more Mum! We don't even know where Mizuki is! What if she's—?" AJ began to cry again.

"I know, darling. I promise your father, Bruce and Siri are looking for her every chance they get. They have a whole team working on it." Leyna looked up at Eva and Archie who were looking awkwardly at AJ. "I feel for you two, out here without your family. You must be so scared."

Archie looked uncomfortable. "We have each other. That's what matters."

"Well, if you ever need anything, my family is here for you. You seem like good kids." Leyna's sympathetic smile only made Archie and Eva more uncomfortable as the weight of their father's atrocities lay before them.

Lunch concluded as a distinctly morbid affair and the students walked wearily back to their camps. The afternoon, at least, was far more light-hearted, with an overview of what each of the camps would be covering.

Camp Tortuga would be the tech camp. These students showed a knack for all things technological and would work on their hacking, coding and programming skills. Camp Loro was more focused on human communication and cooperation, with students gifted in negotiation and collaboration. Siri felt that these skills would be particularly important in uniting the camps and recruiting others. Camp Zorro students were skilled in organisation and strategizing. They would be the brains of the operation, overseeing and managing the missions. Finally, Camp Oro, with the emblem of a mighty bear, was the camp of the fighters. While Siri herself loathed violence, she knew that strong, fearless leaders would be needed. She hoped that they would only need to fight with their words and their actions, but, if necessary, these students would be trained in physical combat. If it came to it, they would need to take on Electi police and bodyguards, which would be no easy task.

AJ paled as her camp leader told them this. Sure, she was great at sports, but this was another matter entirely. She was secretly jealous of Eloy who seemed to have landed himself in the managerial camp — of course — he will love being able to order everybody around, AJ thought to herself. Archie was happy being in the camp where the main goal seemed to be making sure everybody got along and Eva was in her element in a sea of screens and flashing lights. Once the day was over, the four teenagers were feeling in higher spirits and walked to the dining hall with renewed vigour.

"They're going to teach us 'the power of positive communication'," Archie beamed. "Your mum seems to really know what she's talking about. She says we'll be able to talk people into virtually anything!"

"Well, we are the ones who are going to crash the Electi systems," Eva boasted. "Once we're fully trained, they will have enough people to hack into the most top-secret Electi data. We have this girl, she's only seven, but she can already reprogram an Electi drone in under thirty seconds. It's wonderful!"

"We're looking at the best way to infiltrate the government using technology and undercover operatives. We think we can get someone in posing as an Electi member, which will give the tech guys access to the main Electi database." Eloy was animated as he talked about the plan. AJ listened to them all, quietly nervous. "What did you do AJ?" Eloy asked, curious. It wasn't like her to be so quiet.

"Oh." AJ looked at the expectant faces. "We watched some

clips of great leaders. We analysed how they spoke, what they did. Then… then we started some basic combat training." The others fell silent.

"Combat training?" Eva was confused. "Who are we combating exactly? They're not going to send children to actually fight, are they?" AJ didn't reply. She didn't really know the answer. "Sorry AJ. That's awful."

"Well," she began, "it's no more dangerous than being an undercover operative I suppose." She looked at Archie, who confusedly looked at the others. They were all looking at him, waiting for the penny to drop.

"Wait…" he began slowly. "*I'm* the undercover operative? I didn't get that memo!"

"Well, who else would it be?" Eloy stated. "We need people who can talk their way out of difficult situations — you're on team parrot or whatever — that's your job!" Archie looked pale. Suddenly 'team parrot' didn't seem quite as fun after all.

"Nobody said this would be easy," Eva interjected. "But somebody needs to stop this mess, and if not us, then who? If Siri says she needs us, then she must. We must do what we can."

"You're so brave Eva," AJ was impressed. "I wish I was more like you. Although maybe a bit less la-di-dah."

Archie laughed and Eloy chided his sister. Eva smiled weakly as AJ continued. "What's the deal with that, anyway? Are you guys like, part-Electi or something? No judgement of course — we're all here so we must be on the same side. Just, I've never heard a Treb with your fancy accents," she asked with a friendly smile.

Archie and Eva looked at each other as they walked under

the archway and into the dining hall. As Archie tried desperately to come up with a believable but non-incriminatory answer, Siri approached them and beckoned the Kahn children to follow her. Archie and Eva both slowly exhaled and promised to see them when they got back, glad for more time to come up with a story.

"Just in here," Siri pointed. AJ and Eloy walked into a small room with a large table surrounded by chairs. "Sit," she beckoned.

"Okay," AJ obliged warily. Looking around the table there were six other people of about the same age, looking equally confused.

"I'm so glad to have you all here today," Siri began. "I hope you all enjoyed your first day at the education camp?"

AJ nodded as she recognised a blonde-haired boy who had been with her in Camp Oro. Eloy smiled at a dark-haired boy who had worked with him in camp Zorro. "You are all here today because you are special," Siri began. "It's no coincidence that you all ended up here — the Electi have been monitoring you all since you were born and it was only a matter of time before you needed to escape — and here you are."

"With you so far," AJ mumbled, although she hadn't yet connected the dots. She scanned the remaining teenagers but couldn't find anything obviously special about them.

"You were all born in 2047," Siri continued. AJ understood now and let out a quiet 'ah' of realisation. Eloy rolled his eyes — he had, of course, worked this out long before his sister. "You are not the only ones, but there aren't many more of you that we know about. At least not yet. We are trying to track you all down and monitor your abilities as best we can." Some of the table seemed more surprised by this admission than the others.

A girl with the most phenomenal afro AJ had ever seen nodded and said, "Yes, my mum told me about my gift. I can see patterns others cannot. It means I can reprogram things and bypass encryption codes incredibly quickly." Eloy thought this a tad boastful but then, if he could do that, he'd boast too.

"I can read people," announced a small girl with a high-pitched voice. "I know what they are going to do before they do it."

"Hey, me too!" exclaimed a dark-skinned boy with curly hair.

"Some of your abilities do appear to match, yes," Siri interrupted, "and no, we don't yet know how it is you came to have those abilities. It must have something to do with surviving the infertility epidemic though, that much is clear."

"I can run," AJ offered. "Like, really, really fast. And I'm strong."

"Me too," said the boy from Camp Oro.

"I can problem solve," Eloy added shyly. "I can finish logic puzzles in seconds, and I can visualise multiple outcomes and pathways."

"Oh, I think that's like what I can do!" said a girl with long, dark hair and a pink headband.

"But we're in different camps?" she turned to Siri, confused.

"You have very similar abilities, yes, but you, Althea, are also gifted with technology and your abilities are helpful there, as well. You aren't all as straightforward as, say, AJ and Rafe, whose strength and speed naturally puts them in Camp Oro."

The girl nodded in understanding, and everyone turned to the last member of the group, who had yet to speak. He was visibly nervous, wringing his hands. Rafe, who had clearly spent time with this boy before, gave him a friendly nudge.

"It's okay, you can tell them. You're safe here, they can't find you." AJ privately wondered what ordeal this poor boy had gone through to make him so distrustful of others.

"I can do maths," he said quietly. Eloy was expecting something more impressive but tried not to let it show. Rafe continued for his friend,

"He can do *any* maths." The boy blushed.

"Quick, what's seven thousand, three hundred and ninety-one multiplied by two thousand, nine hundred and ten?" AJ asked, making the boy jump.

"AJ don't be a prick," Eloy sighed.

"Twenty-one million, five hundred and seven thousand, eight hundred and ten," the boy whispered. The room fell silent.

"Does anyone have a calculator?" the small girl asked. "I'd use my holophone, but they don't work here."

"Trust me, it's the right answer." Rafe smiled at his friend.

"I'm Mateo," whispered the mathematician.

"I'm Fumiyo," said the small girl. The girl with the afro was called Niah and the boy with curly hair was called João.

"So, we're all Trebs?" Eloy enquired to a sea of nodding heads. "Interesting." He thought for a moment. "And from the looks of it — and I'm hoping not to be out of line here — many of us are at least descended from immigrants?" Everyone in the room except Rafe nodded again.

"We still haven't found a reason for that but it's certainly an interesting point Eloy," Siri mused. "Anyway, each of you will be of vital importance in your relevant camps. We will certainly need your skills when it comes to our mission," Siri continued.

"Yeah, about that," AJ interrupted nervously.

"All in good time, AJ," Siri chided. "For now, just worry about dinner." She walked to the door and the group, heads still spinning, walked back towards the dinner hall. Eloy and AJ quietly collected their dinner plates and found Archie and Eva, who were both hoping the Kahn twins had forgotten their previous curiosities over their accent. Unfortunately for them, AJ was like a dog with a bone, and stared at Eva while munching on a carrot. "So?" she prompted. "Where are you guys from? New Sheffield maybe?"

"AJ, leave them alone," Eloy whispered.

Archie tried to change the subject. "What did Siri want with you guys? Are you in trouble already?"

"No, not yet," AJ replied through a mouthful of pineapple. "We're just part of an elite group of miracle children who all have superpowers. Anyway, what's the deal with you guys?" Eva and Archie stared blankly for a moment.

"Wait... what?" Archie asked. "You have superpowers?"

"It's not in the way you're imagining," Eloy interrupted. "It's more that we have one skill we are especially good at to an unusually high level. AJ can run extremely fast and lift things, whereas I can solve problems in my head very quickly. There are others like us out here too with similar abilities. They were at the education hut with us today and are spread out between the camps."

Archie thought about this for a moment as he chewed on a carrot. "It sounds better when AJ says it, you should stick with 'superpowers' — much more impressive."

"Yeah, like Batman!" AJ smiled and playfully punched her brother in the arm, who was shaking his head in exasperation. "Now if you're not from New Sheffield then—"

"AJ," Eloy warned, sternly.

166

"No, it's fine." Eva looked up. "I don't want to hide it any longer." AJ put down her fork in curiosity. This was going to be good, she thought, as Eva began speaking. "I am… we are—"

"Eva, no." Archie took his sister's hand with pleading eyes. "They won't understand."

"No, they won't," replied Eva. "But they might at least try." Archie looked despondent. He knew he wouldn't be able to change her mind. He might be good with words, but his sister was extremely stubborn.

Eva began again, "We are from an Electi family." Eloy's eyebrow raised and AJ gave him a subtle but triumphant look of 'I told you so'. Eva took a deep breath and continued. "We are from *the* Electi family." Eva paused to let her admission sink in.

AJ looked baffled but Eloy quickly realised why Eva had, at first, given him a false name. "Evangeline Impero-Regnum," he breathed. He turned to Archie. "Archibald, right?" Archie groaned.

"I really hate that name," he mumbled guiltily. AJ gasped, now caught up with her brother. "Holy—"

"Kids! There you are!" Marcus Kahn sat down next to his children, oblivious to their wide eyes and shocked expressions. "How was your first day at jungle school?"

"We have to go," Archie announced as he and Eva both quickly left the table and the dining hall, leaving their uneaten meals behind.

Marcus turned around, perplexed. "Was it something I said?"

Mizuki

Mizuki looked back at the corridor, lined with prison cells, and then out through the hole in the wall, towards the welcoming lights of freedom. She had a choice to make. Should she save her parents or herself? She squinted in the darkness to try and make out where the walls ended, and the cells began but it was so dark.

"Okasan! Dad?" she whispered again, louder this time. In the distance, she heard a distant rumble. She crouched down beside the pile of rubble next to the now-destroyed wall and held in tears. The rumbling grew louder, and Mizuki cursed her inability to make a decision. She crawled towards where she thought her parents' cell to be but was grabbed on the arm by a large figure.

"No!" she called out.

"Quiet, missy!" replied a gruff voice. "I'm not here to hurt you. Where are your parents?" Mizuki cowered as the man's grip on her wrist increased.

"Please, don't hurt them," she pleaded.

"I'm not here to hurt anyone but Electi scum, young miss. Just tell me where they are, and we'll all walk out of here nice and easy." The voice sounded friendlier now. Mizuki had no choice but to trust him. There wasn't much of a chance it could lead to an even worse situation than she was currently in.

"I think they were down here somewhere, but it's so dark." Mizuki gestured meekly down the corridor.

"Step back then, sunshine," replied the voice, and a beam of light suddenly shone from his forehead. "Old-fashioned head-torch," he whispered to her as he tapped his head. "The old gadgets are often the best." Mizuki followed the beam of light down the corridor until she found her parents' cell. She fell to her knees as the beam of light fell upon her father, crumpled in a heap on the floor.

"Dad?" she sobbed. "Dad, please, wake up." Mizuki's mother slowly rose from the body of her husband and ran to her daughter.

"Mizu-chan, what's happening?" Miranda Koizumi held her daughter so tight that she could barely breathe.

"Okasan," she choked through the embrace. "What's wrong with Dad?" Miranda's grip loosened.

"Oh Mizu-chan, I'm so sorry. They beat him so badly. He hasn't moved since yesterday. I tried calling out, but no one came. No one came." Miranda fell back to the floor as her knees gave way. Mizuki howled and tried to reach out for her father but the figure with the headtorch grabbed her again and pulled her away.

"We have to go. They'll be here any minute." Mizuki's mother and the stranger pulled her away, though she fought them.

"Dad... Dad, please." Mizuki's tears fell onto the dust and brick below them as they retreated through the open hole in the wall. The stranger picked up both women and sprinted down more corridors until they saw sunlight. A blare of sirens sounded in the distance and the stranger carried them outside and into a nearby alley. It was here that a police car was waiting for them. Mizuki and Miranda pulled back.

"No," the stranger warned them. "Don't worry, we're on your side. You've got to get in, come on." They had no choice. Hands held, mother and daughter climbed into the police car and were driven away.

Chapter 17

In Too Deep

Eloy & AJ — Archie & Eva

Eva and Archie were hiding in the tortoise enclosure after their recent revelation.

"What now?" Eva asked, still out of breath from their run from the dining hall.

"Well, I don't think you'll be getting a date out of Eloy after this!" Archie said jokingly. Eva kicked him. "Ow! Grief, Eva, can't you take a joke?"

"Not right now, no." She glowered at her brother and stroked a nearby tortoise. Archie read the sign next to them.

"I think that one is called Achilles. Based on this picture, the one over there is called Esio and the one asleep in the dandelion patch is called Boots. There should be another one around here somewhere."

"Yes, Archie, they're very cute," Eva sighed. "But what are we going to do?"

"You're asking me?" Archie raised an eyebrow. "You're the one who outed us!"

"I couldn't keep it inside any more Archie! It was killing me." Eva hung her head, ashamed of her own weakness.

"Yeah, and those people might *actually* kill us." Archie was being sarcastic, but Eva kicked a stone in his direction anyway, accidentally hitting a nearby tortoise, who proceeded to kick dirt passive-aggressively in Eva's direction.

"Oops! So sorry." Achilles the tortoise was highly unimpressed and made a beeline for his shelter.

"Well, we can't exactly live amongst the tortoises forever, Eva. We're going to have to go out there and face the music." The siblings sat for a moment, watching the tortoises and trying to ignore their own situation before a familiar face emerged through the door of Carmen's hut.

"Hey there you two!" Leyna's soothing voice only released some of the tension the siblings were currently feeling. "The kids wondered where you'd run off to."

"Um, Mrs Kahn," Archie began, meekly.

"Please, Archie, call me Leyna." She sat down next to him, silently surveying the scenery with almost an unnatural calmness. As she sat, many of the nearby animals began to gather around her. The disgruntled tortoise, a raccoon, two lizards and a small dog all nuzzled up to her as she smiled reassuringly at the Impero-Regnum children. Eva looked curiously at a pair of foxes curling up at her feet and wondered just how Leyna Kahn was able to attract so much wildlife with her presence alone. Leyna stroked a nearby parrot and began, in a calming voice, "You know we all knew, right? About your parents. Siri didn't exactly keep it low key and your accents kind of gave it away."

Eva blushed and Archie looked visibly relieved. "You mean, you're not going to kill us?" he spluttered.

"Archie, you can't ask her that!" Eva was still unsure.

"Good grief, what kind of people do you think we are?" Leyna replied, slightly hurt and unable to hide it. "We're not violent. What we're doing here, it's frightening, yes, but we don't want anyone to die — Treb or Electi. I know the Electi like to paint us as murdering savages but really..." Leyna trailed off, disappointed.

"Sorry," Archie mumbled guiltily. "I suppose a lifetime of propaganda is hard to undo."

"It's okay, darling," Leyna reassured him. "You're learning and growing just like the rest of us." Archie smiled and looked around, suddenly realising that the group of nearby animals was growing larger by the minute.

"Okay, this is getting silly now." Eva had just been brushed by a passing otter who appeared to be rushing to Leyna's side.

"Yeah, this is weird, Mrs K, how are you doing that?" Archie looked suspiciously at an approaching bear cub.

"Oh my," Leyna exclaimed as she noticed the bear cub. The animal cautiously sauntered towards the group before hiding behind a nearby bush. Leyna smiled at the cub, "We must return this little bundle to its mother. I think Carmen said that her den was just over there, past the trees." As Leyna rose to her feet, the rest of the animals slowly dissipated, leaving the humans alone with the bear cub. The siblings looked nervous.

"You want to walk up to an actual bear, holding its cub?" Eva asked, worriedly. She privately thought Leyna slightly mad, while Archie was honestly impressed by her boldness.

"Of course not, don't be ridiculous,' Leyna replied. "That would be dangerous. We just need to pop the little cutie down close enough for them to find their way home." Leyna approached the bear cub and knelt down. The cub immediately ran into her open arms.

"This is odd, right?" Eva whispered to Archie.

"It's blooming brilliant," Archie replied. "It's like she's Pocahontas or something."

"Mum has always had a thing with animals." Eloy's voice made them both jump and they turned around to see the Kahn children smiling at them. Their parents may have known about Eva and Archie's family tree, but the twins were still in slight shock. As Leyna walked towards the bear cub's home, the four teenagers were left alone with the tortoises. The Impero-Regnums looked sheepishly at the ground, awaiting their judgement.

"I used to imagine what it would be like to be you," admitted AJ. "To eat whatever I wanted — not just those synthetic meal drinks. Real chocolate even."

"I just used to wish we had the opportunities you guys had. The good schools, first-class facilities, respect," Eloy added.

"Mizuki, our friend, is half Electi. We kind of saw what it was like for her but it was nothing compared to your lives." AJ winced as she mentioned Mizuki but carried on. "But you're here. You're living like us now and you're not complaining. You're even training to take down your own family. That takes a heck of a lot of courage." As AJ spoke, Eva looked up to see that Eloy was looking at her with fondness.

"Yeah, had I known who you were before, I think I'd have run in the opposite direction. But now I've seen what you're willing to do." Eloy blushed as he spoke. Archie chuckled under his breath.

"Archie," AJ interrupted, "do you want to go and see the tigers? I hear they've just finished the enclosure — it covers over one hundred square kilometres." Archie looked perplexed.

"If it's that big, how are we going to see any ti—oh wait. Okay, I'm with you." Embarrassed, Archie quickly followed AJ, to leave Eloy and Eva to talk in private.

"I'm sorry," Eva spoke barely above a whisper. "I didn't

mean to deceive you, Eloy."

"I know," he looked kindly at her and reached out his hand. Eva took it.

"Whatever happens, Eloy," she stammered. "I want you to know. I really like—" She stopped suddenly, squinting bemusedly at something over Eloy's shoulder. Leyna was running towards them across the field and waving her arms. She was shouting something. Eloy turned around to see what had snatched Eva's attention away from him. Of course, it was his mother, he sighed to himself.

"What?" Eloy shouted at Leyna. "We can't hear you!" At this point, the pair realised they were still holding hands and dropped them, blushing. Leyna was getting closer.

"The bear!" she shouted. "The bear is angry!" As Leyna ran towards them, Eloy could see flashing lights in the distance. The animal welfare team appeared to be coercing a large grizzly bear back into her cave. As Leyna reached them, she took both of their hands and dragged them into Carmen's hut, panting. "Maybe... I don't have... such a way with... *all* the animals." She panted, as she sunk to the floor. Eloy looked nervously at Eva.

"I think I'm going to go and find Archie," she said quietly, before darting out of the hut. Eloy sat down, deflated.

"Everything all right, petal?" Leyna asked, still breathing heavily.

Eloy sighed. "It's nothing, Mum. Are you okay?"

Leyna stood shakily. "Yes, dear, just a little out of practice. You know I used to work at an ape rescue centre? Those monkeys were quick." Eloy smiled as he remembered his mother's wild stories about her time working at 'Monkey World'. Swapping monkeys for children had seemed like a natural career progression for her at the time, but she often missed working with animals.

"I just have such an affinity with them," she reminisced. "Something about their souls just calls to me. When the war happened, I was just as sad for the animals as I was for the people. I didn't dare tell anyone that, but I felt it. They're so innocent. They didn't cause any of this, but this is the world they're forced to live in now. If they're even lucky enough to be living." She gazed out of the window at the now docile bear, retreating with her cub.

"What was it like?" Eloy asked. "When it happened?" He had never really asked before.

They had learned about it over and over again at school but that was just numbers and statistics.

They never taught him what it felt like to live through it.

"It was hell, my darling." Leyna sat down next to her son. "Everyone thought it was the end of days, which, in a way, it was. Not at first, of course. People went about their lives as tensions built — certain that nothing could really happen. As danger grew more imminent, however, some people began to panic.

"There were food shortages as people hoarded supplies from the supermarkets, not that there was any reason for it at the time. In many ways, people create their own problems. Then the bombs hit and everyone really started to lose it. People began looting and rioting. I was at a shopping centre when it happened and my mother and I had to run home. That was when I met your father — we took shelter in his house with his parents."

Eloy paled; he remembered this part of the story now. His parents had told him a long time ago, in order to explain why he

175

didn't have any surviving grandparents. They had died to save their children — Eloy's parents.

"Anyway, that's when society began to crumble," Leyna worked hard to prevent her voice from cracking, but it was difficult. "Our parents, as you know, weren't let into the shelter as they were immigrants. But your father and I, being children, managed to get in before the shockwaves and radiation reached Anglia." She paused and inhaled deeply. "After that, we were taken in by this sweet little Hungarian family until we were old enough to go to university.

"The world was different by then, though. People weren't as friendly as before. They were more cautious, more guarded. My foster mother said she hadn't seen anything like it since the pandemic of 2020 but of course, I wasn't quite born then. She always talked about it though. She said disasters bring out the very best in some people but the very worst in others. Then the infertility crisis hit in 2046 and it just got worse. People stopped looking to religion to save them and just seemed to accept their fate. Human kindness seemed to disappear as people fought over supplies and argued over politics. The Electi and Treb system just made a broken country more divided and it became every man for himself, so to speak. The sky remained dark, the people grew more bitter and, of course, there was no such thing as 'fresh air' anymore." Leyna instinctively touched her face, reaching for her respirator, only to remember that she didn't need it here. "Goodness me it's wonderful being on this island and not having to wear masks outdoors — it's just like before the war!" She looked out of the window and pointed at the lush jungle. "And nature is taking the earth back, just as she should. Nature always finds a way." Leyna smiled and rested her head against her son's.

"I love you, Mum," Eloy murmured. Leyna kissed his head.

"I love you too, petal. We're going to fix this. We're going to reset the whole world. One corrupt government at a time. Just you wait. We'll fix it all."

The next day, a new aura of calm settled around the Imper-Regnum children, as they no longer had to hide who they were.

"Honestly it's so freeing," sang Eva as they walked towards the education hut.

"Yeah, we're sorry we weren't honest with you before," Archie added. "We just thought you might throw us in the ocean." AJ shook her head.

"Don't be stupid," she laughed. "I only use my powers for good, remember?" Archie smiled at her. As the days went on, however, AJ was discovering more and more about her powers, and it was beginning to frighten her.

Once they arrived at the hut, Siri informed them that it was time for their first practice mission — nice and simple — just to test the waters. The teachers had turned a spare hut into a fake Electi stronghold. They had borrowed tech from the central tower to kit it out with a full security system including cameras, fingerprint scanners and lasers. AJ winced. This seemed a lot trickier than just winning at disuku. She had never been tested like this. Eloy and the rest of Team Zorro stayed in the education hut and spoke to the others through earpieces. They would instruct them where to go, warn them about any guards (played by some other members of Camp Oro) as well as providing moral support. Eva would also be at a safe distance with the rest of Team Tortuga, challenged with the task of turning off the cameras and lasers remotely. Archie and some other Team Loro students would need to either distract or

177

convince the fake guards to leave the area or, better still, lend them their fingerprints. This was the hardest thing to stage as, of course, their fellow students were never actually going to hurt them. In real life, this could be a different story. Finally, AJ, Rafe and the rest of Team Oro were the people on the ground. It was a fairly large hut so they each had a different entry point to try. The target inside the hut was a heavily encrypted computer. Once retrieved, it would be Team Torruga's job to decrypt it and retrieve the information within. AJ and Archie were both positioned at the rear of the hut, behind a grassy bank. A guard from Team Oro waited for them on the other side.

Archie whispered to AJ, "So is cutting their fingers off to get their fingerprint a little too much, would you say?" AJ glared at him. "Okay, not a time for jokes, sure, got it." Archie looked at the ground. It was then he spotted something glistening in the dirt.

"Wait here," he whispered. "I have an idea." AJ was not reassured but watched Archie with interest. He skirted around the edge of the bank before appearing a few feet behind the guard. Nonchalantly, he tapped the boy on the shoulder and held out the shiny object. "Did you drop this?" he asked with a smile.

The guard was momentarily confused, giving Archie enough time to catch the sun at just the right angle and reflect it into the boy's eyes using his newly discovered piece of glass. "Sorry, mate," he said as he whipped out his fake pepper spray and blasted the poor student's face with water. "You're out." The Camp Oro student was embarrassed but gracious in defeat and melodramatically sunk to the floor. AJ then leapt over the bank and gave Archie a high five. "Nice," she nodded, genuinely impressed.

"For the real thing I reckon chloroform would be less messy than pepper spray, but I forgot which pocket I put everything in," he shrugged. Together, they dragged the guard (who helped a little by walking his feet along with them — he didn't fancy being dragged) to the fingerprint scanner at the back door.

"Excellent work you two," Eloy's voice suddenly appeared in their ears. "Wait there though, the lasers and cameras are still on."

"What on earth is Evie playing at?" Archie grumbled. "She has one job!"

"I'm trying," hissed Eva in their earpieces. "Puffles is being difficult! He's still learning how to do all this stuff and he wants some sort of virtual compensation for his time." It was hard not to laugh at the ridiculousness of the situation and Archie couldn't help giggling to himself.

"Quiet," reminded Eloy in his ear. "There's a guard around the corner.

"Well, that one is Rafe's responsibility — we're the only ones pulling our weight here," added AJ. Archie nodded in agreement. Through the window, AJ could see the almost hypnotic dance of lasers filling the rooms of the hut. It made her think of disuku and she felt a pang of loss. What had her life become? She didn't have time to wonder however as the lasers suddenly stopped.

"You've got three minutes until they turn back on — the cameras too — go, go, go!" Eloy shouted. AJ swiftly opened the door and pressed her back against the inner wall. She gestured to Archie that there was a guard in the next room. Nodding, Archie walked around the outside of the hut until he could see the guard through an open window.

"Oi, guard man, I'm over here!" he called pathetically. The guard laughed before remembering her role and quickly ran for the window to pursue the idiotic intruder. This left AJ free to dash for the computer, which she reached at almost exactly the same time as Rafe.

"Well done," he commented as they both went to grab the device.

"Thanks," beamed AJ as she quickly snatched it and ran back out of the hut.

"That was mean!" Rafe called after her, before jumping out a window to avoid the returning lasers. As AJ left the hut, however, there was a new obstacle. In the time it had taken her to retrieve the computer, Siri and her team had pulled in a twenty-foot wall surrounded by yet more guards.

"You've got to avoid them, not hurt them," Eloy instructed. "Your objective is to escape with the device." AJ privately wished she had let Rafe take the laptop and subsequent glory before dashing past two approaching guards, tucking the computer into her combat trousers and launching herself at the wall. One of the guards tried to grab her foot as she climbed but she kicked it away.

"Sorry!" she called down while scrambling up. "Oh, you have got to be kidding me…" At the top of the wall, members of Team Loro were standing ready to hurl cardboard boxes at her.

"Obviously we're imagining these are somewhat heavier — if one hits you, you're out," Eloy informed a now slightly panicked AJ. Her classmates were giving her sympathetic smiles of apology as they readied themselves to pelt her with cardboard boxes. AJ took a deep breath, focussed her eyes on the top of the wall and jumped. As she reached out for the top ledge of the wall, her classmates all stared, eyes wide and open-mouthed. AJ waited for her body to succumb to gravity, but it didn't. She cleared the top of the wall and landed, surprised, on the top ledge. For a moment, nobody said anything. Fumiyo even dropped her box by accident. "How did you do that?" asked João. AJ looked back down the wall and tried to wrap her head around it. She thought it would take her at least four jumps to get to the top but she must have cleared around fifteen feet in one leap.

"I... I don't know," she stuttered.

"Well, it was blooming brilliant!" Archie yelled up from the ground. AJ smiled at him but inside she was shaking.

"Are you okay?" asked Eloy through AJ's earpiece. She breathed slowly.

"Yeah, um... I just cleared fifteen feet in a single jump," she whispered, although hiding this fact was now impossible.

"Wow," Eloy replied, unsure what else to say. "Did you know you could do that?" AJ steadied herself as the others began climbing down.

"No," she replied, privately scared of what else she might be capable of without even knowing.

Chapter 18

A Welcome Distraction

Eloy & AJ — Archie & Eva

The next few weeks passed in a blur. Spring brought beautiful weather and even more vegetation to the already stunning valley. The young people of the camp went to the education hut every day after breakfast and spent the day honing their specific skill sets. Eva learned how to hack her way through the toughest Electi firewalls; Archie learned how to use his gift of the gab for good; Eloy learned how to lead simulation missions; and AJ trained in low-level breaking and entering. After one of her more morally dubious practice missions, however, AJ was beginning to feel conflicted.

"Do you ever think we're on the wrong side?" she asked as they began their walk back to their respective huts. "It just seems a bit dodgy to me."

"Definitely dodgy," Archie replied. "I had to pretend to convince an Electi official to risk his own life and defect. We could do some real damage here."

"But that's the point, isn't it?" Eva chimed in. "The Electi have taken so many Treb lives, on purpose and without any regret. We must do something, and we're not being trained to actively hurt anyone. Well, unless you count AJ."

"It's self-defence!" AJ replied hotly.

"Sorry, yes, of course." Eva blushed. She wouldn't admit it, but AJ scared her a bit. How one little person could be so strong amazed her. On top of this, tensions in the camp were running high. They had been staying there for several months with no contact from the outside world, no working holophones and — for Archie and Eva at least — with a severe decrease in comfort and luxuries. Bathing in a jungle clearing seemed cool at first, but Eva couldn't remember the last time she actually felt clean. AJ was enjoying the adventure somewhat but Mizuki was still missing. Eloy felt out of his depth without his books and he was struggling with the new concept of never having any time alone, although he didn't show it. Archie and Eva had no idea how their family were faring and all the while they were being trained to overthrow them. It was a complex time and all four of the teenagers really needed a break. Luckily, Siri could sense that emotions were frayed among her four favourite pupils, so she invited them up to the central tower that evening after dinner.

"Well, if it isn't my star students?" She beamed as they entered her private apartment. It wasn't much — wooden walls like the rest of the structure were lined with tapestries and tie-dyed cloth hangings. There was a tortoise asleep in the corner which Archie recognised as Boots from the enclosure in which he and his sister had previously hidden. "You've all been working so hard, and I know it must be difficult living here. The same food day in, day out and no technology outside of the education hut, it's rough, I know." The four teenagers looked blankly at her, waiting for the next revelation — it was never just idle chit-chat with Siri. "Yes, well you're probably wondering why I called you up here," she continued. "It's um…" She looked uncharacteristically nervous. "It's time."

"Time for what?" Archie asked. Eva elbowed him.

"Time for the real mission, cretin," she whispered.

"Oh…" Archie nodded, then realised what she meant. "Oh!"

"Calm down, Archie, we've got a month of preparation to do," Siri began. "But after that, we will all be travelling back to the mainland. Our mission is to retrieve vital Electi information. We've tried accessing it remotely, but their security is just too powerful. We will need to access the President's computer itself."

"But…" Archie winced. "That's my father's computer… you'll never get to it. I managed once, but that was when I lived there!"

"We need to extract the data onto one of our devices, it's the only way. We won't be putting you in any danger, but you will need to hone your skills. Most of my adult operatives are tech-based and next to useless when it comes to strategising or negotiating. I'm going to need all of you to pull this off." As Siri dismissed them, their heads were collectively spinning. Back to the mainland — but wasn't that dangerous? Eloy and AJ walked back to the hut they shared with their parents to break the news.

"Siri told us she'd be taking you with her," Marcus sighed. "I asked to go too, of course, but she said it was too dangerous and I was needed here in her place."

"Siri won't put you in harm's way," Leyna reassured, although neither Eloy nor AJ fully believed that. Meanwhile, Archie and Eva had wandered towards the animal enclosures and were sitting outside Carmen's hut.

"This is where they brought me on my first day here," Eva said quietly. "Carmen, the lady who looks after the animals, escaped from Belgium when the Electi sent the army in to destroy their base. Her whole family was killed except for her. I just keep thinking, are we responsible for all of this? We're so close to it."

Archie was uncharacteristically quiet. He too felt the overwhelming sense of guilt every day as he realised more and more how privileged his life had been. Every time he craved real meat or a disuku game with genuine lasers, he remembered that very few people in Anglia had ever experienced those things. He hated himself for having taken them for granted and worse, even resented them at times. All his life he'd been taught that the Trebs were the enemy — that the Electi government had been generous to them, but they had just thrown it back in their faces. He should have seen it, but he was on the inside and the windows were all mirrored.

"I just keep thinking, if we ever have to look our father in the eyes again — how can we forgive him? I don't think I can. But Mother — she must have known."

"I don't blame Mother," Archie finally spoke. "I've seen Father hit her, you know. She's just as trapped as the Trebs. She didn't want this, you can see it in her eyes." Eva was surprised by her brother's uncharacteristic perceptiveness.

"I always thought only I had seen that," she replied.

"No. I act like I'm not paying attention sometimes because I don't want to see." Archie looked at his sister. "It was the day I ran away, it was your birthday and—"

"Oh!" Eva's eyes widened as she remembered. "Oh no, I missed it." Eva looked forlornly at the sky. "I missed my birthday."

"Your sixteenth birthday!" Archie jumped up. "Evie we should have a party!"

"Oh but Archie it was nearly a month ago — it's nearer to your birthday now than it is to mine!"

"YES!" Archie fist-pumped the air. "Double party! Woooooo!" Eva laughed as Archie danced around the lake.

"I'm not sure this is the right time," she said doubtfully.

"Are you kidding?" Archie grabbed Eva's hands, "It's a perfect time — we're about to go on an actual mission, we don't know if we'll ever make it back, it'll be an epic send-off!" Eva considered this. "Come *on* Evie," Archie gave his sister his biggest, widest eyes.

"Ugh, okay, fine!" she conceded, trying to hide a smile. Archie did another little dance of glee while his sister stifled a giggle.

"Come on, let's go and tell the others. I want the tortoises wearing party hats at the very least." Archie joyfully grabbed his sister by the hand and skipped towards the Kahn's hut.

The Kahn family were playing with an old pack of playing cards when Archie and Eva burst in.

"We're having a party and the tortoises are going to fly in on drones!" Archie shouted.

"We said no to the drones, but a 'maybe' to the party hats," Eva clarified. "We missed my birthday, and Archie turns fifteen on Sunday."

The Kahn twins exchanged looks. "Actually, now that you mention it…" Eloy started.

"Oh petals, it's your birthday on the seventh — we *should* have a party!" Leyna smiled and kissed her daughter on the forehead."

"Way to steal my thunder, Mrs K," muttered Archie. "I guess you'll want tortoise party hats too…"

"Actually, I think I might knit some scarves for the flamingos," Leyna mused, mostly to herself. "They seemed chilly the other day." Marcus looked lovingly at his wife. She was quirky, sure, but he found it especially endearing.

The rest of the day was spent gathering whatever the teenagers could loosely class as 'party decor'. AJ found a collection of colourful feathers in the parrot enclosure and her mother helped her tie them to a string, creating colourful bunting. Eva had programmed the security searchlights to shine in an array of colours, creating a sort of 'disco' vibe. Archie, never to be outdone, was leading a pack of llamas in party hats towards the main hall, until Leyna politely told him, that this bordered on animal cruelty, and he was forced to return them, removing the party hats in the process. Just before dinner, the main hall was ready, and Siri stood on one of the central tables, to explain the occasion to the gathering crowd.

"It seems," she began in a booming, soulful voice, "that we have a cluster of spring birthdays in our midst!" She gestured to the four teenagers who stepped forwards, Eloy and Eva fairly bashfully, while AJ and Archie practically jumped onto the table themselves. "Do we have any more March or April birthdays?" Siri asked the room. Slowly, a smattering of children and adults began to step forwards. Eventually, there were around thirty people in the centre of the room. "Well isn't that wonderful? We are here today to celebrate you all! The camp cooks have made the largest beetroot chocolate cake you've ever seen and I for one am famished! We've got bright lights and music which is loud enough to dance to, but not loud enough to be heard from far away so let's party!" With that, Siri did an impressive pike jump off the table and landed with an elegant bow. Applause filled the dining hall as the camp cooks brought out the mightiest feast they had seen since they arrived.

"They must have used all of their best ingredients!" AJ swooned as she took a deep sniff of her magnificent vegetable and nut roast. Leyna was in food heaven and even Archie, usually one of the fussiest members of the group, was happily tucking into a coconut milkshake.

"Isn't that more of a pudding?" Eva asked him, sceptically.

"My party, my rules!" Archie spat through a mouthful of milkshake. "Oops, sorry." Eva wiped the excess milkshake from her cheek with a look of disgust.

"Delightful." Eloy smiled, weakening Eva's scowl just a little. Under the table, he tentatively took her hand. Eva smiled and turned slightly pink. AJ was about to say something but a stern look from her mother told her to 'just pretend you didn't see anything'.

The nut and vegetable roasts were followed by a course of freshly caught fish from the nearby fishery, wrapped in banana leaves and steamed. Nothing in the ocean was safe to eat any more, not that there was much left, but part of Project Libertas' Nature Division had taken on the task of sourcing and breeding healthy, sustainable sea life. A rare treat, and while Leyna declined, the rest of the group relished the taste of fresh, real, fish. For Archie and Eva, it tasted even better than at home. For dessert, the beetroot chocolate cake was heavenly and both AJ and Archie had second helpings before sinking down into their seats, full but extremely happy. After some more singing and an impromptu conga line, the group headed outside for some fresh air. AJ almost screamed when she saw what had been set up in an open area of the camp.

"A disuku court!" she squealed. Archie tilted his head to the side and squinted. Sticks had been used to mark out a large rectangle and there were some old school frisbees piled in the corner but this hardly constituted a disuku court.

"It's not much, I grant you," Marcus said shyly, "but I thought some of us could wave these palm leaves around and pretend to be the lasers. Then you could use these boxes for the goals." He looked down, embarrassed at his poor attempt to replicate something usually requiring a great deal of electricity and metal, but AJ took his hand.

"Dad, I love it!" her words brought a smile to his face and his heart as his daughter rushed towards the pile of frisbees. "Archie we've got to be on opposite teams, I know you play nearly as well as me."

"Nearly as well?" Archie scoffed, mockingly, but was fairly certain AJ could beat him blindfolded. Eloy, Eva and Marcus decided to play as the lasers while Leyna assigned herself the role of referee. AJ looked around, disheartened.

"We need more players," she sighed. Luckily, at that moment the rest of the camp's children had decided they were too full of cake and needed a walk.

"Hey, what are you lot doing?" yelled Rafe as he caught sight of them.

"Rafe, come play disuku with us!" AJ shouted back. Rafe smiled and grabbed Mateo, Niah, Althea, Fumiyo and João. Feeling that it would be unfair to have two teenagers with super speed and strength on the same team, Rafe joined Archie, along with Mateo and Fumiyo. Niah, Althea and João joined AJ's team, feeling pretty confident that they had the better captain.

"Well, it's not quite a team of five but we can work with this," AJ smiled.

"Ready?" Leyna asked as she held the frisbee, ready to throw it into the air. AJ and Archie nodded, already taking it much too seriously. Eloy and Eva rolled their eyes. This couldn't end well. "Go!" Leyna threw the flying disc into the air. AJ leapt so high she almost cleared Archie's head and triumphantly caught the frisbee. She had considered holding back her newly discovered leaping abilities, but she was just too competitive. As soon as she'd snatched the disc, however, Eloy was making a beeline for his sister, waving his palm-leaf in determination.

"Oh, now that's not fair, Eloy, the lasers are supposed to be random!" she cried as a stray leaf brushed her and she was forced to toss the disc into the air, ready to be claimed by another player. Rafe grabbed it with amazing speed and darted straight for the goal. Eva tried to swipe him with her palm-leaf laser, but he was too fast and expertly threw the disc into the wooden box.

"Wey!" Archie punched the air. "Nice one, Rafe!" Leyna took the frisbee back into the centre of the court and tossed it into the air. This time AJ was ready. She grabbed the disc then barely dodged Eloy's palm fronds before pelting it into the opposing team's goal.

"Yes!" AJ shouted jubilantly. A sneaky goal from Archie, however, put the opposing team back in the lead, and as they all felt the weight of their birthday feasts slowing them down, AJ knew she didn't have long left. She huddled with her team and tried to come up with a plan. "I can't get the disc or Eloy will be right on me with his stupid green laser," she muttered. "So, we need to be strategic. If I hang back, one of you can grab the disc and chuck it to me."

"But AJ, none of us can beat Rafe," Niah pointed out. "He's too fast, like you."

AJ thought about this. "Fumiyo, you're really small," she

began.

"Er, thanks?" replied Fumiyo, who was a good foot shorter than most of the other players.

"Sorry, I just mean you can sneak past undetected. If I get the disc, then immediately pass it to you..."

"No one will be guarding me?" Fumiyo offered.

"Exactly," replied AJ. Leyna pointedly cleared her throat. "Yeah, sorry, Mum, we're ready." AJ strolled back into the centre of the court. As Leyna threw the disc into the air, AJ swiped it. Just before Eloy could reach her, she threw it to Fumiyo who somewhat surprised herself by catching it. Before anyone could realise what happened, she skipped to the goal and delicately placed it in.

"Teamwork!" cheered AJ as she gave Fumiyo a high five.

"Ouch!" squeaked the girl — AJ's high five was a little stronger than she was used to.

"Oops, sorry," AJ smiled apologetically. Leyna blew a final whistle, much to everyone's relief as they all had stitches in their sides, and everyone happily wandered back to their huts for the night. It was the nicest day they'd had in a long time. AJ had even forgotten to worry about Mizuki for a little bit, just for a little bit. Then, of course, she remembered again and felt twice as guilty.

Chapter 19

Lost London

Eloy & AJ — Archie & Eva

A month after Project Libertas' first-ever joint birthday celebration, it was time to leave the island. Despite training at Project Libertas for nearly two months, none of the students quite felt ready for the mammoth task ahead of them. After an unbelievably early start (it was the first time Archie had seen three o'clock in the morning for many years), the teenagers had assembled on the beach where they had first arrived.

"Will we be back?" AJ asked Siri, nervously.

"Of course we will! Blink and you'll miss it," Siri replied with her usual peppiness. AJ turned to look back towards the jungle and the hidden base concealed within it. It looked even more beautiful, if that was possible, in this light. The trees cast beautiful shadows and moonlight lit up pools of water like glistening puddles of silver.

"Hello, are you coming?" Eloy's voice rang out from the deck of the boat. AJ sighed and took one last look at the island before boarding the slowly bobbing vessel. She was always the brave one, but even she was feeling nervous. It was going to be a long journey back, across the sea and up to New London via the Southern villages of Anglia. Marcus and Leyna waved from the shore as the boat pulled away, and AJ squeezed her brother's arm. Archie and Eva waved too, grateful for all that the Kahns had done for them during their time on the island.

"To New London!" Siri cried out, pointing dramatically at the horizon. The teenagers half-heartedly replied with a weak cheer before retreating below deck for some much-needed sleep.

Archie was once again relieved to see dry land as their dingy reached the southern shores of Anglia. He didn't think he'd ever get used to ocean travel. A long journey lay in front of them, however, as several off-road vehicles drove to meet them. Eloy and Eva decided to climb into one of the smaller jeeps, earning raised eyebrows from AJ and Archie, who climbed into the jeep behind them with Rafe and Mateo.

"Do you think they'll mind us ditching them?" Eloy asked Eva nervously.

"I love my brother, and I know you love AJ, but we've been stuck with them twenty-four hours a day for the past month. I just needed a break," she sighed.

"But not from me?" Eloy asked quietly, trying his hardest not to blush. Eva smiled at him and whispered, keeping her voice low enough not to be overheard by their driver.

"Not from you."

The air was thick with smog and sacrifice as the party approached the outskirts of New London. Eloy and AJ stared in wonder at the distant glass monoliths of the city while Archie and Eva felt pangs of guilt as they remembered their mother, most likely still scouring the city for any trace of them. After their long journey together in the jeep, Eloy and Eva were trying to avoid each other to prevent any sarcastic comments from their siblings. "The entrance to the lost city is just up ahead," Siri whispered. "It's guarded by some of our best, so we shouldn't have any trouble getting in."

"I still don't understand," began a boy with spiky green hair, "how there can be an entire city underneath the Electi capital without them even knowing it."

Siri bent down to meet his eyes. "It's very clever. Aidan. You see, the safest places to be are the places the Electi don't want to see. They know about the maintenance tunnels used by their Treb workers to keep the city running but why on earth would they ever want to go down there themselves? It's literally beneath them." Aidan smiled as he began to understand. They had all heard about the tunnels underneath the city, used by Treb workers for cleaning, rubbish collection and general maintenance. They never knew they had another purpose, however. They passed several old, abandoned supermarkets which were now used by the many homeless Trebs displaced by increasing poverty. A crumbling library seemed to be the home of a large group of families and several cats.

"How are they all surviving out here without respirators?" Archie asked in awe. AJ looked and gasped.

"And how are those animals alive? We can only let Sully out for ten minutes at a time or he would get sick from the radiation," she paused, suddenly remembering that Sully was, in fact, a robot and therefore might have been fine after all. "Well, at least for real pets I'm pretty sure that's the rule."

"Look closer," Eloy urged. Archie and AJ squinted at the feral cats climbing through the holes in the walls of the old building and recoiled. On closer inspection, Archie could see that the cats were horribly misshapen — tumours were growing all over their frail bodies and restricting their movement. He was almost afraid to look at the kneeling child behind them, but

194

he needed to know. As he shifted his gaze, the child looked up. Through a gap in the brickwork, she could see the passing group and cast curious eyes over them. Curious, milky white eyes. Archie realised in horror that this child was blind, with a tumour growing across her forehead and another on her cheek. He tried to keep his reaction internal, but his knees buckled and he managed to pull off his respirator just before throwing up on the dirt at his feet. AJ fought to hold back shocked tears. Siri heard the noise and looked anxiously behind her.

"What's wrong with him?" she asked sternly. "We have to keep moving." Eloy grabbed Archie gently by the arm and hauled him up.

"He's okay, he's just not used to this." Eloy gave a pointed look at the library and Siri nodded. She couldn't imagine what it must be like to see this for the first time, especially when your own father was largely responsible. Eva, meanwhile, was staring fixedly at the ground. She didn't want to see. She didn't want to know what it looked like to live like this.

"Eva," Archie whimpered. "You have to look. We can't keep hiding behind privilege." Eva shook her head.

"I know, I'm awful," she whispered. "I know I'm weak and pathetic and part of the problem, but I don't want to see what we caused."

"We didn't cause it," Archie interrupted. "Our father did."

"We were complicit," Eva replied darkly. "Every roast dinner; every Latin lesson; every private transport filled with all the food and entertainment we could ever want, while people lived... like this." Eva forced the tears not to fall — she didn't deserve to be the one crying. Not after everything she had been given.

"We're fixing that now," Archie reassured her. "We are

going to help them."

"How?" Eva was louder now, "How are we going to help *these* people? Will they even last another week?" Siri turned around again at the commotion.

"You two shut it! If anyone gets wind of us, we're done — do you hear me?" The siblings were silent. "Good. Now be quiet and keep moving."

The entrance to Lost London wasn't as dramatic as AJ expected. In the rubble of a bombed-out shopping centre sat two, unassuming Trebs in standard-issue respirators, playing with an old-fashioned chess set. Siri signalled for the group to stay behind as she approached them.

"Looks like the bishop's seen better days," she remarked.

"Which one?" replied one of the players without looking up.

"The green one." At Siri's reply, the man looked up.

"I knew it was you," he smiled. "I just had to follow the procedure, you understand."

"Of course," Siri replied with a smile, and she ushered everyone across the debris to her side. The two men picked up the chess pieces and looked around before turning the table upside-down. On the underside of the chess table, Eva was fascinated to see a mess of circuitry and buttons. Each man began detaching and reattaching wires in various places and pressing a complicated sequence of buttons. When they had finished, AJ gasped. An old elevator, previously disguised by the rubble around it, had lit up and opened its doors. Siri led them all inside.

"Cool," AJ remarked. "It's bigger on the inside!"

"No, it isn't," Siri chuckled. "It just looks smaller from out there because it's hidden by all the rubble." As the doors closed and the elevator began its descent, Eva looked thoughtful. "I can't believe these tunnels were underneath us the whole time…" Siri smiled at her.

"Not just the tunnels — they've built an entire city down here." The elevator doors opened, and they walked out into a dark room with a strong smell of damp. Siri removed her respirator and took a deep breath.

"We're safe from the radiation down here," she told them, and they slowly removed their respirators, many grimacing at the unpleasant smell.

"That's natural stone, that is!" An old man with a grey beard appeared as if from nowhere. He had a thick accent and neither Archie nor Eva had any idea what he was saying. "Best smell in all the world! You won't find it much no more." Eva looked confusedly at Archie, who shrugged. AJ chuckled under her breath and smirked at her brother. "Now you must be Miss Siri." The man took Siri's hand and beamed at her. "We're all so glad you're 'ere with us, Miss."

"Please," Siri pleaded. "Just Siri is fine."

"Nonsense, Miss." The man admonished, "You're a very important person down 'ere. You deserve respect."

"Well, in that case, please respect me enough to just call me by my name." Eva and Archie continued to look around in confusion. AJ was finding this more and more hilarious.

"Is he speaking in a different language?" Archie asked.

"No, you posh idiots, he's just from the West Country." AJ tried to keep her amusement under control, for fear of insulting the man. Archie looked even more confused. "Which country is that? Is it near the ESA?"

Eloy rolled his eyes. "Finest education money can buy and you're still completely stupid," he mocked. Just as Eva was about to chime in defensively, Siri turned to the group.

"Bert here is going to show us where we'll stay tonight. Stay close. This is a Treb city but it's..." she paused. "It's not the safest place in the world, I'll just say that. People here are pretty desperate and they don't all have faith that we can save them." The group exchanged nervous glances. "Archie, Eva — wear these." She threw what looked like old curtains towards the Impero-Regnum siblings who quickly heaved from the smell. They unfolded the garments to reveal hooded cloaks, covered in a mixture of dirt and what looked like blood. "I know they're not the nicest, but we can't risk you being spotted down here. You'd be kidnapped for ransom money before we saw anyone coming. Let's go." Archie and Eva looked at each other in horror before hastily running after Siri and the group. Eloy tried to stay as far away as possible from the hideous-smelling cloaks, but Eva seemed keen to run beside him. Once or twice their hands brushed together as they ran, making Eloy feel something between nausea and butterflies. As they approached a large metal door, Eva tentatively took Eloy's hand.

"It's... it's okay," he stammered. "We'll be okay, I'll keep you safe." Eloy smiled at Eva and tried to ignore his twin sister making mocking kissy faces behind Eva's shrouded head. Archie spotted AJ, however, and was quick to laugh along.

"Behind this door is the Lost City." Siri's severe tone snapped them all out of their mirth. "Stay close. I mean it." The group instinctively took a step closer together, many of them stepping on each other's toes but no one really minding. Siri inputted a code into a keypad and a small opening in the metal door slowly swung open, releasing a gut-wrenching smell. Eyes watering, the group walked through the gap and into a dimly lit but bustling underground street. Rows of shops were carved out of the stone walls, selling anything from black market foodstuffs to weaponry. Dark alleyways seemed to conceal questionable interactions and stagnant water flowed down the uneven stone pathways. Eloy was fascinated.

"It's like something from history," he whispered to Eva. "Like Victorian London — everything is so primitive and... dirty. Very, very dirty." He sidestepped to avoid a particularly deep puddle of brown water while Eva held her nose and tried not to faint. The old man leading them seemed to know everyone and nodded and waved at various passers-by. They carried on through a maze of similarly depraved-looking streets and courtyards for around ten minutes before arriving at a metal-walled building with a sign reading 'H-t-l'.

"Ere you are," the man announced proudly. "Finest 'otel in Lost London this is!" Many of the group seemed largely unimpressed. Archie had no idea what he had said but was very confused as to why they had stopped.

"Is that meant to be a hotel?" he asked, curiously. "Who on earth would want to *stay* down here?"

"That would be us," Siri scolded. "Thank you so much, Bert, we owe you one." With a threatening glance back at Archie she led the group inside and bid farewell to their friendly guide. She approached the sullen-looking man at the reception desk and produced a red flower from her pocket. The man's eyes widened, and a surge of colour flushed to his sallow cheeks.

"My goodness, it's you!" He looked up at Siri in awe. "I told them you'd come, you know. I never lost hope!" The man seemed giddy with excitement as he pulled down an assortment of keys from the wall behind him. "This way, please, follow me!"

"What are those dangly things?" AJ asked her brother.

"Keys," he replied. "They let you into doors and stuff in the olden days."

"Why don't they use their chips?" AJ asked, confused. "What if they lose the key, then they'll be stuck?"

"There's no technology down here, Miss," the man replied. "The Electi could track it." He paused to open a door with one of the larger keys. "And yes," he continued, "we do sometimes lose keys. The noble art of locksmithing is still alive and well in Lost London though, thank heavens."

AJ privately thought that this man was either very confused or downright delusional, but kept those thoughts to herself. She did object to the sheer amount that people down here seemed to insist on calling women 'Miss' however. "Your rooms are all along this corridor," he continued. He turned to Siri. "Madam, it's been an honour. I hope we meet again." He gave a strange sort of gesture with his hand to his head and walked back down the corridor, leaving AJ more confused than ever.

"What a weirdo," she mumbled under her breath.

"Right?" Archie agreed. There was a tentative rush to various doorways as Eloy, AJ, Eva and Archie all headed for a room together. "Get some rest everyone," Siri shouted down the hall. "We've got important work to do tomorrow." Now safely in their damp, dark room, the four teenagers sat quietly for a few moments, contemplating their fate.

"Well," AJ began, trying to lighten the mood, "who wants to have a look around?"

Chapter 20

Who Will Buy?

Eloy & AJ — Archie & Eva

Although they were all exhausted from the long journey, none of the teenagers felt much like resting and it was AJ who boldly suggested they explore Lost London.

"Are you mad?" Eva asked incredulously. "Didn't you smell what it was like out there? There are vagrants around every corner!" AJ scoffed,

"Look, I have no idea what you just said, but it doesn't exactly smell much better in here. I'm going."

"Wait," cried Eloy, "I'm coming too." Eva looked at him in surprise.

"It'll be cool, Eva — it's like a city out of time. Imagine you're in Oliver Twist."

"Who's Oliver Twist?" Archie asked, confused.

"It's one of the old paper books he loves," AJ replied as she pulled on her boots. "Anyone who wants to come with me has about thirty seconds to make up their mind." Eloy pulled on his coat and Archie, after some careful thought, zipped up his hoody and pulled the hood low over his head.

"What if someone recognises you?" Eva asked, concerned.

"I'll be careful!" Archie urged. "Now come with us, you're being boring."

Eva let out a long, overly dramatic sigh before grabbing a hat and large jumper. "I'm going to boil out there," she muttered.

"It's better than being spotted," Eloy reassured her and took her hand, prompting a shy smile. AJ peered out the door to make sure Siri wasn't there, before gesturing to the rest of them to follow her. She led them out of the hotel and back towards the main thoroughfare. The streets seemed to have been carved into rectangular blocks, Eva noticed, reminiscent of New Moon City in the ESA.

"We need to remember which way we've been," she reminded AJ. "We don't want to get lost."

"Good point," Eloy nodded. "I'll keep track." Eloy's abilities proved useful in areas such as this, but he was soon distracted by a nearby shop. "Oh wow," he breathed. AJ followed his gaze.

"It is pretty cool how they've made all these old-fashioned shops down here," she agreed. "I suppose they had to — I doubt Zoom2U delivers down here." Eloy slowly approached the shop, still holding Eva's hand.

"Oh, it's a book shop," Eva realised. "Wow, do people actually still buy these?"

"It must be because they don't have that much electricity down here. Remember that strange man was telling us it could be tracked?" AJ added.

"Goodness, imagine being so bored you have to resort to reading paper books," Archie exclaimed. Eloy shot him a disapproving look before tentatively opening the door of the shop. As the others followed him inside, they couldn't believe their eyes. Rows and rows of not only books but seemingly all kinds of knick-knacks and curiosities the owner could get his hands on filled the many rooms before them. Smaller rooms seemed to jut off to the side and Eva even spotted a small, rickety staircase leading down to another floor. Fairy lights hung precariously from a section marked 'True Crime' while strange hand-carved figures were dotted between piles and piles of maps.

"Good lord," Archie breathed. "What is this place?"

"A treasure trove," Eloy replied, smiling. As he disappeared into the clutter, AJ and Archie both stared in fascination at the maps on a nearby table.

"Look, Archie, they just keep unfolding! They're huge!" AJ could barely hold up a particularly large map of the Lake District while Archie pored over one labelled New York City.

"That's New Moon City," Eva pointed out. "President Moon changed the name after the war."

"Oh yeah, I remember Mrs Totterton told us something about that," Archie replied unconvincingly. From further back in the shop, AJ could hear a strange noise. Unable to re-fold the map she had been investigating, she looked around to check that no one was looking before placing it precariously on top of the others. She had to walk sideways to get through some of the narrower aisles and passed statues, paintings and even musical instruments as she retreated further into the depths of the mysterious shop. It was almost like a museum, really, she thought as she carefully descended the rickety stairs into the basement level. The sound was louder now, and AJ followed another string of flickering fairy lights to find a large box with a rotating disc inside of it. It was spinning round underneath a metal arm. An electric generator hummed loudly behind the machine and it was hard to hear exactly what was coming from this mysterious disc. AJ listened intently and could vaguely make out what seemed to be a radio broadcast. She could make out the words, 'war' and 'bombings' but it didn't sound like the war she knew about. Then she heard something about a blitz, and she was even more confused, as she was pretty sure that this was some sort of sports manoeuvre. Eloy found her staring blankly at the noise-emitting disc and chuckled.

"It's a record player," Eloy told her. "This is how people listened to music before music was digital. Well, actually, this is a very old medium — you had cassette tapes after this and CDs of course."

"Of course," AJ agreed, pretending to remember her history lessons.

"Good grief it's like a mausoleum in here." Archie almost fell down the stairs in his excitement. "I have never seen such a weird assortment of artefacts in my entire life, and Father has his own private museum!"

"Of course he does," AJ's words dripped with distain as she went to climb back to the main floor of the store.

"Buying anything?" Archie asked Eloy, curiously.

"I wish," Eloy sighed. "But they only take old paper money down here — I wouldn't even know how to get that."

They retreated back up the stairs in search of Eva, who was in one of the side rooms. She was hastily stuffing something into her pockets when AJ walked in. "It's n-not what it looks like," Eva stuttered, seeing AJ's curious expression. "I dropped my tissues, that's all. I was um, startled by this peculiar looking doll."

"Woah," AJ recoiled as she saw what Eva was gesturing at. "That doll is truly terrifying. Is it missing an eye? Why is its dress covered in red stuff?"

"It's blood," came a chilling voice from behind them.

"Um, excuse me?" Eva replied, turning around slowly to see an old, bearded man wearing a blood-stained apron.

"It's cursed," he continued, "and if you don't get out or buy something, that curse will follow you to your grave." Eva stood there shaking, unable to move. AJ grabbed her arm.

"I'm so sorry, we were just leaving," she remarked, attempting a smile, as she grabbed Eva's arm and pulled her back into the main room of the store.

"AJ, what are you—" Eloy began before noticing the menacing stranger.

"We're just leaving, *aren't* we boys?" AJ replied pointedly. Eloy and Archie nodded hastily before quickly following the girls back out into the main street. Feeling the aggrieved shopkeeper behind them, the teenagers ducked into a nearby alleyway. Eva tried desperately to avoid the suspicious brown puddles as they sidled down the ever-narrowing passageway. Just before hitting a dead end, a hand-pulled Eloy into a courtyard. The others looked around for a moment before finding the entrance hidden behind a hanging curtain. They emerged into a small walled garden adorned with colourful flags and resilient climbing plants, growing towards the light of a collection of tiny candles.

"'Ello again," smiled the friendly guide who had shown them to their hotel. "Sorry if I startled ye, but Bill's not the best bloke to get on the wrong side of, so I thought ye could lay low in my garden for a bit."

"Oh thank you," Eva breathed, relieved.

"Anytime," the man smiled again. "Name's Bert by the way. An' I think it's amazon' what you kids are doing. 'Specially considerin' yer age. Got a daughter just a bit older than ye' and…" He paused. "I'd dread to think of her riskin' her life like you lot are." There was an uncomfortable pause as the group looked nervously at each other.

"Dad, you're freaking them out." A tall girl who, AJ assumed was responsible for the beautiful courtyard decor, ducked under the curtain and waved at the group. "Go make them some tea or something," she urged.

"Right you are, Reva." Bert nodded and retreated inside the stone house.

"I'm sorry about him," Reva began. "He means well. I'm sorry if he frightened you."

"No, it's, um, no problem," Archie flustered, trying to hide his blushes. Eva smirked. Archie clearly had a crush.

"Do you really think we might die?" AJ asked, nervously. An uneasy silence returned to the group at AJ's question.

"We're here to support the main team," Eloy added nervously. "They've got trained adults carrying out the main mission, we were just brought along in case of emergency and to support behind the scenes. There's no way we're going to be put in any real danger." He almost sounded convincing, and the others were slightly reassured as Bert returned with tea. The already small garden was now dangerously crowded, so after politely sipping their tea, they headed back to the hotel. Reva walked with them, in case they ran into Bill the blood-covered shopkeeper.

"What is it like to live down here?" Eloy asked Reva with genuine interest.

"It's not as bad as it looks," Reva replied thoughtfully. "We have schools and doctors, and once a month we get to go up to the surface if it's safe."

"Do you miss all the technology?" Eva asked. Reva smiled.

"I was only young when we moved here — my parents

were caught up in the protests and it was either get deported or hide down here. So I don't really miss what I don't know. We're getting better facilities all the time though — we've just had a whole sports area dug out — we can play football and basketball in our sports lessons now." AJ smiled although she felt sorry for Reva. Imagine not being able to play disuku or browse the internet. "I love reading," Reva added. "I think that's an advantage of being down here — books are everywhere!" Eloy beamed.

"I love reading too, I'd love to be able to get this kind of access to paper books." Eva and Archie both looked slightly disgruntled at Eloy and Reva's sudden moment of connection. They were immediately distracted, however, as they approached the hotel, narrowly avoiding a flustered looking Siri who burst out of the front door holding what Eloy thought looked like an old walkie-talkie. They hid behind a pile of bin bags as she ran back towards the entrance of the city, as they knew they weren't meant to have left the hotel.

"What do you think that was about?" AJ asked suspiciously.

"I don't know," Eloy mused, "but it didn't look good." The group said goodbye to Reva and headed back to their room. After a meagre dinner of some soft fruit and crumbling biscuits brought with them from Project Libertas, the four teenagers decided to go to bed early. They never knew what Siri was planning, but they were fairly sure that resting would be a wise idea. As they climbed into the creaking beds, Eva removed a handful of papers from her pocket.

"I thought you said those were tissues?" AJ asked, suspiciously. Eva blushed.

"I saw my name," she explained. "I think it's our family

tree."

"What would our family tree be doing in an old underground book shop?" Archie asked, suddenly interested.

"Well, we *are* a famous family, Archie," Eva chided.

They looked at the papers for a few moments, following the lines up from their own names to their ancestors. They paused as their fingers settled on someone unfamiliar.

"Who the heck is Ciaran Doyle?" Archie asked, incredulous. Dad's father was called Atticus the first, wasn't he? That's why our brother has that stupid name."

"That is very strange," Eva mused. This Ciaran seems to be descended from Irish immigrants. But Father has always said our bloodline goes back centuries through British nobility."

"Look," Eloy picked up another piece of paper that had fallen from Eva's pocket.

"It is supposed," Eva read aloud, "that the acquisition of the name Atticus Imper-Regnum occurred in 1964, when Ciaran Doyle was nineteen years old. His decision to change his name and identity may stem from his desire to better assimilate into his prestigious British university and gain societal momentum." The siblings looked at each other for a moment.

"Has anything we've been told ever been true?" Archie asked, despondent.

"I doubt it," Eva sighed.

"This is cool, in a way," Eloy offered. "Now you're children of immigrants too – we have something in common!" Eva smiled at him, grateful for his attempt to find a silver lining. She tucked the papers back into her pockets and yawned. Despite their dingy surroundings and the Impero-Regnum's spinning heads, all four teenagers slept soundly that night, exhausted from the long journey and baffling new experiences.

They were woken at five a.m. the next morning by an unusually agitated Siri.

"Kids! Kids wake up," Siri whispered urgently, shaking Archie gently.

"Oi, who are you calling a kid?" Archie grumbled.

"Yeah, we're grown-up heroes now," AJ yawned, still half-asleep, reaching for her glasses.

"There's been a problem." Siri's revelation suddenly shattered all remaining pretence of sleep. "Our operatives up top have been captured. We're... you're all that's left." The room was silent. "This is why we brought you — they knew the risks, and you have all been training for this. We didn't think you'd be needed like this so soon but... get up, get dressed and meet me outside." The group hastily dressed and made themselves vaguely presentable before heading outside. Eva had fashioned a large curtain out of sheets so that she could change in relative privacy, whereas AJ decided to change in the bathroom — a choice she later regretted as she slipped soaking wet socks into her shoes. Siri beckoned them around a small table covered in paper plans. It was like something out of an old-fashioned spy movie, Eva thought.

"Eloy, you'll man the radios — nobody moves unless you say so," Siri began. Eloy nodded and swallowed hard. "Eva, you're on tech. We've got a computer lab set up for you with all the infiltration software you'll need." Eva tried to suppress her excitement as the timing didn't seem quite appropriate. "AJ and Archie, you'll be going into the President's house itself." They both paled and AJ instantly regretted her 'grown-up heroes' comment.

"I can't go in there — it's *my* house! I'll be caught in seconds!" Archie protested.

"That's exactly why you need to go — you're the distraction. If anyone senses trouble you just pop out and say you found your way home and no one will be any the wiser about AJ." Archie looked unconvinced.

"But, what if I don't *want* to go home? Now I know what kind of a monster Father really is. I'm…" He paused and dropped his voice to an embarrassed murmur, "I'm afraid of him." Siri put a reassuring hand on his shoulder.

"We will get you out again. We won't leave you anywhere you don't want to be." Archie exhaled slowly and nodded.

"Okay," Archie conceded, "but Wendoline is going to smell me a mile off and start barking — that dog's a liability."

"I'll send someone from Team Loro down to one of the shops here to get you some dog treats. Now assemble your teams and brief them on the mission," Siri instructed.

By half-past five all the students had been ushered into their respective teams and were somewhat ready and willing. AJ and many others were still yawning. The four camp leaders had all gathered in various rooms of the hotel and were briefing their teams. Eva nervously relayed the details to her fellow students.

"I know this might seem a bit strange, but we're just doing what we've been doing in the hut back at Project Libertas. Charlie, you'll take the lead on chip control — I've seen you deactivate chips like it's child's play and, well, you are only ten, so I suppose it is child's play for you." The boy called Charlie gave a playful grin and nodded. "Fumiyo, you take physical security — any gates, doors, invisible lasers — whatever they've got, I want it down. I know where most of them are so I'll draw you a map, but I'm sure Father will have increased security since we left."

In the next room over, Eloy was instructing his team on the plan.

"We are their eyes and ears, people. Just like we practised back at the base. We watch Team Oro's camera feeds as well as the camera feeds from the mansion, if Camp Tortuga do their jobs, then there shouldn't be anything we don't see. We will be able to track their location as well as warning them of any incoming threats — are we clear?"

In the hotel's modest kitchen, Archie was attempting to make porridge over a gas stove while talking to his team.

"Right, I'm the bait. I'll hang back while AJ sneaks in. We'll listen for Eloy's orders and, if needed, I'll go in. Your jobs are to run interference — if any guards aren't where they should be and the other teams can't get rid of them, we stage a distraction. Maybe you pretend you've been hit by an E-Car or something." Archie gestured to a girl with pigtails. "You're adorable, it'll work. I'll find you some jam if I can — we can pretend it's blood." Archie looked around the kitchen but, unfortunately, the only food he could find was a bag of mouldy meal drinks. "Okay new plan, where can one find paint around here?"

In the corridor, AJ was holding back her yawns as well as her nerves.

"I don't want to say we're the most important team," AJ began modestly. "But we definitely are." Heads nodded in anxious agreement. "I am going inside the president's mansion and my one job is to reach his computer and get the data we need. All I need to do is plug in this drive and wait for the transfer."

A small boy with glasses looked sceptically at the drive. "Bit antiquated, isn't it? I thought everything was in the cloud."

"The president's paranoid — he doesn't store his data remotely in case people like us manage to hack it. So, he's also quite smart. Because that would have made this entire operation unnecessary."

"What about us?" the small boy prompted.

"Well, we can't all go in, or we'd be spotted. However, should anything happen to me, one of you will have to take my place, and so on." The group collectively swallowed at the thought of all the many things that could 'happen' to each of them, before following AJ out of the hotel. Siri was there to meet them outside.

"I just want you to know, I'm really proud of you all," she said in a moment of uncharacteristic seriousness. "You've all agreed to do something I never thought kids your age would ever even consider, for the sake of your country and humanity itself." She let her words sink in for a moment, hoping to inspire her team. "Now let's move out."

Chapter 21

Home Invasion

Eloy & AJ — Archie & Eva

Siri led the anxious adolescents and cautiously confident children deeper into Lost London. Eventually, they passed another large metal door and entered a dark, dusty elevator. This ascended into a long corridor.

"Team Tortuga, you get off here. Down the hall to the left is a small control room. It's not our main base of technical operations and it's all run off a generator, but it works. It's surrounded by several walls and doors to prevent any signals from being detected so you'll need the codes — I've sent them to your holophones which should activate again as you approach the control room." Eva nodded at Siri's instructions and led her team out of the elevator, which then continued its ascent, finally emerging into an abandoned petrol station. Siri went out first, to check the perimeter, before nodding to the others to follow.

"So, how are we getting to my father's house?" Archie asked, tentatively. "We're still in the outskirts, our house is right in the centre of New London."

"Don't you remember your history lessons Archie?" Siri asked with a wry smile.

"Well, you taught us technology and were a lot more

engaging than Mrs Totterton, let me tell you!" Archie chuckled to hide his blushing cheeks.

"Well thank you, but you're missing the point. We're going to be using the river."

"River? What river?" Archie was nonplussed. There was no river in New London that he knew about.

"He really doesn't remember his history lessons, does he?" Eloy whispered to AJ, who was presently pretending to know what Siri was talking about.

"After the war, the River Thames became so polluted that the President ordered it to be drained and filled in. Shortly afterwards, New London was built on top of the ruins of Old London and the river was largely forgotten about," Siri explained.

"Okay," AJ nodded, still pretending that she knew about the River Thames all along, "but if they filled it in, how do we use it?"

"Oh," Eloy interjected. "I know this! They never got round to filling it in because they ended up using it as part of the underground tunnel system for the Treb workers!"

"That's right, Eloy. The river is, or was, part of the service corridors that prevented the Treb workers from 'polluting New London with their presence' as your father would say, but still allowing them to do their menial jobs such as cleaning and catering for the Electi citizens who lived in the city. In recent years it has developed, shall we say, a mould problem, and has been closed off. However, I know a guy with a set of quad bikes who can ride us up that thing in no time at all!" Siri explained. AJ's eyes widened.

"What are quad bikes and are they as awesome as they sound?" Siri laughed and nodded to AJ. "Cool."

After around thirty minutes of walking, a couple of the younger children were growing tired, and AJ was carrying one on her back.

"Here we are." Siri gestured to a sign that read 'Treb's Municipal Entrance: New London'.

"Classy," Archie commented. AJ and Eloy glared at him. "Oh, um, sorry guys." They were led into a dingy room lined with a thick layer of black mould.

"Keep your respirators on," Eloy warned the others. "This stuff is dangerous."

"There's an office over here with some equipment our team brought with them earlier," Siri said to Eloy. "You can monitor us from here. We wanted you far away enough so that if we got into trouble, you wouldn't be caught up in it." The rest of the teams looked at her, dumbfounded. "Which," she continued optimistically, "definitely won't happen. Don't worry." Siri smiled, slightly unconvincingly. Eloy led his team to the temporary office while Siri and the others walked down the mouldy corridor, at the end of which stood a large shadowy figure. Some of the children flinched but Siri's smile was warm. As they grew closer, she threw her arms out wide. "Brucie!" she called.

"Siri!" called a gruff voice familiar to AJ.

"Hey!" AJ called, "Bruce — it's you!"

"Little Alejandra!" Bruce scooped AJ up in his arms just like he used to when she was little.

Eloy beamed at their family friend; it was so encouraging to see a familiar face.

"Have I got some good news for you," Bruce began and AJ's eyes widened in hope.

"Is it Mizuki?" AJ couldn't even bear to hope. She knew Bruce had been working on her rescue, but he couldn't have actually pulled it off, surely?

"I got her out, and her mum." AJ's eyes filled with tears and she fell to the floor. "Hey, it's all right, she's safe, she's okay." AJ held Bruce's hand tightly in silent thanks. Eloy tried to hold back his emotions as his sister wept, but the relief was overwhelming. He put his hand on his sister's shoulder and smiled at Bruce. AJ was still sobbing on the floor as Siri gave an impatient cough.

"There you go, now you've really got something to fight for, eh?" Siri smiled and coaxed AJ and the others towards the quad bikes, each equipped with small trailers. Eloy and AJ gave a grateful wave to Bruce before being ushered onto a quad bike. AJ hardly had time to process this news before being thrown into the next stage of the mission and her head was spinning.

Still shaken, she straddled a quad bike with a mix of fear and excitement. She'd never driven anything before let alone something like this. Siri gave her a quick tutorial before encouraging her to just go slowly to start with. Unbeknownst to Siri however, AJ didn't have a 'slow' speed setting and rocketed off down the mouldy riverbed. "Everyone, follow AJ!" Siri shouted before starting her own bike, as they sped off towards the centre of New London.

"I'm pretty sure I just saw a dead crocodile," Archie wrinkled his nose as they dismounted their quad bikes, now deep in the depths of the dredged River Thames.

"Don't be ridiculous," Eloy scoffed. "There were never any crocodiles in the River Thames." Archie was unconvinced.

"Right, Team Tortuga have unlocked a couple of the

secured tunnels underneath the president's mansion. Once we're through those, the exit will take us above ground where we can get Team Loro in position. Their job will be to distract any guards or Electi officials in our way — although hopefully Team Tortuga and Team Zorro will have made that job a little easier for us by distracting them with fake security breaches at the other end of the perimeter. Rafe and the rest of Team Oso will hang back here and wait for my signal in case they are needed. AJ, Archie, you're with me."

After navigating the secure tunnels with relative ease, the group took a deep breath and adjusted their respirators, ready for the harsh outdoor air.

Shielding their eyes from the sudden sunlight, the party ascended a ladder, through a disused manhole cover in the alley near the president's mansion, where the family's food was usually delivered. Archie felt his entire body grow tense. This was suddenly feeling too real. The rest of Team Loro turned on their communications equipment and were guided by Team Zorro, still safely below ground, to their positions. "If they all do their jobs, we shouldn't have anything to worry about," Siri whispered. Somehow, AJ and Archie were still worried. "Eva says there's a safe entrance at the back, behind the greenhouses. Once you're in the garden, you won't need your respirators." AJ looked confused.

"Our house is in a sort of… bubble," Archie explained. "So we can be outside without actually being outside, if you know what I mean." AJ was fascinated. She'd never experienced such a phenomenon. Siri urged them to follow her and they silently left the alley. The huge presence of the mansion could be seen for miles around as it towered over the surrounding city.

Though not as tall as the skyscrapers of New London, it was infinitely statelier, with old fashioned but pristinely maintained structures and gardens. It was more like a palace than a home. AJ couldn't help staring which only made Archie feel guilty. Siri noticed him look away and reminded them to "remember why you're here, no distractions." The teenagers nodded and ducked down behind the back wall of the garden. "Eva and Team Tortuga should be disabling the perimeter security in three, two..." Before Siri could reach 'one' they heard a slight hiss and the bubble around the garden seemed to change colour. In their ears they could hear Eloy's voice.

"Over the wall, now!" Without having time to consider the implications of what they were about to do, or indeed to consider whether it was an appropriate mission for a fifteen- and sixteen-year-old, the pair leapfrogged the wall and were safely tucked away behind the greenhouses. Luckily, both AJ and Archie excelled athletically, making this a fairly easy task, although Archie was still impressed to see quite how high AJ could leap from standing.

"Nice," he whispered. She smiled back.

Eloy's voice was still in their ears, "There is a guard to your left, so you need to go around the right side of the greenhouse. Stay low or he'll spot you. I'll get Team Tortuga on a distraction. Eva, can you make the exterior gate open to draw him away?"

"On it," came Eva's voice through their ears. "Come on Puffles, work with me here," she pleaded quietly. AJ and Archie waited for the guard to turn away from them before running alongside the greenhouses. Archie pulled AJ around the fountains so that they were still hidden from the house.

"Good thinking, Archie," Eloy's voice continued. "Your

mum is in the kitchen and, as planned, your dad is out so you've got a clear run to his office. Unfortunately, your younger sisters are currently in the playroom and their nannies aren't doing a great job at watching them." Archie swallowed. He hadn't seen his sisters in months and knew just how loudly they would shriek if they saw him.

"You have younger sisters?" AJ enquired.

"Yeah, but they've spent most of their lives at boarding school. Mother hates children," Archie mumbled. "Their nannies, Constance and Patience, are pretty useless to be honest. Everyone knows Father only hired them because they were pretty, if you like that sort of thing," he grimaced. AJ patted his shoulder sympathetically, but privately thought this wasn't really the time for family stories. Eloy was back in their ears with further instructions and Archie suddenly found his focus again.

"The girls are distracted by a dragon cartoon; this is your window!" At Eloy's words, AJ followed Archie into the house and up the stairs. She tried not to be distracted by the marble staircase, gold handrails or what looked like a full-size disuku pitch in the mansion itself. Archie pointed to a door at the end of a long corridor. AJ nodded and sprinted ahead. Archie followed behind, trying to avoid looking in his bedroom and experiencing the pangs of familiarity and loss. AJ stopped suddenly outside the door.

"What?" Archie whispered. "Go in, quick!"

"I can't," AJ replied, "It's locked, look!" AJ pointed to a retinal scanner beside the door frame.

"Sh—" Archie began but was cut off by Eloy.

"Eva, we need that scanner disabled or something — we can't go any further!"

"It's new!" Eva was mildly panicked. "He never had that before, why would he upgrade security like this?"

"Oh, I don't know," Archie whispered back, "maybe because of situations exactly like this?" Eva's sigh in their ears made her annoyance clear.

"One minute," she muttered, frantically trying to bypass the scanner remotely. Archie kept peering round corners and jumping at slight noises while AJ stood calm, eyes closed, awaiting her next instruction. The shrill voices of young children and frustrated caregivers were still ringing up the stairs.

"How do you stay so chilled out?" Archie asked her, anxiously.

"My mum taught me to meditate," AJ replied in a hushed whisper. "It helps my dad with his panic attacks, but it's also useful for times like this." She inhaled deeply before slowly exhaling. Archie tried to copy her, but the noise of his sisters downstairs, was making him increasingly nervous. Suddenly, he froze. At the opposite end of the hallway, guiltily emerging from the master bedroom, came Wendoline the sausage dog.

"Oh cr—" AJ covered Archie's mouth just in time, before Wendoline could recognise her owner's voice.

"Eva," he whispered at a level that was almost inaudible. "We're really going to need to get in there now."

"I'm trying," she hissed.

"But," Archie protested, "Wendy is here…" Eva gasped and her audible typing grew quicker. Wendoline was going in and out of the bedrooms, presumably in pursuit of snacks.

"Just, one more minute," Eva pleaded. Archie tried to hold his breath as he hid round a corner behind AJ. Wendoline seemed to be at least momentarily distracted in Eva's room, giving AJ time to think of a plan.

"We need to snatch the dog."

"Excuse me?" Archie asked, bemused.

"She's going to get here before we can get in and we can't risk her alerting everyone to our presence. We need to grab her."

"Are you mad! Don't you think that grabbing her might alert everyone to our presence?"

"Keep your voice down!" AJ urged. "Look, if you coax her over maybe she won't bark?" Wendoline strutted out of Eva's room with a bag of fudge in-between her teeth, grinning proudly as she waddled towards them.

"Oh no, that's Eva's special fudge, she was saving that."

"Bigger problems, Archie!" AJ muttered frantically. Archie sighed and peered around the corner. Wendoline saw him out of the corner of her eye and turned, tail wagging madly, towards him. Archie wore his best pleading expression, placed a finger to his lips and beckoned her forwards. In her excitement, Wendoline dropped the packet of fudge and bounded towards Archie. She was so excited by her master's presence that she failed to accurately measure the distance between them and crashed headlong into his legs, letting out a small welp as Archie scooped her up into his arms. He quickly held her close and started stroking her head, hoping that nobody had heard the commotion.

"Do you think anyone heard that?" he asked AJ.

"Your sisters are still screaming, I think we're good," AJ whispered reassuringly.

"You're in!" Eva's voice sounded triumphantly through their ears as the door clicked open beside them. Still holding Wendoline, the pair dashed into the office and closed the door behind them.

"You've got company on the stairs," Eloy warned. "One of the nannies."

"It's okay," Eva replied, "she won't be able to get into the office."

"If she can't get in," Archie began, concernedly, "then why is her cardigan in here?" AJ looked at the crimson cardigan sprawled across the sofa. On a table beside it sat two empty wine glasses.

"It... must be mother's?" Eva asked through the earpiece.

"No, Mother doesn't wear cardigans, remember? She says they look frumpy. And Constance always wears this, don't you remember?" There was a pause as Archie realised why Constance had been in his father's private locked office. With their father. And two wine glasses. "Eva..."

"Just focus on the mission, Archie." There were tears in her eyes though she tried to hide it in her voice. "And just try not to be surprised by any other horrible things that Father seems to be doing from this point on." AJ patted Archie on the shoulder before approaching the wall of screens and keyboards.

"The main computer is under the desk." Archie pointed, still staring at the cardigan. "That man... my poor mother."

"Archie, I need you to focus," Eloy prompted. The nanny has found the fudge and is coming your way. I may need to send someone in to make a distraction.

"Way ahead of you," Eva interjected. Suddenly an alarm began blaring downstairs. "I've set off the fire alarm in the kitchen, but you still need to hurry," she instructed. AJ had found the USB port and was now transferring the files they needed but the outdated technology was taking longer than anticipated.

"I don't understand it," AJ mused. "There's like a bar and

222

it's going up but it's so slow. I thought data transfer was instant."

"Not in 2025, which is roughly when this particular model was built. He doesn't store anything important on the newer machines for security reasons."

"Madness," AJ muttered, still staring at the little green bar in bemusement.

"Hey, AJ, what do you suppose this is?" Archie asked, gesturing to a metal cubicle in the corner of the room. Inside it there were several wires and a small stool. "I saw it last time I was in here, but I've never seen anything like it before."

"No idea," AJ replied. "They look sort of like the AI charging stations we have at school for the robot staff, but it's different. This one's probably the newest model. Do you have robot servants?" Archie thought for a moment. It was possible, he supposed, that one of their servants could have been an artificially intelligent robot. He'd never asked them such a personal question.

"Maybe? But then, they'd be very realistic and that sounds more expensive than just hiring regular humans," Archie mused.

AJ returned her attention to the computer, which had now finished the data transfer. "I've also installed a backdoor program which allows us to monitor Father's files remotely," Eva explained. AJ removed the USB stick and tucked it securely in her pocket before approaching the door of the office.

"Which way, Eloy?" she asked, tentatively.

"Okay, you're going to want to go back down the stairs and then turn left. You need to avoid the kitchen as that's where everyone is gathered. Do you…" Eloy paused. "Do you have a dog in there with you?" Archie paled and frantically looked around. At his feet, staring dutifully up at him was Wendoline.

"Oh thank goodness, I'd forgotten all about you." Archie picked her up and tickled her chin. "Arch, you can't bring her with you. They'll know we were here."

"I know, AJ," replied Archie. "I guess I just missed her more than I thought I would." The pair silently exited the office and Archie put Wendoline down. "Don't follow us, okay?" he whispered to her.

"She's a dog, she can't understand you, Genius," Eva said sarcastically. Archie scowled and lured Wendoline into his old room with a treat before closing the door.

"I knew those would come in handy." He sighed sadly, before following AJ down the stairs. From the lower level, they could see through to the kitchen where Lady Margot, the girls and the nannies were all gathered, trying to find the reason for the fire alarm. Turning left, they ran through the children's playroom and past the disuku court. AJ nearly had to pick her jaw up off the floor as she saw it.

"You have this in your *house*?" she asked, amazed.

"Guys, stop!" Eloy's voice boomed in their ears and AJ almost shouted back at him before realising the danger. "There's a kid in the next room, he's arguing with what looks like the butler. Honestly you guys are like an old movie, I didn't know people even had butlers any more…"

"Just tell us where to go," AJ snapped.

"Go out the doors to your right, that will take you through the conservatory to the garden and then you just go out the way you came in. You've only got about three minutes until the security perimeter turns back on though, so hurry!" AJ began running towards the conservatory, but when she turned around, Archie wasn't behind her. Looking around the room, she suddenly saw a tuft of ginger hair poking out from behind a chaise lounge.

"Archie, what are you—" But she was cut off by a cold, drawling voice.

"Who in the hell are you?" Atticus Impero-Regnum the second stood in the doorway and glowered at AJ.

"I…" AJ froze.

"Tell him you're hired help," Eva whispered to AJ.

"I, um, I'm the help. I'm here to help. That is to say…"

"Oh do shut up, Treb." Atticus snapped and waved his hand. "A little ethnic for our service, aren't you?" AJ felt her blood boil as Atticus distastefully surveyed her warm amber skin. "Just go and get me a drink will you, it's terribly warm today and Samuel has gotten me all hot and bothered with his irksome fussing." The butler, whom AJ presumed to be Samuel, shuffled nervously away. "And will somebody turn off that wretched alarm, it's giving me a headache!"

"Of course, sir," AJ replied, trying her best to keep her distaste for Atticus in check.

"Where are you going?" Atticus asked, as AJ proceeded to the conservatory. "The kitchen is that way." AJ nodded, apologised and began walking towards the kitchen, which was still full of people. "Stupid girl, why does Father always hire the idiots?" Atticus mumbled to himself as he walked away. As soon as he had gone from sight, AJ turned around and sprinted to the conservatory, dragging Archie behind her. They tore through the double doors and dashed through the garden.

"Twenty seconds!" Eloy warned. Archie wondered what would happen if he was caught in the perimeter at the exact moment their security system turned back on and began to feel sick.

"Keep going!" AJ called back to him as she leapt over the

wall with ease. Archie jumped up and grabbed AJ's hand, but something was caught on his foot.

"Oh no, Wendy get *off!*" Wendoline was biting his shoe and refusing to let go.

"Five seconds!" Eloy shouted. AJ pulled as hard as she could and Archie came tumbling over the wall seconds before the perimeter bubble changed back to its original electric-blue hue. The pair of them sat with their backs against the wall, breathing a sigh of relief. Suddenly, AJ saw something that made her heart sink.

"Oh no," she breathed. In Archie's lap, wagging her tail and beaming with undeserved pride, was Wendoline.

Chapter 22

Black Holes and Revelations

Eloy & AJ — Archie & Eva

After another terrifying quad-bike ride down the empty River Thames, followed by a tentative walk through mouldy corridors, the four teenagers were finally reunited. There was, however, one unexpected addition.

"Wendoline, what on earth are you doing here?" Eva gasped as Wendoline attempted to leap into her arms, managing to make it only to her shins before crashing inelegantly to the floor.

"Funny story," Archie began.

"Save it," Siri interrupted. "That was great work back there but Eloy's right, they will know something's up now the dog is missing, and it could mean serious trouble for us. We need to get back to the hotel immediately." As the adrenaline wore off and reality set in, the group made a hasty retreat to Lost London. Once they arrived back at the hotel, Eloy and AJ headed straight back out to find some food, leaving Eva and Archie to talk about what Archie had found in their father's office. The red cardigan and empty wine glasses were still prominently on Archie's mind.

"Eva, do you remember when AJ and I were in the study?" Archie began, delicately. Eva nodded. "Well, I saw something. I saw a lot of things, actually. But I saw Constance's cardigan. It was on the sofa next to two empty wine glasses. I just thought it was odd, you know?" He paused, waiting for Eva to connect the dots, which, of course, she had already done.

"How long do you think he's been having an affair?" Eva asked, quietly

"Who knows?" Archie shrugged, with a hollowness in his throat that only seemed to come when he was talking about his father. "Constance and Patience have been Antoinette and Euridice's nannies ever since they were born... so perhaps as long as that." He steadied himself for a moment before concluding, "I feel sick."

"I'm just angry," Eva added coolly. "I mean, all the awful things he has put Mother through and now this. Why doesn't she just leave?"

"Do you really think she could?" Archie asked. "I wouldn't be surprised if he would have her killed for less."

"Archie!" Eva slammed the side of the bed. "Don't say that."

"But don't you think he would?" Archie asked, trying to stay strong.

"I..." Eva paused, also trying to keep her emotions under control. They were both taught from a young age that showing any emotion was beneath a true Electi, but it was difficult to hold it in at times like this. "I don't know what to think any more." Eva swallowed hard. "I just don't want to be part of the problem anymore." Wendoline gave a low whine. She wasn't used to going this long without food, particularly the gourmet kind, and there was none of that to be found in Lost London. Eloy and AJ returned with limited supplies, but even after a can of simulated meat, Wendoline wasn't happy.

"It's your own fault for coming with me!" Archie told her as he stroked her belly.

"It was all we could find," Eloy apologised. "I got the impression that all of the higher quality items required... more nefarious means in order to obtain them."

"Oh goodness, are you okay, Eloy?" asked Eva, concerned. "You weren't threatened, were you?"

"I was there too, you know," AJ pointed out. Eva blushed. "In one shop, a guy offered to buy my hair *and* my glasses." AJ dramatically placed her hand to her head and pretended to faint.

"Oh good grief!" Eva laughed at AJ's thoroughly over-the-top rendition. "Are you both all right?"

"Hm." AJ looked down and her smile faded. "We're used to the rougher side of town. At least nobody down here has hurled racist abuse at me yet," she muttered darkly. Archie and Eva turned red.

"I'm so sorry about our brother, AJ," Archie apologised. "There's nothing we can say to defend him, he's awful — he's always been awful. He's like a miniature version of Father." Eva nodded in agreement.

"We don't see colour," Eva added. "We just see our friends." AJ sighed.

"It's not enough to 'not see colour'," Eloy explained. "You need to see it — to see the difference in our treatment, to acknowledge it and actively work to change it." Archie and Eva nodded, eager to show that they were hearing what Eloy was saying. Eva gently placed her pale hand on Eloy's. She thought his golden skin was beautiful, but she was too shy to say it. Eloy smiled delicately at her while AJ and Archie made pretend vomiting noises behind them. Before Eloy could respond, Siri Perl burst in without knocking, as usual. Eva snatched her hand away and turned a deep shade of pink.

"Sheesh, Siri, do you have to do that every time?" Eloy gasped, clutching his chest. "It makes me jump."

"Sorry, Eloy, but this is important. Our off-site tech team should be analysing the data as we speak, which will enable us to make our next move."

"Shouldn't we let the grown-ups go on the next mission?" Archie pleaded.

"We could have died, you know?" Siri scoffed at him.

"Don't be ridiculous, you were fine. In fact, you were better than fine, which is exactly why we need you! Adults aren't as good at quick decision making. They get all wrapped up in consequences and moral compasses, but you kids, just do what needs to be done," Siri explained. Eva wasn't sure what was so wrong with having a moral compass and was about to ask Siri when one of her assistants walked in.

"Miss Perl, we need you a moment."

"If one more person calls me 'Miss' anything I am going to lose it. Do you have any idea how undermining it sounds?" Siri muttered as she strode after the nervous-looking man. She nodded at the others to follow her. They were led out of the hotel, down a street and out of one of the large metal doors on the outskirts of the settlement.

"Are we going above-ground again?" Eloy asked, nervously.

"I expect the tech team has found something. With minimal electricity down here, the main tech base had to be located elsewhere." Eloy nodded in understanding as they approached a large elevator that took them to the surface. They emerged in a dilapidated parking structure and once again had to climb over rubble to get out. Eva was less than impressed, although she was used to this sort of thing by now. They were ushered into a black E-car and driven away from London.

"How far away is this tech team, exactly?" Eva asked, concerned.

"Not too far," Siri reassured. "But we couldn't risk any signals being intercepted close to the settlement. It's much bigger than the room you used for the mission." After a forty-minute drive, they arrived at a large reservoir.

"This is it?" asked AJ, unimpressed.

"What were you expecting? A skyscraper? We're undercover, remember?" The man led the party down a disused staircase and along a concrete hallway with mould and mildew clinging to the walls. Eloy privately wondered how many more mould infested tunnels he would have to deal with that day. They walked further and further down the sloping corridor until they were directly beneath the reservoir. There, through a set of creaking, metal doors, the group collectively gasped.

"I really can't believe you're all still surprised by these sorts of things," Siri laughed, as she led them into the glistening white room lined with holographic screens. Eva let out a small squeak — she had never seen so much modern technology in one room before, even in the president's mansion. AJ gave a long whistle.

"This is magic," Eloy exclaimed. The man led them to a central desk where a woman was concernedly looking through data. Out of the corner of her eye, AJ could see the Puffles avatar dancing along a holoscreen with an error message.

"Siri, thanks so much for coming. I didn't feel it was safe just sending a message. You need to see this for yourself." Siri looked at the screen, which was now displaying a government report from 2046. Siri gasped as she read, but the others couldn't see over her shoulder.

"What is it?" Eva asked.

"Eugenics," Siri replied and read on.

"You what now?" Archie tried to read over Siri, but even his tall frame couldn't help him understand what any of it meant.

PROGRESS REPORT: PROJECT PLATO
7.9.2046
For the eyes of President Impero-Regnum only

Sir,

The project is going as planned and our population control measures are looking promising. The altered synthetic food is now fully distributed and the water supply to all Treb settlements has now been compromised. We are seeing positive results, with an increase in Treb miscarriages of 400% and a dramatic reduction in Treb pregnancies. This number is disproportionately higher in ethnically British Trebs which is troubling, but our researchers are looking into resolving this. C. Davenport

"I don't get it," Archie mused. "Why does it seem like the government was happy about the infertility crisis? It was a national disaster!"

"Because it wasn't a disaster," Siri breathed, still in shock. "It was their plan all along." Eloy and AJ both felt the floor fall away from beneath their feet as they realised what this meant. They weren't meant to have been born because the government had tried to stop all the Trebs from having babies. That's why the government was monitoring them. They shouldn't exist.

"I don't understand." Eva was reeling. "Why would they not want Trebs to have babies?" Siri ignored her and continued reading.

"What did they use?" Siri asked the woman at the screen.

"P.U.F.F.L.E.S is still decrypting that information but it appears to be some sort of new compound called Acertine. Undetectable in most cases and very dangerous. They put it into the food and the water supply to Treb houses, schools and hospitals."

"Hospitals?" Eva was shaking now.

"But…" Archie still didn't understand. "The Electi helped *cure* the Trebs. They started having babies again because the government provided the vaccine." Eva, however, was one step ahead of him now.

"Archie, do you remember in history class — the anti-government protests and uprisings of 2044-2045?" Archie nodded slowly, trying to remember. "It was the worst backlash the Electi government had seen since its inception and threatened to topple them altogether. What stopped it?" Eva asked. Archie thought for a moment.

"The infertility crisis… it broke their momentum. They stopped protesting about the government and started protesting for a cure."

"And the government gave it to them," Eva continued. "So they stopped protesting. They were indebted to the Electi for giving them their children back."

"But they are the ones who took them away!" AJ shouted. She couldn't believe it. "And there are still far more miscarriages today than ever before — it must still be in the water."

"Population control," Siri interjected. "Trebs were

reproducing faster than the Electi and they would have been overrun."

"You talk about us like we're rats or something." Eloy was quietly furious.

"That's what we are to them," Siri replied calmly. "So they treated us like rats." The colour had drained from the faces of the four teenagers. They had all been born in the midst of the crisis. "I think you'd all better go and sit down for a while," Siri said, quietly. "This is shocking news for all of us."

Having been ushered into a side room with several chairs and a plant pot, the teenagers sat down in silence. After several minutes, Eva broke the silence. "Nothing we can say will make this any better but we are so, so sorry." She was trembling as she spoke.

"It's not your fault," Eloy reassured her. "You didn't do this."

"How are we alive, Eloy?" AJ asked. "I mean, there were how many other children born during the crisis? Maybe twenty at most? Why did we make it?"

"I… I don't know AJ. Maybe it's because Mum was always so careful about what she ate? I don't know."

"Eloy," AJ added in sudden realisation. "Do you think that's why we have abilities?" Eloy's eyes widened but he couldn't find the words to respond. Silence returned and hung heavy in the air as their heads collectively spun. Siri entered after a few moments, looking forlorn.

"I'm sorry that you had to find out this way," she began, sitting on the floor across from them all. "Unfortunately this is the sort of reality that everyone needs to come to terms with if we are going to have a chance of changing it. We know what your father's government is doing, and the fact is, they have probably done far worse. We may still find greater atrocities the more we look."

"And what if we don't want to know?" Archie asked, with a familiar hollowness in his voice.

"It is our duty to know, Archie," spoke Eva softly. "The first step towards an equal society is being aware of our own privilege." Archie blushed and nodded.

"It's hard to hear Archie but it's far harder for those living on the other side," Eloy added.

"AJ, Eloy." Siri turned to the twins. "We think the reason for your abilities lies in acertine, but we don't yet know enough about the compound to fully understand it. But I promise you, as soon as we know more, you and the other acertine children will be the first to know."

"Acertine children?" AJ queried. "There are worse superhero team names I guess."

"What do we do now?" Eva asked nervously. "We can't just go back to Project Libertas — we have to keep fighting." The others muttered in agreement.

"We think we know what our next steps might be," Siri announced. "The president is planning a trip to the mainland. This is unusual as he normally just sends his army to sort out the factory cities. Something important must be happening and we want to be there when it does. We need to return to the hotel and send the rest of the teams back to Project Libertas for their own safety. I've been thinking—" Siri paused and swallowed. "I've been so wrapped up in the revolution that I've lost my own morality a little." The others listened with interest. "Sending children into a situation like that. Some of them weren't even ten years old — sure they're just as good, if not better than some of my adult teams but at what cost? I can't and

235

I won't put their lives at risk any longer. You four — I'm giving you the choice. You've been with me the whole time and have proved you are more than capable. You're all at least nearly sixteen and, I think, old enough to decide for yourselves. I wouldn't ask if it wasn't important, but we're losing operatives every day and you're some of the best I have right now."

"I'm in." AJ stood without hesitation.

"Me too." Eloy stood beside her, fearful but determined. Eva silently stood to join them and looked imploringly at her brother. Archie winced, grappling with the internal turmoil of guilt and injustice, before slowly standing to meet them.

"You have to be sure," Siri insisted.

"We are." Archie held his sister's hand and squeezed it. "We need to be on the right side of history for once." Siri smiled.

"Then we leave at dawn."

Mizuki

Mizuki and her mother had been driven down to the south coast for safety. Mizuki was desperate to see her friends, but it was enough to know that they were alive. Bruce ushered them onto the ship bound for Project Libertas in the dead of night.

"Okasan?" Mizuki addressed her mother as they sat huddled under a blanket below deck. "What happened to Dad... is it my fault?" Mizuki couldn't hold back the tears as she remembered the image of her father lying motionless on the floor of the prison cell. Miranda held her daughter close.

"No, no Mizu-chan, don't ever think that, okay?" She stroked her daughter's damp cheeks.

"But if I hadn't looked through your files they would

236

never—"

"You can't think like that, Mizuki, you didn't hurt him. *They* did." A darkness came over Miranda's eyes and she inwardly resolved never to refer to herself as an Electi again. "I'm the reason they came for us," Miranda breathed sadly. "I was trying to help the Trebs using my Electi position. They must have found out. I just never understood how people could live like that – just watching so many people being treated so badly and doing nothing about it." Mizuki kissed her mother's cheek in silent admiration.

"What will happen to us now?" Mizuki asked nervously. "You can't go back to being an Electi anymore."

"I wouldn't want to," Miranda sighed. "Not after this. We'll have to stay hidden, like your friends. But at least we have people we know out there; we won't be alone."

"And Bruce says they might be able to fix things," Mizuki added optimistically. Miranda was less convinced than her daughter of four teenagers' abilities to change the world, but she smiled at her daughter anyway.

"Whatever happens, we're safe now. We have each other, and I'm never letting you go again."

Chapter 23

History Repeating

Eloy & AJ — Archie & Eva

They left Lost London before its inhabitants awoke. The long journey to the coast was used mainly as an opportunity to catch up on sleep. When they reached Bournemouth, they led the children and other teenagers into the dinghies that would take them to the boat to Project Libertas. As the last dingy departed, Siri then led AJ, Eloy, Eva and Archie to a wooden rowboat.

"Please tell me we're not rowing ourselves to France?" Archie pleaded.

Siri laughed. "Don't be ridiculous Archie, he is." Siri pointed to a large figure approaching them from the other side of the cliff, now level with the ocean.

"It's Bruce!" AJ exclaimed with a grin. Bruce was smiling as he approached the group, and both AJ and Eloy greeted him with a hug.

"How is she?" AJ asked nervously.

"Mizuki is doing just fine," he reassured her. "She's safe with her mother on the boat to Project Libertas and cannot wait to see you both."

"But wait—" Eloy thought for a moment. "What about Simon, her dad?" Bruce looked down forlornly. AJ gasped.

"I'm sorry to have to tell you this but Simon Grey didn't

make it out."

Eloy clenched his fist. "Those monsters," he shouted, alarming everyone nearby. "Sorry," he quickly corrected.

"No, don't be sorry," Bruce prompted. "It was monstrous what they did to him. Poor guy."

"I'm sorry," Eva whispered respectfully. Eloy held her hand. With everything that was happening he felt, more than ever, that it was important to keep the ones he cared about close.

"Promise me you'll be careful," he whispered to Eva once everyone else had begun boarding the rowboat. "I really want to take you out for dinner once all of this is over." Eva smiled and blushed.

"How very dignified," Eva giggled.

"Oh," Eloy stammered. "It might not be what you're used to... I mean, it will probably just be Burger Moon, but, you know."

Eva shushed Eloy with a finger to his stammering lips. "Sounds perfect." She kissed him on the cheek and joined the others, leaving Eloy swooning at the cliff edge. After a moment, he could hear AJ mocking him from the boat and promptly snapped out of his temporary stupor, quickly scrambling into the boat with the others.

Bruce rowed them out to sea with impressive speed. Archie was just beginning to think that maybe Bruce was going to row them all the way to France when the Project Libertas boat sounded a distant horn.

"That's our ride," Siri announced. "You didn't really think we were rowing to France, did you? The main boat will drop us off and float around the coast of France for our extraction before heading back to Project Libertas."

AJ's heart leapt. "Mizuki's on that boat!" she exclaimed. They excitedly awaited the approaching vessel, bobbing silently on the waves. Archie tried to take deep breaths to keep his growing seasickness at bay and was relieved to finally board a marginally more stable vessel. He leant against a faded orange lifeboat with Eva while, below deck, AJ and Eloy were dashing around, trying desperately to find Mizuki.

"AJ! Eloy!" The twins turned, hearts full, to see their best friend slumped against the wall of the boat with her mother. AJ ran over and threw her arms around the relieved girl.

"I missed you so much," Mizuki whispered into AJ's hair.

"I was so worried, Miz!" AJ felt tears of relief falling down her cheeks. "I didn't know if I'd ever see you again."

Miranda Koizumi placed a gentle hand on AJ's shoulder.

"We can't thank your family enough for saving us, AJ. If your friend Bruce hadn't got to us… I don't know what would have happened." AJ finally let Mizuki go and sat back next to her brother. It was then she noticed the two women's faces, scarred and peeling.

"What happened?" she asked. "What did they do to you?" Mizuki squeezed her mother's hand and took a deep breath.

"They tortured us. With acid rain." There was stunned silence.

"That's—" Eloy swallowed hard. "That's inhumane." AJ punched the floor of the boat which responded with loud a metallic clang. Archie and Eva heard the noise and came over to join them. Archie was looking paler by the minute. AJ looked at him with concern.

"You're really not a boat guy, are you?" Archie declined to respond, instead preferring to keep all his fluids inside of his body.

"You must be Mizuki." Eva extended her hand politely. Mizuki delicately returned her handshake with burned and blistered hands. AJ winced to see Mizuki in such pain. Eva was about to introduce Archie and herself but a warning look from Eloy made her change her mind. He didn't think it was a great time to reveal them as the offspring of Mizuki's chief torturer.

"Team Tortuga, what do you have for me?" Siri made a typically dramatic entrance below deck as she approached the group of children on E-Scrolls.

Niah stood to meet her, confident as ever. "Chatter on the Electi channels points to some sort of big shakeup at the main factory city. There have been minor uprisings by the prisoners there."

"There is also talk of a brand-new factory city opening in the south of the Electi Controlled Territories, towards what used to be Spain," added Althea. "The previous inhabitants, not that there were many, have been sent to another factory while they build the new city. We believe that they too have been enslaved." Siri nodded as she listened.

"That's bad news for us," she mused. "We may have to relocate Project Libertas earlier than planned. They are getting too close."

"Siri." Charlie, the ten-year-old tech whizz presented Siri with his E-Scroll. "We've just found this." Sir's eyes flitted over the screen as the teenagers tried to interpret her facial expressions.

"That's why he's come," Siri whispered and silently passed the E-Scroll to the Impero-Regnum siblings. Eva gasped.

PROGRESS REPORT: PROJECT FILII ABSENTIS 20.4.2063

241

For the eyes of President Impero-Regnum only

"Sheesh, always with the Latin," Archie grumbled.

"I know right?" sighed Puffles as his avatar popped out from the corner of the screen. "It's the worst."

"Puffles, not now," Siri hissed, as he guiltily popped back off screen.

Sir,

There is mounting evidence that both assets are being held somewhere within the ECT by the
rebels. With our new factory city planned for the south-east and our others virtually drained
of resources, we have little option but to use the army to round up our existing workers in preparation
to relocate. Our main city on the coast can house our entire workforce short-term. We can then use this as leverage to lure out the rebels. We have a surplus of workers and threatening to demolish a small selection of the
camps with workers still inside may draw the rebels out. If they let the workers die then they will
undoubtedly lose Treb support. The new city will be up and running within days, and any
surviving workers can be moved there.
    C. Christie

The siblings exhaled slowly as they passed the E-Scroll back to Siri.

"We have to give ourselves up," Eva stated calmly. Eloy took a step towards her.

"No, you can't," he pleaded.

"They're talking about killing hundreds of people in order to find us, Eloy. I will not have that blood on our hands."

"Wait, am I missing something here?" Mizuki interrupted. "You're the president's children?"

Archie and Eva looked appropriately guilty and nodded.

"They're with us though," Eloy quickly reassured her. "They've helped us break into the president's mansion and steal important intel. They risked their lives." Eva squeezed Eloy's hand gratefully. Mizuki looked pensive.

"Do they know what he's done?" she asked, her eyes searching the pair for any signs of deception. The Impero-Regnum siblings nodded sadly. "We know now, and I know nothing we can do will ever make up for his crimes," Eva admitted.

"And he's not finished yet," Siri added. "Mateo, tell us what you've found." Mateo nervously stepped forwards.

"The factory cities," he began slowly, "they're not what you've been led to believe." The group all nodded, unsurprised at this point by revelations such as these. Mateo continued, "I think we all knew that any Treb dissenters, protesters and anyone the Electi classed as criminals ended up in these cities, but we didn't know how bad the conditions were." While daily news reports painted the factory cities as 'new opportunities' for willing volunteers, most Trebs were aware that this was far from the truth. Eva and Archie, however, were not.

"What kind of conditions are we talking about?" Eva asked, preparing herself for the worst.

"One of the workers recently managed to escape and flee to Project Libertas," Mateo continued. "He told us that they're all crammed together in shacks stacked high with bunk beds and no air treatment systems. They're given poor quality second-hand respirators; only fed once a day; and any dissension or attempted escape leads to…" Mateo swallowed.

"Leads to?" Archie prompted, not really wanting to know the answer.

"To death," Mateo whispered, barely loud enough to be heard. Siri patted him gently on the back.

"It's all right Mateo, you can go now." Mateo gave her a grateful smile before scurrying shyly back towards Team Zorro.

"There is good news though," Siri added, aware of the falling morale in the room.

"Really?" Eloy asked, doubtfully.

"Their factories are failing," Siri explained. "They're draining the mainland of natural resources before they've really had the chance to grow back which means they're going to struggle to keep supplies flowing to Anglia — this weakens their position. Not only that, but they're moving all their workers into one city, ready for the new factory."

"So in theory," Eloy surmised, "if we liberate one city—"

"We liberate them all!" AJ now realised the advantage of their current position.

"Exactly," Siri pumped the air with her fist before regaining a more serious demeanour. "Now, we had to leave some operatives behind in Anglia. If we succeed, we'll need people over there to set everything off for the final revolt."

"I see where this is going," Archie began. "You're sending us into the city, aren't you?" Siri smiled weakly.

"How can the four of us save an entire city from his army?" Eva asked, her voice full of fear. "I know how strong his soldiers are, I've seen them at demonstrations."

"It won't just be the four of you." Rafe came to join them, followed by Fumiyo, João, Niah, Althea and a somewhat reluctant Mateo.

"We trained alongside you," Niah added. "We're coming too."

"Is this really a good idea?" Eva asked, concerned. "Sending all of the acertine children in together?"

"You're the best chance we have." Siri looked gratefully at the group. "I really can't say enough how proud I am of all of you. When we get through this, I promise to never put any of you in harm's way again."

Eloy was unconvinced by this. "If we get through this," he corrected.

"I have a plan that should keep you all safe," Siri explained calmly. "I believe that a more undercover approach is the way forward. They expect to be met with an army of rebels, but they aren't expecting you." AJ tried to look confident as she privately wondered when and if she was going to see her parents again. "The burden I have placed on you all is beyond what you should carry, I know." Siri sat next to AJ as the others gathered around them. Archie rested his head on his sister's shoulder as he tried to hold down a fresh wave of nausea. "We too are building a new city — in Poland. Everyone from our base as well as the factory cities can live there in peace, far away from the nearest Electi Controlled Territory. Once we're there we can train up new operatives to replace the ones we've lost."

"You can't just replace people," Mizuki croaked, horrified. She wasn't yet used to how blunt Siri could be.

"No, you're right, I'm sorry." Siri looked away. "I never wanted it to be this way." They were quiet for a moment before Eloy decided to try and lighten the mood.

"Did you say the new camp would be in Poland, Siri?

Which part? Our mum was born there, it would be amazing to see it." Siri smiled gratefully at him.

"I'm afraid it won't be the same as it was before the war, but I hear Zakopane is still quite beautiful, especially up in the mountains." AJ and Eloy smiled. Their mother had told them stories of visiting Zakopane and its picturesque streets amongst the mountains.

"Mum will be so happy to be back," AJ grinned.

"But first we need people to help build it," Siri added. "The people on Project Libertas are being transported there now. We knew the Electi Controlled Territories were moving eastward; we just didn't anticipate it to be this soon. We will need people from those factories to help us."

"From one rough job to another," Eva wondered aloud.

"But this time they will be working for themselves," Siri interjected pointedly. "Not for the Electi. They will be building their own houses and infrastructure. I think you'll find them a lot more eager to work this way." Eva blushed, ashamed of her origins again.

"So what do we do?" Eloy asked, always practical. Siri stood up and paced, thinking, for a few minutes.

"The president will be waiting in the centre of the city, within the nuclear plant itself. It's the safest place in the city and he can be easily extracted once he gets you two back — or at least that will be his plan. I imagine he's come all the way here to personally enact vengeance on some rebels, undoubtedly me," Siri paused and swallowed. "But we're not going to let that happen. If we could somehow disable their main power plant, that would cripple their infrastructure. Without the new factory up and running, Anglia would be in chaos and the true nature of their 'perfect factory cities' would be revealed. If we

246

can do that and somehow get access to the president, then we would call all the shots. We can't let the plant fall back into their hands, though. If it malfunctions it could release a dangerous amount of radiation and the world already has far too much of that." The group nodded in agreement. "We should reach land and be ready by nightfall. After dark, we go in."

"What's the plan?" asked Eloy. Siri smiled that familiar, mischievous smile, and ushered them into the boat's brand-new control-room. AJ gave Mizuki another quick hug before following them. On a large holoscreen, Siri brought up the plans of the city, highlighting, specifically, the sewer system. Archie turned a deeper shade of green as a virtual Puffles indicated the route they would need to take.

"Oh no, not again. Why must everything always be underground? It's so dark and smelly and…" he retched. Eva patted him gently on the back.

"Because that way we won't be seen, Archie. Just stick a handkerchief up your nose or something."

"You think I have a handkerchief with me?" Archie scoffed. "Eva, we've been on a boat or in a dilapidated, subterranean, lawless town for the past four days! I haven't even brushed my teeth since we left Spain and I haven't brushed my hair since I escaped from home — the first time, not the second time." He retched again, prompting AJ to shuffle a few paces away from him.

"The sewers are our best way in and out, they lead right from the ocean. As long as we don't bring the boat too close to the shore, we should be undetected. Team Tortuga are scrambling their scanning systems so they won't see us coming." Siri went on to show them the various settlements within the city — some for exiled criminals from Anglia; some protesters and activists; some for defected soldiers and one for—

"No!" AJ gasped as she saw it. Near the city's nuclear power plant was a settlement marked 'Minorities'.

"You're kidding me." Eloy was furious.

"Unfortunately not," Siri replied sadly. "Any dissenting citizen of colour or 'alternative' sexual orientation or gender identity ends up here," she explained. AJ winced. "And it takes a lot less for them to get shipped out than their majority counterparts, let me tell you. The Electi calculated that they were far less likely to vote for them than 'non-alternative-lifestyle-citizens' which is why they take such a tough stance on the issue."

"I knew there was a reason the number of LGBTQ+ people kept going down," AJ sighed. "I just thought it was because of all the conversion camps the Electi had set up." Eloy put his arm around his sister. Eva gave them both a sympathetic look and clenched her fist. She had never understood her father's aversion to minority communities, but she never realised it was this bad.

"They, um—" Siri tried to suppress her natural bluntness as she wasn't used to seeing AJ so vulnerable. "They send the stubborn ones they can't convert out here. I'm so sorry, AJ." AJ sniffled. She had only come out to her family, but she never realised how dangerous being gay could be. Her family was so accepting that she always felt safe to be herself. "Do you want to hear something cool though?" Siri offered kindly. AJ tentatively raised her head. "You know the Anglian Angels captain, Natasha Jay?"

"Of course," AJ mumbled. "She's my hero."

"Well," Siri smiled and continued, "she's secretly engaged

to Emily Chel, the singer." AJ's eyes widened.

"No way! That's so cool." AJ was really smiling now.

"They'd be married if they were allowed, and they live in this beautiful little house by the sea." AJ sat up.

"How come nobody knows?"

"Well, they tried to tell people — lead protests, get their rights back, that sort of thing. But the Electi government arrested them — quietly of course — and explained that if they wanted to remain in Anglia and not out here, they would need to keep their relationship a secret. They knew they couldn't make waves from the factory cities so they're biding their time. At least until I tell them to." Siri winked. "Anyway, I owe them one. They took care of my little sister for a long time after she came out as trans. She wasn't safe anywhere and their house is fairly remote, for obvious reasons." A look of pain crossed Siri's face that seemed unnatural on the usually unshakable woman. "That was until… well, she was just shopping one day. As profitable as being an international sports star and singer might be, they were still Trebs so they had to go to the nearest town to shop and… someone reported Omolara, my sister." Siri paused to regain her composure. "Police officers were there before she even knew what was happening. Natasha tried to fight them off, but they shot her in the arm. That's why she was out for the 2061 season. I know my sister's out here though, somewhere. Alive, I hope."

"I'm so sorry Siri," Eva replied, gently. "What about your parents? Are they…" Eva immediately regretted asking the question, seeing another look of pain cross her mentor's face.

"Well, as you know, the vast majority of arrests are on people of colour," Siri began, shakily. "My parents were rounded up when I was ten. They were just out for a run together, but the police thought they were running from a crime scene and that was enough." Eloy swore under his breath. AJ felt conflicted. Her own father worked for the police. In such a corrupt and discriminatory institution, could he really be the man she thought he was?

"Of course we have our agents on the inside, like your dad, trying to change the system," Siri continued as if reading AJ's mind, "but it's so widespread and systemic now, it's hard. But we cannot stop trying to change these things for the better." The group nodded and now collectively understood why Siri was so passionate and, at times, downright dangerous in her battle for equality. She had a personal stake and one larger than most, in the fight. Over the course of the journey, the teenagers were mostly subdued — planning their mission, finding scraps to eat and comforting an increasingly hungry Wendoline, who was far from satisfied with their meagre attempts at food. AJ and Mizuki played snap while Eloy went over the mission plan with the rest of Team Zorro. Archie and Eva tried to focus on what was about to happen but neither of them could shake the feeling of shame over yet another of their father's atrocities. As far as they had been told, the factory cities were Treb utopias, but Mateo made them sound more like concentration camps. Archie could no longer tell whether his feelings of queasiness were from seasickness or from guilt. As the sun set and the boat bobbed around in place, Siri approached the group.

"It's time."

Chapter 24

Look at the Fireworks

Eloy & AJ — Archie & Eva

Once they reached France, the twins bade a hopefully temporary goodbye to Mizuki, who agreed to look after Wendoline until the Impero-Regnum children returned. A choppy journey to shore in the dinghy only increased Archie's sea-sickness and he vomited onto the sand as soon as they reached land.

"Sorry," he spluttered in between retches. "I'm just not a boat guy." Eva winced. Once he had settled himself, Siri led them through the tunnels into the sewage system. Even with their respirators on, the smell was still extremely unpleasant. It was a long walk, but several members of Team Zorro were guiding them from the boat and members of Team Tortuga were ensuring that they weren't swept away by redirecting the flow of water within the underground pipes.

Siri had some of the older members of Team Loro ready to receive any escaped citizens while a select group of Team Oso were on hand in case things went wrong. Anyone under the age of sixteen, however, was banned from the mission, with the exception of Archie. Siri motioned to a ladder to their left. Through their earpieces, AJ and Archie were instructed to climb it, find the first settlement and release the prisoners, while Eloy and Eva hung back to direct them back towards the boat. Rafe, Fumiyo and João climbed a ladder further down the pipe, with bags full of fireworks.

"They're your distraction," explained Althea, as she, Niah and Mateo hung back to manually override the sewer system if necessary. Siri climbed a ladder to their right and explained that she would be meeting up with some of Project Libertas' finest scientists in an attempt to disarm and decommission the nuclear plant at the centre of the city. This would give them leverage over the Electi as well as cutting power to their all-important new factory. Eloy and Eva waited with bated breath for any sign of success or failure, at the bottom of the ladder. "I just can't stand doing nothing," Eva whispered. "There must be something we can do?"

"We're doing it," Eloy reassured her. "If we're not here when the prisoners get down here, they might end up running straight into another settlement — we need to show them the way out." Eva nodded reluctantly. The silence was deafening, and Eloy privately wondered whether having his first kiss in a sewer would be a good or bad story further down the line.

On the surface, AJ had taken position behind a truck opposite the first settlement. There was a guard directly outside the gate, but it was her teammates' job to distract him. Right on cue, an explosion of fireworks in the distance made AJ almost jump out of her skin.

"For goodness' sake, Rafe," she muttered beneath the sound of exploding gunpowder. "You were meant to save some for the next camp!" As the guard ran towards the commotion, AJ dashed towards the gate, wire-cutters in hand and Archie just behind her. There was a retinal scanner as well as a fingerprint scanner on the side of the gate, but AJ wasn't waiting for Team

Tortuga and Puffles — she'd seen enough old movies to know a faster way through.

"Good idea," Archie whispered as AJ expertly cut a hole in the fence. Once she had climbed through, they sprinted silently to the first bunkhouse. They waited for Team Tortuga to tell them that the security cameras were down before cautiously opening the door. Hundreds of curious eyes, awoken by the sound of explosions and fearful of their meaning, stared at AJ and Archie.

"We are here to free you," AJ whispered as loudly as she could. "We're with the rebels. You need to silently and quickly follow Archie, please." Many of the people began whispering but nobody moved.

"Listen, we don't have time — we are from Project Libertas and this is your chance to get out, it's not a trick. Please!" One of the men cautiously approached AJ.

"Forgive us if we aren't inclined to follow a teenager into a sea of armed guards," he offered. "We are wary of our lives."

"I know," AJ pleaded, "but we have a way out — underground — and the guards are distracted by the fireworks, but they won't be for long, please!" The man examined AJ. Her desperate expression and tattered clothes seemed enough to convince him that she wasn't an Electi. He nodded to his peers and they silently followed Archie out of the bunkhouse and back towards the tunnels.

Stealthily, AJ made her way around each of the houses in the camp and sent each group of prisoners back with Archie, who led them to where Eloy and Eva were waiting to receive them in the tunnels. At the last bunkhouse, a voice came through their earpieces. "AJ, there's a guard, you need to take him out, he's behind the building on your left." AJ's heart practically stopped. Take him out, were they serious? She thought all the guards were distracted by the fireworks — that was the plan.

"AJ," her brother's voice hissed urgently in her ear. She had trained for this but... "If he finds out anyone escaped, he will raise the alarm. AJ, you have to do it, now!" Heart beating like the wings of a hummingbird, AJ tiptoed around the building and located her target. She had been given non-lethal tranquiliser darts, but she couldn't stop her hands from shaking. From behind her, Archie gently placed a steadying hand on her shoulder. This was enough to remind AJ to breathe. With a deep inhale, she aimed the gun. On her exhale, she pulled the trigger. The man leapt to his feet and the pair pulled themselves behind the building out of sight. They heard a reassuring crash and peered round to see that he had indeed hit the floor. AJ sunk to the ground.

"You did it, you're amazing, you did it!" Archie reassured her in an excited whisper.

"I can't believe I just did that," AJ breathed.

"Come on, AJ, there's only one group left!" They quickly dashed towards the final crumbling structure, the power plant now looming over them menacingly. AJ heaved the doors open as another set of fireworks exploded behind them.

"Great job team," AJ whispered to herself as even more soldiers were drawn away from their location. After they had liberated the last of the workers, Archie and AJ ran back with them to the tunnels. As they were descending the ladder, a deafening sound reached their ears.

"They've sounded the alarm," shouted a voice in their ears.

"Yes, I think we got that," Archie quipped back sarcastically, as he showed the final prisoners where to go.

"Now what?" asked Archie, breathless.

"Siri and her team managed to liberate two other camps — I'm pretty sure they took out about a dozen guards to do it — so that only leaves the camp near the reactor. But now they know we're here, it's going to be nearly impossible. You have to retreat!" Before he had finished, however, AJ was already gone. "AJ what are you doing? You're going to get yourself killed!" Eloy shouted after her. The three teenagers looked at each other before reluctantly sprinting after her. AJ quickly reached the end of the tunnel and listened to Team Zorro's nervous instructions.

"If you're going to do this then you need to be careful, AJ. To get to the central camp, you need to take the tunnel to the right and then go up. There are six guards outside the settlement, so you need to wait for backup." AJ ignored the final warning and ran to the ladder. Silently removing the grate at the top, she looked around her. Beneath a stationary van, she could see the feet of three guards outside the main gate. Where the other three were was anyone's guess. Suddenly she felt a tug on her foot and looked down. The other three were at the bottom of the ladder. Slowly, AJ climbed down.

"What?" she hissed, "I have to go!"

"Not on your own, you don't, are you mad?" Eloy grabbed AJ by the elbow. "You could die, AJ, they have real guns out there. Machine guns! You'd be dead in seconds." AJ swallowed. She had been trying not to think about that.

"Some of the rebels from the main plant are coming to help you, stay in position!" Mateo pleaded in her ear.

"They could be ages away," she protested. "We've trained, there's no one else here and we're so close!"

"Team Tortuga can set off a motion sensor alarm down a side street," Eva whispered. "That should draw them away for long enough to get us in and out. You stay here and shoot any guard that comes close. I've seen you back at camp — your aim is second to none, you can do this." Eloy looked at Eva, mouth open.

"You're encouraging this?" he asked, aghast.

"She's strong enough, Eloy, trust your sister," Eva insisted.

"Okay, fine, but we're going with her."

Before AJ could argue, a siren wailed from a nearby alley, distracting the remaining guards, and the four teenagers climbed the ladder and ran towards the final camp. Suddenly, a soldier rounded the corner and came face to face with Eva, who froze. AJ was too far ahead of her to see what was happening but Rafe, fresh from setting off his final round of fireworks, was close enough to slide tackle the man to the ground, giving AJ time to realise what was happening, and hit him with a tranquiliser dart.

"Thank you," Eva squeaked at Rafe as she shook in place. Eloy took her hand.

"Come on," he urged, "The sooner we save these people, the sooner we can get to safety."

Eva had watched her whole life seemingly flash before her eyes and was starting to wonder whether she should have stayed on the boat with the rest of her team. Maybe she wasn't cut out for field work.

As the group reached the final camp, Team Tortuga bypassed the scanners and the gate opened, but before they could run in, a mass of people burst from the bunkhouses and ran towards them. "Wow, these guys were ready, huh?" Archie whispered, impressed. "The alarms were probably a clue that something was up, and they just took their chance to escape."

"Well let's make sure it's not wasted," AJ added and waved

at the crowd, ushering the prisoners towards them. Leading the charge of factory workers was the most beautiful woman Archie had ever seen. Tall, strong and with stunning curls down to her waist, she sprinted towards them with more grace than a ballerina. Archie didn't even notice his sister trying to drag him away.

"Archie! Archie, they've got this, we need to go — now!" Archie snapped out of his stupor to follow his sister. The group ran back through the gate and hastily climbed down the ladder to the tunnels, to where Fumiyo and João were already leading the prisoners to safety. There were so many of them, though, and the ladder was struggling under the weight.

"We need more time," Eva shouted up to AJ.

AJ desperately looked around and had an idea. The vacant guard tower next to the settlement would provide a higher vantage point. She darted over and swiftly climbed the ladder. As she climbed higher, she could see more and more guards, all rushing towards the escaped prisoners, though they didn't yet know it. Leaping the final few feet, AJ dashed to the edge of the tower and gently grasped the Gatling gun mounted to the edge. Raising it up, away from the guards, she began firing at a nearby building. Archie stared up at the source of the gunfire in frightened confusion.

"What is she playing at?" he shouted over the noise. "The guards are down here!"

"She doesn't want to kill anyone!" Eloy shouted back.

"Well, sure," Archie continued as he helped lower more prisoners, "but they're going to kill us if she doesn't."

Suddenly Eva caught sight of what AJ was shooting at.

"Can everybody swim?" she yelled down the tunnel. Archie looked at her as though she had lost her mind. But there was no time to explain, AJ had shot enough holes in a rooftop water tower to send a torrent of water into the streets below, instantly toppling any remaining guards and prisoners alike.

"Just jump in!" Eloy shouted to the last few prisoners as the cascade of water turned the manhole into a waterslide. After leaping back down the ladder of the guard tower, AJ sprinted to the tunnel and, swiping the grate, jumped in feet first. As she descended, she let go of the grate at just the right time to return it to its rightful spot, cleverly concealing their escape route.

"Nice touch," shouted a soaking wet Archie. The alarms were deafening now, but as the group raced back towards the coast, a voice in their earpieces stopped them dead in their tracks.

"I don't know who you are, and I don't know how you're doing this, but I will find you, and I will kill you."

AJ and Eloy froze. That voice sounded so familiar, but where had they heard it before? Who had hacked into their system and why? They turned to see Archie and Eva collapsed on the floor, clutching each other.

"It's our father," Eva confirmed, shaking. "You need to get the others out of here, quickly. We can distract him until they're safe. If they're not down here yet then they haven't regained control of their systems, but it's only a matter of time until they work it out."

"I'm not leaving you," Eloy took her hand. "The others are taking care of the prisoners — I'm coming with you." AJ helped Archie to his feet. "Me too." A welcome, familiar voice met their ears now.

"Teams, it's Siri. The president is here. Puffles has kicked him out of our system for now but if he gets back in, they'll find out you're in the tunnels. Once the prisoners are safely out we're going to flood the sewers. Get out as soon as you can, we will deal with the president. Follow the prisoners and get to safety."

The group looked at each other.

"Yeah, we're not going to do that, are we?" Archie joked, shakily. The others shook their heads and headed back towards the centre of the city.

"How do we know where your father will be?" asked Eloy, as they climbed the ladder back up to the surface.

"My father always keeps himself safe as a priority," Eva began. "He will be at the most heavily guarded place in the city."

AJ paled. "Super."

The scene that greeted them as they raised their heads through the manhole was nothing short of chaos. Scores of armed guards were running from building to building, unsure where to go but sure of their orders to kill any intruder on site. A nearby camp was set ablaze and the cooling towers at the nuclear plant were emitting a cloud of strange black smoke. They ducked back down to come up with a plan.

"Well, that cannot be good," Archie commented as black smoke began seeping in through the tunnel walls. As they tried to figure out their next move, their respirators began beeping in unison.

"What now?" AJ despaired as she removed her respirator. The warning light indicated electrical damage as the mask gave a final, feeble beep.

"It must be water-damaged," Eloy suggested. "We all got soaked when you flooded the tunnel."

"We have to go back," Eva sighed, "We won't be able to keep breathing that air for long, especially with whatever is billowing out of the power plant." But AJ had come too far to go back now.

"I once spent two hours without my respirator and I was fine," she said, resolutely. "A bully at school stood on it and I wasn't allowed to go home until the end of the day."

"Yeah, I remember that," Eloy added. "Mum and Dad were so cross we moved schools — they could have killed you!"

"But it didn't kill me," AJ insisted.

"Yeah but..." Archie began. "Do you really want to risk taking that chance again? We're already exposed right now and it's at least twenty minutes back to the boat." They all looked doubtfully at AJ, but she remained steadfast.

"I'm going, but I won't ask any of you to come with me. I just have to take this monster down if I can. He's right here." She looked at the grate above them. "He tortured Mizuki, he killed her father and thousands more. We're so close."

"Are you out of there yet?" Siri's voice in their ears cut through the tension. "Althea's about to flood the tunnels and there's a fire in the transformer switchyard. We're not sure the plant is going to remain stable for long. You need to get to the boat, now!"

AJ looked behind her. They would never make it back to the boat in time — their only choice was to get to the surface. Nervously, they each climbed the ladder and emerged in a dark alley. Moments later, a gush of water flowed beneath them, taking with it the ladder they had just climbed. Archie exhaled slowly.

"This way!" AJ gestured towards the power plant's main complex.

Chapter 25

Better, Stronger, Faster

Eloy & AJ — Archie & Eva

An explosion within the nuclear plant's complex seemed to draw the guards inward, leaving the exterior unguarded and eerily silent.

"That must have been Siri's team," Eloy commented. "And Team Tortuga must have disabled the alarm. Finally, I can hear myself shake in fear again," he muttered.

"My father will be in there," Eva insisted. "That must be why we encountered so few guards at the camps — he will have them all protecting him."

Cautiously, they followed a group of soldiers at a distance, into the inner walls of the power plant. It was a large area containing several smaller buildings, but the black smoke from the cooling towers lay thick in the air and it was hard to see specific details. A group of guards rushed past on their left and they took shelter behind a stack of crates.

"The president wants a full report," barked one of the guards.

"But we haven't found the prisoners — they're like ghosts! We sent all our best troops to the tunnels, but they drowned them out," protested another guard. "And the rebels have locked themselves in the pump room — through two walls of bulletproof metal!"

"Do *you* want to be the one to tell the president that?" asked the first man. "He's waiting in the office now." As the group of soldiers retreated to a side building, AJ assessed the situation.

"So, assuming they've just come from there." She gestured. "We need to go that way." She pointed towards the middle of the complex, currently teeming with guards.

"Super," Archie quipped.

"If we stick to this wall we can get around the edge unseen, but we'll need to make a break for it once we get around this building," Eloy observed.

The group nodded and followed AJ despite their fear. As the explosions continued, more soldiers began to peel away towards the commotion, giving AJ her window.

"I'm going to run in." She pointed to the central building. "Once I know it's safe, I'll call you guys up."

Eloy wasn't sure. "AJ, I can't just let you run into an ambush! Besides, what are you even going to do once you find him? You can't kill the president!"

AJ looked down at her tranquiliser gun. "I can't kill him, but I can make him really sleepy." She tried to smile but she couldn't hide her fear. "You can come with me Eloy, but if anything happens to you, I'll never forgive myself. You're not as fast as me and I can't protect both of us."

"Then I'll have to protect myself," he interrupted her. "I know you're better, stronger and faster than me but I can't let you go alone." Eloy's mind was made up, AJ knew that. Nodding in understanding, Archie and Eva retreated against the wall and waited for their cue. Eva clutched her chest and steadied herself — it was getting harder and harder to breathe.

Archie took her hand. With one final scan for soldiers, AJ nodded to her brother and they both sprinted across the forecourt. AJ reached the building first and skidded to a halt, looking back for her brother. He was running, but so was a guard who had spotted him. Instinctively, AJ took out her tranquiliser gun and aimed at the guard, but it was too late. Time moved in slow motion as the bullet left the soldier's gun, flew through the air and embedded itself in Eloy's leg. With a shout, Eloy fell to the floor, followed by the now-unconscious man, having been hit by AJ's dart only seconds too late. Eva and Archie rushed towards Eloy and carried him to where AJ stood, paralysed, still aiming at the fallen soldier. Eloy, trying to balance on one leg, held AJ's shaking hands, still clasped around her gun.

"AJ, I'm okay, put it down," Eloy's rasping words did little to reassure AJ as blood soaked through his trouser leg.

"Get inside, quickly," Eva prompted. Before they could approach the door of the building, however, a team of soldiers flew through it, having heard the gunshot. The group took shelter around the side of the building, dashing in only when the soldiers were distracted by their sleeping comrade. Eva locked the door behind them by rewiring the scanners and they dragged Eloy into a room with tinted windows marked 'airlock'. Once inside, Eva was able to flush the black smoke from the room and fill it with treated air, giving the group a welcome moment to breathe.

"Oh, thank you, Evie," Archie breathed deeply. "I was really struggling back there." They all regained their breath for a few moments before Eva turned her attention to Eloy. She gently pulled up his trouser leg and held in a gasp.

"How does it look?" he asked, weakly.

Eva had studied biology and hoped to become a doctor one day, not that her father would ever have allowed it, but anyone could see Eloy was in trouble. The bullet had hit his shinbone and, judging by the unpleasant angle of his ankle, broken it in several places. AJ leant over her brother.

"You won't be walking out of here, but we can carry you. I think, maybe, we need to think about escaping," AJ admitted, defeated. Eva agreed although going back the way they came was no longer an option. Guards were pouring in, trying to find whoever had shot their tranquilised colleague. Archie looked through the furthest window and saw more buildings past the cooling towers. As he searched through the mist, he could faintly see a waving mass of blue and purple hair running across the complex.

"Siri!" he cried although she was too far away to have heard him. His heart sank as he saw that she and her team were also spotted by nearby guards, who chased them into a nearby building. On the plus side, it left no guards in the way of their next planned move.

"This might be our only window," he advised, before returning to Eloy to check on him.

Eva squinted through the smoke to try and spot Siri, but something else caught her eye. A glint of gold, she knew she'd seen before. She slowly stood up, her face pressed against the window, willing the smoke to clear. The gold shone brighter, and she suddenly realised what she was looking at. Her father's respirator. She was so close. She felt all of the rage, the hurt, the injustice building inside of her. This was it. She could end it all right now. He was right there. She turned hesitantly around to face the others, but they were still helping Eloy. She glanced at the console by the door, took one look back at her friends, and pressed it. The room filled with the black haze once more, but Eva was out and closed the door behind her before anyone could stop her.

As the air cleared inside the room, Archie rushed to the window to see Eva striding purposefully towards their father. "Evie, what are you doing?" he shouted, but she couldn't hear him now. AJ looked around for her tranquiliser gun but it had gone.

As Eva approached her father, she felt her lungs begin to ache as they filled with poisonous fumes. Just a little further and she'd have him. All she would need to do would be to shoot him with a dart and take off his respirator. He would choke to death as she herself soon would. But it would be worth it, she thought to herself, to rid the world of this monster. Her father's back was turned, she approached slowly but it was getting harder and harder to breathe. Everything sounded far away, and her vision was becoming increasingly blurred. She felt herself falling. No, not now, she was so close. She had come so far. A hand reached out and pulled her back. Eva turned to see AJ's panicked face.

"No!" Eva shouted through the fog. AJ tried to pull her away again, but Ignatius heard the commotion and turned to face them. In a final rush of desperation, Eva launched herself at her father and tore off his respirator. As she did so, she succumbed to her final, strangled breath and fell to the floor. With Ignatius distracted, AJ quickly picked Eva up and sprinted back to the others.

"We've got to go!" AJ shouted at them as she re-entered the room. "Come on! Archie, you carry Eloy. We're going to have to run for it."

"But, AJ," Archie stammered, "there are soldiers

everywhere!"

"There's no time, the president is just in there and we'll have a world of guards on us in minutes!"

Archie looked down at his sister to see, grasped in her hand, their father's golden respirator. Archie recoiled in horror and shrieked.

"Archie, this is no time to freak out — we have to go!" AJ urged.

"But, AJ, look!" Archie was pointing to the respirator. As AJ reluctantly looked down at Eva's unconscious hand, she gasped. Attached to the golden respirator was a face. A thin, silicone face with holes where eyes, nostrils and a mouth should be. "What the—"

"That's my father's face," Archie spluttered. "Why is… why is it not *on* his face?" AJ grabbed his wrist firmly.

"Archie, I have no idea, but I can hear them coming for us. We need to work this out later — not now." Archie swallowed hard and nodded. Struggling to pick up Eloy, he followed AJ out of their shelter and back towards the outskirts of the complex. They stayed hidden, skirting the edges of the buildings and hiding in shadows. Archie tried not to inhale but carrying a boy a year older than him made it very difficult to hold his breath.

"AJ, this is hard," he gasped, trying to conserve oxygen. AJ looked at him. He was pale and his eyes were turning red. Why wasn't she struggling like him? She felt fine other than the rush of adrenaline coursing through her bloodstream. There was a way out, but it was blocked by Electi troops.

"I'll distract them," AJ whispered. You take Eva over past that wall there, come back for Eloy and then you should have a clear path out. There's a guard station through there which should have respirators. I'll run amongst them and keep them away from you. They'll never catch me."

"No, AJ, it's way too dangerous," Archie protested. AJ looked at him and winked.

"I know," she smiled.

Archie was amazed by her for a moment, then terrified as she dropped his sister gently to the ground and ran out towards the troops, sending them running in her direction.

Archie paused for a moment — who should he take first? His heart prevailed and he rested Eloy against the wall, hauling his sister onto his shoulders and sprinting for the opposite wall. Through the corner of his eye, he could see AJ leading the soldiers on a chase through the rubble. How was she managing this with so little oxygen? He reached the gap in the wall and felt his heart lift when he reached the guard station. He quickly lay his sister on a bench and took four respirators. After putting one on his sister, he put his own on, took a deep, dizzying breath and ran back for Eloy.

This time, he couldn't see AJ anywhere. He picked Eloy up, stronger now, and carried him to where he had left his sister. With the last respirator, he went back for AJ. Where had she gone? She must know where they would be. Why wasn't she coming? To his left, he saw an observation tower that appeared to be unmanned. Cautiously, he approached it and climbed the ladder to the summit. Peering over the side, he could see that all available guards were gathered in a nearby courtyard, shooting madly at a wall behind which — he paled at the sight — AJ was trapped. He looked around him for anything that might help — anything that might distract them. He tried frantically to read the signs, but they were all in French and his father had forbidden any language learning other than Latin as it 'wouldn't be necessary in the new world'. He did, however, see one familiar word. 'Alarme!' Archie pushed the button beneath it and suddenly a fresh wave of noise burst through his eardrums. In the confusion, AJ was able to slip through the soldiers and sprint back towards their escape route. Archie ran to the ladder of the guard tower so fast that he nearly fell over the side and ended up sliding down rather than climbing.

AJ, thinking he had done this deliberately, was extremely impressed. "Smooth moves, Electi!"

Archie blushed and hid his stinging hands as they ran towards the guard station. While waiting for their return, Eloy had managed to find a way back down into the sewers through the guards' bathroom. He hoped that the water Siri sent had been enough to clear their escape route of soldiers, as it didn't look as though there was any other way out. They managed to lower the still-unconscious Eva into the tunnels before the guards realised where AJ had gone, but they couldn't stay there long. "Here, take this. Not that you need it... for some reason." Archie passed AJ the respirator.

"Yeah," she held it in her hands. Her breathing was still unaffected — if you didn't count the effects of fear and sprinting. She put the respirator on anyway and followed Archie, carrying Eloy on her back. As the stronger out of the two of them, AJ had diplomatically volunteered to carry the heaviest wounded ally.

"I found a map in the observation tower," Archie began. "There's a tunnel out of here that leads to the ocean. We'll be able to radio the others to come and get us on the boat — they can't be far from where we'll end up."

AJ nodded and followed Archie down the ladder into the underground tunnels. Behind them, they could hear swarms of soldiers and gunfire.

"Are you injured?" Archie asked as they jogged along the passageway.

AJ hadn't really had time to check herself over. Her arm stung but she assumed that was from carrying Eloy. She glanced at her right bicep and winced. That was definitely going to hurt once the adrenaline had worn off. "Just a scratch," she lied, as she tried to ignore the blood soaking through her shirt.

As the end of the tunnel grew closer, Archie pulled the radio out from Eva's bag. "How on earth does this work then?" he asked, nervously.

"Give it here." A weak voice made Archie jump and he nearly dropped his now-conscious sister.

"Good grief, Eva, don't do that!" Archie breathed. "I'm so glad you're okay."

"Give me the radio, Archie." Eva took the device and adjusted the frequency. "Eva to base, Eva to base, do you read me?" The familiar static of the radio hung in the air. Eva tried again. They were approaching the end of the tunnel now. As the daylight grew clearer, so did the sound of the radio.

"Ev... Marcus... locati..."

"Keep trying," Archie urged.

"Eva to base. We are heading for the ocean around three kilometres east of the drop point, over." More static, then silence. Suddenly the roar of an engine filled their ears as a group of jet skis rounded the corner and pulled up at the end of the tunnel.

"Dear lord, I hope they're on our side," Eva whispered.

"Kids, kids, is that you?"

AJ's heart skipped a beat.

"It's my dad! It's my dad!" She waved frantically from the

269

tunnel entrance, still balancing Eloy on her back. After manoeuvring the jet skis closer to shore, Marcus rested his son on the back of his jet ski and motioned the others to take the rest of the teenagers. AJ leapt onto the back of the furthest jet ski while Archie gently hauled Eva onto the side of Bruce's boat before sitting behind her.

"We've been riding around all the pipeline exits hoping you would use one to escape! You are so clever, my girl." Marcus beamed.

"Actually, that was Archie's idea," AJ admitted. "He found the map that showed us the way out."

"Well colour me impressed, Master Regnum." Marcus nodded approvingly at Archie who smiled weakly as the jet skis roared away. He still didn't care much for ocean travel.

The convoy travelled along the coast of France for a few kilometres before reaching the main boat. Mizuki personally welcomed them aboard and immediately took Eva and Eloy to the medical room.

AJ and Archie were welcomed like heroes with applause and cheers from the crew and Marcus beamed with pride at his daughter. After they had all settled down and the adrenaline was beginning to wear off, Siri heaved herself over the side of the boat, dripping and exhausted. She had a black eye and was bleeding from her ear but reassured everyone that she was fine. The boat was now overflowing with released prisoners and several other boats came to meet them to lighten the load.

After AJ had been treated for the injury to her arm, she found Siri embracing the young girl who had led the charge from the final camp.

"My sister, Omolara," Siri choked through tears. "My beautiful baby sister." AJ smiled and Archie blushed uncontrollably. He had been captivated by her beauty at the factories but had no idea that she was Siri's little sister.

"You really do have a type," AJ whispered, teasingly.

"I'm Lara." The girl approached Archie and AJ. "I can never thank you enough for saving me." Archie blushed again.

"It's really okay," he stuttered. AJ giggled. Soon pain began to replace the adrenaline that had previously filled their bodies and AJ and Archie headed down to the medical room. Eva was feeling much better, having been given oxygen and Eloy's gunshot wound had finally stopped bleeding. That didn't mean he was out of the woods, however, and AJ remained by his side for the rest of the journey, her father beside her.

"He's going to be okay," Marcus reassured, mainly to himself. "You've both been so brave. When I found out what you'd been sent into, I was furious." He shook his head. "But then you did so much better than anyone else ever could have." He beamed at his daughter once again. "You've used your gifts for good AJ and I'm so proud."

AJ squeezed her father's hand. She looked out at the hundreds of freed Trebs laughing and singing and felt an enormous sense of pride. These people could be free now and she had been a part of that. With that final, peaceful thought in her mind, AJ allowed her eyes to close and her body to rest at last. They were going home.

Chapter 26

Viva La Revolución!

Eloy & AJ — Archie & Eva

Everyone had made it back safely to Project Libertas and spirits were high. All of the imprisoned factory workers had made it to the escape boats and were now settled either at Project Libertas or at their new camp location in Poland. Eva had mostly recovered from her ordeal but needed regular doses of oxygen to get her lungs back on track, while Eloy hopped around on crutches, his leg in a cast but now back at the correct angle.

"We're really building a resistance now," Siri nodded, smiling. "All that's left to do is for our agents in Anglia to kick start the revolution."

"But I thought that was it," AJ replied. "I thought we'd got the president and... that was it — we won?"

"It's a little more complicated than that, AJ, but it's a hugely important start. With the factories destroyed and their president... well, I've actually got some news about that. But for now, it's just for Archie and Eva." Siri beckoned the two Impero-Regnum children into her private office, while AJ turned discreetly to Eloy.

"It's about his face," she told him in a hushed whisper. "It sort of came off with his respirator when Eva pulled it away."

"Wait, what?" Eloy looked queasy. "Came off?"

Inside the office, Siri sat the siblings down.

"It's about Father, isn't it?" Archie was pale. "Eva, you didn't see what happened when you removed his respirator, did you?" He looked meekly at his sister.

"No, I... I passed out. Why? Is he..." Eva looked away. She was so sure, at that moment, that killing her father was the right thing to do. Now, however, guilt filled her like a sickness, and she felt dizzy.

"He's not dead," Siri quickly interrupted. "But, he's not exactly alive either." The siblings exchanged confused glances. "Archie, I know you saw... Well, what you saw was a synthetic face." Eva looked, if possible, even more confused. "We were able to recover the model number and it comes back to a company in the ESA that makes synthetic humans. Incredibly lifelike ones at that — not like the artificially intelligent robots you get in restaurants — you wouldn't even know these machines weren't alive."

"Oh yes, I know about those," Eva added thoughtfully. "I've read that they can make them frighteningly realistic now. Mother always wanted one instead of our butler, Samuel. Father wasn't keen though, he said there was no replacing flesh and bone."

"Well," Siri began, awkwardly, "that was deeply ironic of him." She looked at the pair, wondering whether they were going to catch on.

"Did Father... have a robot decoy?" Archie offered. Siri shook her head.

"That's what we thought, at first. It would make sense for security and while they are inordinately expensive, your father certainly has the money." She paused. "But when we traced the order from the model number, we found more orders with a whole host of parts and technologies purchased by your father. This then led us to a company specialising in human consciousness transference."

"Human, what?" Archie's head was beginning to hurt.

"They were pioneers when it came to preserving one's mind inside a computer, although, due to skyrocketing costs and concerns around legality, the program was kept quiet and never gained public recognition," Siri explained, although Archie didn't think this really explained anything at all. "Records indicate that your father's account began paying for their services as far back as 2005." Eva's face scrunched up in thought.

"But that's the year father was born," she inquired with a raised eyebrow. "So that doesn't make any sense!"

Siri looked apologetically at the pair before delivering her bombshell. "Eva, Archie. We have reason to believe that your father is a synthetic human."

"Come again?" Archie almost choked on his own saliva. "That's not possible. We definitely would have known that. Right, Evie? We'd have known." Eva, however, was beginning to realise.

"He can't swim. He's afraid of water. Didn't you always find that odd, Archie? Father is afraid of nothing, but the concept of water freaks him out."

Archie shook his head. "No, no you're being ridiculous. Father is not a robot!"

"No," Siri interjected. "Not a robot. A synthetic human. A humanoid robot controlled by artificial intelligence. Your father is alive but only in data form. His consciousness belongs to a real person, who transferred his mind into a computer, back in 2005."

"Wait!" Archie flapped his hands around for silence. "So our father might not even *be* our father?"

"The concept of your father simply doesn't exist," Siri replied gravely. "Have you ever seen any childhood photographs of him?" They paused, desperately thinking back to any memories of home.

"Technically," Archie mused, "no. But then Father isn't sentimental. He was shipped off to boarding school practically as soon as he was born and then he worked in the ESA until..."

"Until?" Siri prompted.

"Until grandfather Atticus died," Eva replied. "Just before the war." Eva looked at Siri, fully realising now. "Siri, could Grandfather..."

"That's what we thought too," Siri confirmed.

"Will someone please tell me what in heaven's name is going on?" Archie stood up. "Are you telling me that Grandfather did something to Father? Did he clone him or something?"

Eva took her brother's hands and sat him down, without breaking eye contact. "Archie. Think about it. There are no photographs of Father and Grandfather together. No photographs of him before he was twenty. He never gets ill."

"We have good doctors!" Archie protested. "We're very well off!"

"We think that your grandfather became an AI before his death and implanted himself in a synthetic human, thus taking the role of your father," Siri explained calmly. "That's what the tube you found in his office was for. It's a synthetic human charging and repair pod."

"Nope." Archie shook his head. "No that doesn't make sense." But as he said it, he realised that it did make sense. His

275

father never hugged him or even touched him; never seemed to age; and looked so frighteningly like his own father, Atticus I, or as they now knew him, Ciaran Doyle. Could it be possible?

"But, wait." Archie was quiet now. "What about us? Synthetic humans can't have children." Siri nodded.

"We looked into that too. But we have concluded that your mother must be human and aware of the operation — she must have known from the beginning. You saw her carry your sisters so we can assume you are your mother's children; however, we think your grandfather may have preserved elements of his own biology, shall we say; in order to carry on his genetic line.

"Therefore—" She paused, waiting for Archie's brain to catch up. "Your mother is your mother, but your grandfather is actually your father."

"Ew." Archie reached for the nearest bin and heaved.

"I'm so sorry to break this to you, although, Eva, I hope this alleviates your feelings of guilt over your father's death. I mean, not death, because he wasn't ever actually alive." Siri gave Eva a weak smile, but she too was trying not to vomit. "There is some good news, though," Siri offered. The siblings didn't look particularly relieved as they turned varying shades of green.

"Evie! Archie!" Eva and Archie's heads flipped round as the familiar sound of their young sisters hit their ears. Antoinette ran straight into Eva's arms as Euridice toddled tentatively towards Archie. Behind them, wearing a blindingly white fur coat and a forlorn expression, was their mother.

"Mother!" Eva called out as she held her sister. "Are you okay?" Lady Margot Impero-Regnum sat carefully beside her children. She wasn't used to sofas made of synthetic fibres and worried about the implications for her fur coat. She inhaled deeply before looking solemnly at her children.

"Can you forgive me?" she asked, gravely.

"For what?" Archie asked, Euridice now napping in his lap like a kitten.

"For deceiving you. I assume Ms Perl has told you the truth by now. But I want you to know that I had no choice. Your grandfather bought me, you see, from my parents. They had invested poorly and lost their entire fortune. Your grandfather promised them that I would continue living the life of luxury in which I had been raised. I was told that if I ever tried to leave, or revealed that your father was, in fact, your grandfather..." She paused and looked down at her vintage patent leather boots, wondering to herself if her life of designer clothes and restricted food had been worth it.

"He would have killed you," Eva said, quietly.

"Yes," replied Margot, still staring at her shoes. Siri stood up to leave the family with some privacy.

"One of our teams rescued your mother and sisters from the house as soon as your father fell. We knew they wouldn't be safe there. She knew too much."

"Thank you," Archie breathed, fighting back tears. It was all so much. The disconnect he had felt with his father his whole life suddenly made sense. The fear and sadness he felt from his mother had been real. Their whole lives were part of an elaborate scheme concocted by an old man desperate to cling to power for as long as possible. Archie held his sister close to his heart and sighed. At least his family were together again. Well, the ones he liked at least. As he smiled at Eva, they were both wondering the same thing — where was Atticus?

In the dining hall, Mizuki and the Kahn family were enjoying a well-deserved meal while Sully and Wendoline teamed up to search for scraps. As they were tucking into a freshly dropped chunk of pineapple, the diner's rarely used holovision screen flickered into life with a small, waving Puffles telling everyone to pay attention. The diners all jumped — the holovision was never used, except in emergencies to conserve power. Scenes of chaos filled the screen as a familiar face stepped into view.

"Reva," Archie exclaimed as his family came to join the Kahns. "From Lost London!"

"I'm here in New London," Reva's voice rang out over the noise behind her, as her colleague tried desperately to steady the camera. "The president has fallen and Treb rebels have released damning evidence that the Electi government has broken countless laws and kidnapped its own citizens. Many Electi citizens have cancelled their membership and reverted to Treb citizens while higher-up Electi officials have been seen fleeing major cities!" she shouted, as hundreds of excited Trebs ran behind her, covering Electi propaganda with their own posters of protest. "The majority of the Treb-led police force have turned on their Electi bosses and are assisting the thousands of Trebs now marching on government headquarters, demanding answers and justice. Electi supplies from the mainland have been cut off, but rebels are redistributing their existing food and medicine to Treb community centres and homeless camps. The media is silent, so we've come out here to tell you all — there is hope, this is the time — resist!" Reva raised her fist in the air.

"Where is this broadcasting?" Eva asked, amazed.

"Everywhere," Siri replied, smiling.

"Do they know it was us?" Archie asked, optimistic for public glory.

"Not yet," Siri shook her head, "but if you want people to

278

know, I'm sure that can be arranged."

"No." AJ looked at Siri. "I think everyone should get the credit — those captured operatives back home deserve just at much credit as us for risking their lives. Archie was disappointed but knew that AJ was right. Now was not the time for fanfare.

"The Electi government has disbanded and thousands of Treb prisoners have been released," Reva continued. "The factory cities — which we now know to be illegal Electi-run prison camps — have been liberated and the workers rescued."

Siri squeezed her sister's hand in hers, silently vowing never to let her out of her sight again.

Reva took a deep breath before continuing. "The citizens of Lost London can finally live on the surface again." Tears filled her eyes now as she addressed her fellow citizens. "We are free."

Leyna squeezed her son's hand as they all stared at the screen in silent amazement. "We are free."

After what felt like a week-long party, only a few members of Project Libertas were left on the island. Most of the inhabitants had either moved on to the new base in Poland or returned to Anglia to be with their families, now that the rebels were in charge and they were safe from persecution. While Siri explained that a temporary rebel government was not a permanent solution, they were confident that with time and a lot of work, they could re-build Anglia into a fair and equal society. Everyone had been thinking long and hard about what their next move might be, and it wasn't an easy decision. The group had gathered on the beach to take in the view one last time before the base was shut down. Siri had considered staying now that

President Ignatius was gone, but there was still a last, desperate collection of Electi troops determined to wipe out any remaining rebels, and so she had decided to move ahead with their new base in Poland.

"What will you do now?" Mizuki asked AJ, as they sat by the ocean, hands held against the soft sand.

"I want to go to the new base," AJ announced. "There are still scores of Electi troops all over the place and Siri says that some of the higher-ranking Electi players have fled Anglia, heading to the mainland. We'll need to keep them from gaining a foothold over here — we don't want a new Electi government on the continent." Eloy nodded in agreement.

"I'm with AJ. With everything that's going on in Anglia, the situation is still far from over. We need to make the mainland safe so that people can live here again in peace. We can reintroduce the wildlife and change the world back to the way it was before the war, but better!" Marcus smiled at his son.

"That'll be no small task," he admitted reluctantly.

"You're right," Eloy agreed. "But it will be worth it. And to do it, they're going to need people with experience."

Marcus sceptically raised an eyebrow. "Oh, and that's you, is it?" he chided.

"It's all of us," Eva announced. "I've heard the president of the ESA isn't too happy about the situation in Anglia and you'll need my help if they decide to act. Their technology is second to none, but I know how to get past it."

"I want to help Carmen with the animals," AJ smiled. "Mizuki, you won't believe all the different creatures they've managed to rescue!" Mizuki's eyes lit up.

"My mum says she wants to use her knowledge of the

Electi to help keep them out of power," Mizuki explained. "So, we're coming too!"

"And I'm also useful!" cried Archie, jokingly. The group laughed.

"Well," Leyna began, "I suppose there's not much for us back home anymore and I would love to see Poland again." She smiled at her husband.

"I…" Marcus paused. "I never wanted this for you kids. I just wanted you to have normal lives."
AJ took her father's hand.

"But this is so much better," she grinned. "We're heroes!"

Marcus smiled proudly at his daughter. "Yes," he nodded. "I suppose you are."

After packing up the little possessions they had acquired during their time on the island, the Impero-Regnum children bade a tearful farewell to their mother and sisters. It was now safe for them to return to Anglia, and a rebel base was no place for two little girls.

"Promise me you'll be careful," Eva pleaded with her mother. "Don't try to find Atticus, he won't understand." Lady Margot shook her head.

"He won't," she agreed, "but he's still my son. I must try and find him."

Eva reluctantly nodded before letting her family board the boat back home.

"We'll see them again," Archie reassured her, his hand on her shoulder. "Besides, we'll be having too much fun to miss them." He grinned and went to collect the rest of his belongings, leaving Eva standing sadly on the shore.

"Are you okay?" Eloy asked her as he tentatively

approached, still getting used to his crutches. Eva jumped slightly.

"Oh, Eloy," she smiled. "I'm fine. My whole life is a little upside down but it's going to be okay." Eloy looked at her kindly.

"Maybe," he wondered aloud, "for the first time in your life, you're the right way up?" Eva blushed. As AJ peered over to see what she could mock her brother for next, she softened. He looked happier than she had ever seen him, holding her hand. He leaned forwards on his crutches, wobbling slightly. Eva held him steady as he gently kissed her. AJ giggled to herself before leaving them to their moment. Eventually, they joined her back by the trucks.

"You're right, Eloy," AJ laughed at him as they loaded their belongings into trucks that would board the boats for the mainland. "Having your first kiss on the beach was a much better choice than having it in the sewers!" She grinned mischievously at her brother. Eva turned even redder.

"AJ, leave us alone!" Eloy playfully kicked his sister with his good leg.

"It was romantic," Eva blushed.

"Yeah, see, I'm romantic," Eloy boasted to hide his shyness. "Anyway, you've got a girlfriend now too, AJ. Prepare for a taste of your own medicine!" But AJ was still teasing him when the rest of the acertine children came to join them.

"Are you coming with us?" AJ asked, hopefully.

"We wouldn't miss it," Rafe smiled. "Besides, most of us don't have families to go back to — all we have now is each other."

Mateo smiled encouragingly at his friend. "I heard Dr Kyap is going to find out more about how acertine gave us our abilities," he said shyly. "And I definitely want to be there when she finds out." The rest of them nodded, before loading their bags onto the trucks.

"Well, team." Marcus beamed proudly at the remaining five teenagers. "It's time for another adventure. Are you ready?"

AJ squeezed Mizuki's hand and looked inquiringly at her. "What do you say, Miz? Fancy joining our team of heroes? I know you've got a million skills you could bring to our team!"

Mizuki looked around at the smiling faces before her. Eloy and Eva, hands held, were staring kindly at her while Archie grinned excitedly.

"I don't know much about being a hero," Mizuki began, "but I'd be really glad to call you all my friends."

The group took one final, longing look at the beautiful beach and tropical paradise they had lovingly called home, before climbing into the trucks that would take them to Poland.

"Ready?" Siri shouted from the front of the convoy. The group all shouted back in resolute unison.

"Ready!" And with the collective hum of electric engines, they held their breaths, ready for their next adventure, as heroes and as friends.